Francis Parkman

The old régime in Canada. France and England in North America

Part fourth. Vol. 1

Francis Parkman

The old régime in Canada. France and England in North America
Part fourth. Vol. 1

ISBN/EAN: 9783337208349

Printed in Europe, USA, Canada, Australia, Japan

Cover: Foto ©Andreas Hilbeck / pixelio.de

More available books at **www.hansebooks.com**

EDITION DE LUXE.

THE WORKS

OF

FRANCIS PARKMAN.

VOLUME VII.

Figure of Chomedey de Maisonneuve.

THE OLD RÉGIME IN CANADA

FRANCE AND ENGLAND IN NORTH AMERICA · Part Fourth

BY FRANCIS PARKMAN

IN TWO VOLUMES

VOL. I.

BOSTON · LITTLE · BROWN AND · COMPANY · MDCCCXCVII

𝔘𝔫𝔦𝔳𝔢𝔯𝔰𝔦𝔱𝔶 𝔓𝔯𝔢𝔰𝔰 :
JOHN WILSON AND SON, CAMBRIDGE, U.S.A.

TO

GEORGE EDWARD ELLIS, D.D.

My Dear Dr. Ellis:

When, in my youth, I proposed to write a series of books on the French in America, you encouraged the attempt, and your helpful kindness has followed it from that day to this. Pray accept the dedication of this volume in token of the grateful regard of

Very faithfully yours,

FRANCIS PARKMAN.

NOTE TO REVISED EDITION.

When this book was written, I was unable to gain access to certain indispensable papers relating to the rival claimants to Acadia, — La Tour and D'Aunay, — and therefore deferred all attempts to treat that subject. The papers having at length come to hand, the missing chapters are supplied in the present edition, which also contains some additional matter of less prominence.

The title of " The Old Régime in Canada " is derived from the third and principal of the three sections into which the book is divided.

June 16, 1893.

PREFACE.

"The physiognomy of a government," says De Tocqueville, "can best be judged in its colonies, for there its characteristic traits usually appear larger and more distinct. When I wish to judge of the spirit and the faults of the administration of Louis XIV., I must go to Canada. Its deformity is there seen as through a microscope."

The monarchical administration of France, at the height of its power and at the moment of its supreme triumph, stretched an arm across the Atlantic and grasped the North American continent. This volume attempts to show by what methods it strove to make good its hold, why it achieved a certain kind of success, and why it failed at last. The political system which has fallen, and the antagonistic system which has prevailed, seem, at first sight, to offer nothing but contrasts; yet out of the tomb of Canadian absolutism come voices not without suggestion even to us. Extremes meet, and Autocracy and Democracy often touch hands, at least in their vices.

The means of knowing the Canada of the past are ample. The pen was always busy in this outpost of the old monarchy. The king and the minister demanded to know everything; and officials of high and low degree, soldiers and civilians, friends and foes, poured letters, despatches, and memorials, on both sides of every question, into the lap of government. These masses of paper have in the main survived the perils of revolutions and the incendiary torch of the Commune. Add to them the voluminous records of the Superior Council of Quebec, and numerous other documents preserved in the civil and ecclesiastical depositories of Canada.

The governments of New York and of Canada have caused a large part of the papers in the French archives relating to their early history to be copied and brought to America, and valuable contributions of material from the same quarter have been made by the State of Massachusetts and by private Canadian investigators. Nevertheless, a great deal has still remained in France uncopied and unexplored. In the course of several visits to that country, I have availed myself of these supplementary papers, as well as of those which had before been copied, sparing neither time nor pains to explore every part of the field. With the help of a system of classified notes, I have collated the evidence of the various writers, and set down without reserve all the results of the examination, whether favorable or unfavorable. Some of them are of a character which I regret, since they cannot be agreeable to persons for whom I have a very cordial regard. The conclusions drawn from the facts may be matter of opinion, but it will be remembered that the facts themselves can be overthrown only by overthrowing the evidence on which they rest, or bringing forward counter-evidence of equal or greater strength ; and neither task will be found an easy one.[1]

I have received most valuable aid in my inquiries from the great knowledge and experience of M. Pierre Margry, Chief of the Archives of the Marine and Colonies at Paris. I beg also warmly to acknowledge the kind offices of Abbé Henri Raymond Casgrain and Grand

[1] Those who wish to see the subject from a point of view opposite to mine cannot do better than consult the work of the Jesuit Charlevoix, with the excellent annotation of Mr. Shea. (History and General Description of New France, by the Rev. P. F. X. de Charlevoix, S.J., translated with notes by John Gilmary Shea. 6 vols. New York: 1866–1872.)

Vicar Cazeau, of Quebec ; together with those of
James Le Moine, Esq., M. Eugène Taché, Hon.
P. J. O. Chauveau, and other eminent Canadians,
and Henry Harrisse, Esq.

The few extracts from original documents
which are printed in the Appendix may serve as
samples of the material out of which the work
has been constructed. In some instances their
testimony might be multiplied twenty-fold.
When the place of deposit of the documents
cited in the margin is not otherwise indicated,
they will, in nearly all cases, be found in the
Archives of the Marine and Colonies.

In the present book we examine the political
and social machine; in the next volume of the
series we shall see this machine in action.

Boston, July 1, 1874.

CONTENTS.

SECTION FIRST.

THE FEUDAL CHIEFS OF ACADIA.

CHAPTER I.

1497–1643.

LA TOUR AND D'AUNAY.

CHAPTER II.

1643–1645.

LA TOUR AND THE PURITANS.

CHAPTER III.

1645–1710.

THE VICTOR VANQUISHED.

SECTION SECOND.

CANADA A MISSION.

CHAPTER IV.

1653–1658.

THE JESUITS AT ONONDAGA.

CHAPTER V.

1642–1661.

THE HOLY WARS OF MONTREAL.

CHAPTER VI.

1660, 1661.

THE HEROES OF THE LONG SAUT.

CONTENTS. XV

CHAPTER VII.
1657–1668.
THE DISPUTED BISHOPRIC.

CHAPTER VIII.
1659, 1660.
LAVAL AND ARGENSON.

CHAPTER IX.
1658–1663.
LAVAL AND AVAUGOUR.

CHAPTER X.
1661–1664
LAVAL AND DUMESNIL.

CHAPTER XI.
1657–1665.
LAVAL AND MÉZY.

CHAPTER XII.

1662–1680.

LAVAL AND THE SEMINARY.

SECTION THIRD.

THE COLONY AND THE KING.

CHAPTER XIII.

1661–1665.

ROYAL INTERVENTION.

CHAPTER XIV.

1666, 1667.

THE MOHAWKS CHASTISED.

LIST OF ILLUSTRATIONS.

VOLUME ONE.

THE OLD RÉGIME IN CANADA.

CANADA

ND ADJACENT COUNTRIES
towards the close
OF THE
17TH CENTURY.

Nipissings
GEORGIAN Bay
LAC HURON
R. des Ontous
(Ottawa)
Ft Frontenac
Kenté
Ganneious
LAC ONTARIO
La Famine
Niagara
Trondequoit Bay
Senecas
Cayugas
Onondagas
Oneidas
IROQUOIS
LAC ERIE
NE
YOI

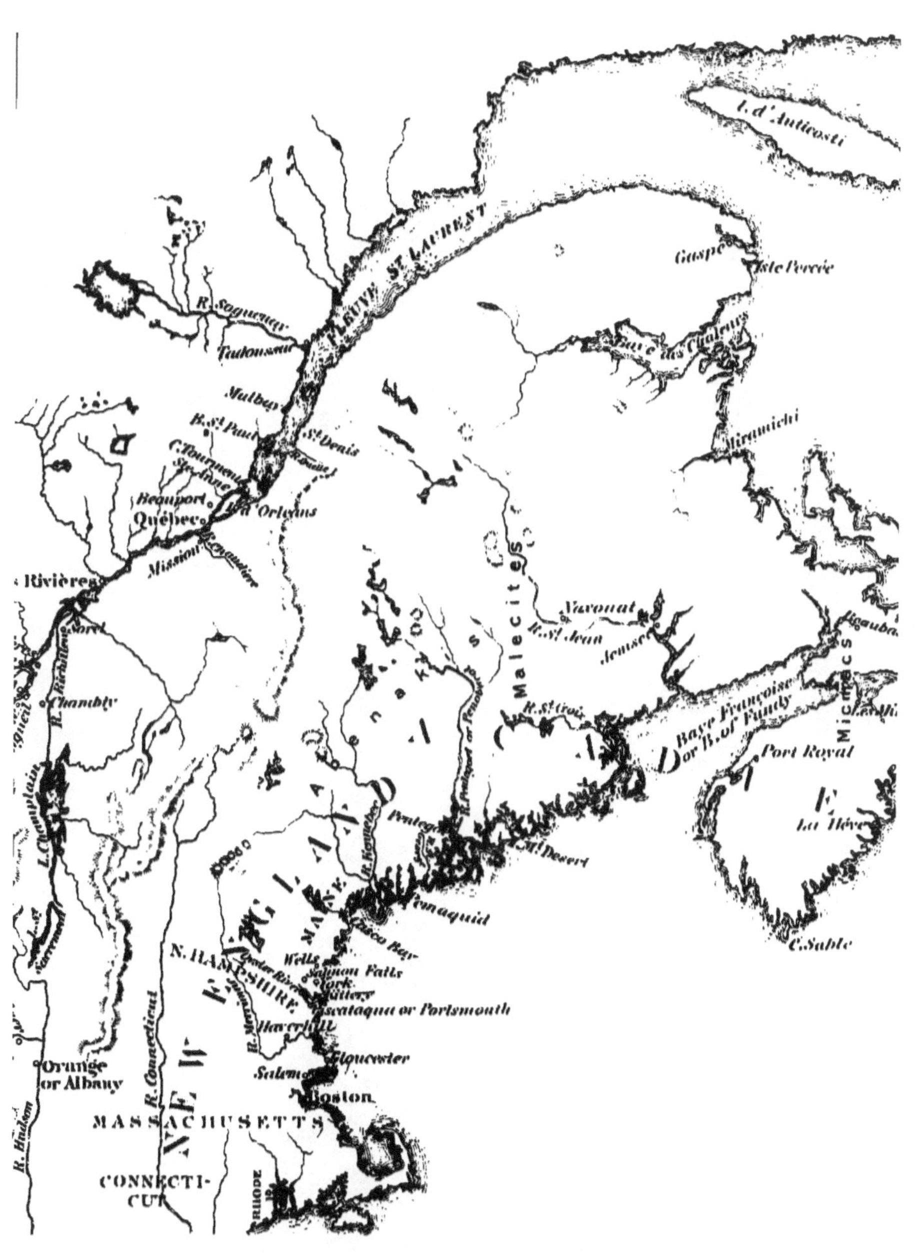
I. d'Anticosti
FLEUVE ST LAURENT
Gaspé
Isle Percée
R. Saguenay
Tadoussac
Baye des Chaleurs
Mulbay
B. St Paul
St Denis
C. Tourment
Ste Anne
Miramichi
Beauport
I. d'Orleans
Québec
Malecites
Navonat
R. St Jean
Jemseck
Rivière
Mission
Sorel
R. St Croix
R. Richilieu
Baye Françoise
or B. or Fundy
Micmacs
Chambly
Port Royal
L. Champlain
Pentagoet
Penobscot or Pemaquid
Mt Desert
La Hève
Pemaquid
Casco Bay
MAINE
N. HAMPSHIRE
Wells
Salmon Falls
York
Kittery
Piscataqua or Portsmouth
Haverhill
C. Sable
NEW ENGLAND
R. Connecticut
Gloucester
Salem
Boston
Orange
or Albany
MASSACHUSETTS
R. Hudson
CONNECTI-
CUT
RHODE

SECTION FIRST.

THE FEUDAL CHIEFS OF ACADIA.

CHAPTER I.

1497–1643.

LA TOUR AND D'AUNAY.

The Acadian Quarrel. — Biencourt — Claude and Charles de la Tour. — Sir William Alexander. — Claude de Razilly. — Charles de Menou d'Aunay Charnisay. — Cape Sable. — Port Royal. — The Heretics of Boston and Plymouth. — Madame de la Tour. — War and Litigation. — La Tour worsted: he asks Help from the Boston Puritans.

With the opening of the seventeenth century began that contest for the ownership of North America which was to remain undecided for a century and a half. England claimed the continent through the discovery by the Cabots in 1497 and 1498, and France claimed it through the voyage of Verrazzano in 1524. Each resented the claim of the other; and each snatched such fragments of the prize as she could reach, and kept them if she could. In 1604, Henry IV. of France gave to De Monts all America from the 40th to the 46th degree of north latitude,

including the sites of Philadelphia on the one hand
and Montreal on the other;[1] while, eight years after,
Louis XIII. gave to Madame de Guercheville and
the Jesuits the whole continent from Florida to the
St. Lawrence, — that is, the whole of the future
British colonies.   Again, in 1621, James I. of England made over a part of this generous domain to a
subject of his own, Sir William Alexander, — to
whom he gave, under the name of Nova Scotia, the
peninsula which is now so called, together with a
vast adjacent wilderness, to be held forever as a fief
of the Scottish Crown.[2]   Sir William, not yet satisfied, soon got an additional grant of the "River and
Gulf of Canada," along with a belt of land three
hundred miles wide, reaching across the continent.[3]
Thus the King of France gave to Frenchmen the
sites of Boston, New York, and Washington, and
the King of England gave to a Scotchman the sites
of Quebec and Montreal.   But while the seeds of
international war were thus sown broadcast over the
continent, an obscure corner of the vast regions in
dispute became the scene of an intestine strife like
the bloody conflicts of two feudal chiefs in the depths
of the Middle Ages.

After the lawless inroads of Argall, the French,
with young Biencourt at their head, still kept a

---

[1] See "Pioneers of France in the New World," ii. 65.

[2] *Charter of New Scotland in favour of Sir William Alexander.*

[3] *Charter of the Country and Lordship of Canada in America*, 2 *Feb.*,
1628–29, in *Publications of the Prince Society*, 1873.

feeble hold on Acadia. After the death of his father, Poutrincourt, Biencourt took his name, by which thenceforth he is usually known. In his distress he lived much like an Indian, roaming the woods with a few followers, and subsisting on fish, game, roots, and lichens. He seems, however, to have found means to build a small fort among the rocks and fogs of Cape Sable. He named it Fort Loméron, and here he appears to have maintained himself for a time by fishing and the fur-trade.

Many years before, a French boy of fourteen years, Charles Saint-Étienne de la Tour, was brought to Acadia by his father, Claude de la Tour, where he became attached to the service of Biencourt (Poutrincourt), and, as he himself says, served as his ensign and lieutenant. He says, further, that Biencourt on his death left him all his property in Acadia. It was thus, it seems, that La Tour became owner of Fort Loméron and its dependencies at Cape Sable, whereupon he begged the King to give him help against his enemies, especially the English, who, as he thought, meant to seize the country; and he begged also for a commission to command in Acadia for his Majesty.[1]

In fact, Sir William Alexander soon tried to dispossess him and seize his fort. Charles de la Tour's father had been captured at sea by the privateer "Kirke," and carried to England. Here, being a widower, he married a lady of honor of the Queen,

---

[1] *La Tour au Roy, 25 July,* 1627.

and, being a Protestant, renounced his French allegiance.

Alexander made him a baronet of Nova Scotia, a new title which King James had authorized Sir William to confer on persons of consideration aiding him in his work of colonizing Acadia. Alexander now fitted out two ships, with which he sent the elder La Tour to Cape Sable. On arriving, the father, says the story, made the most brilliant offers to his son if he would give up Fort Loméron to the English, — to which young La Tour is reported to have answered in a burst of patriotism, that he would take no favors except from his sovereign, the King of France. On this, the English are said to have attacked the fort, and to have been beaten off. As the elder La Tour could not keep his promise to deliver the place to the English, they would have no more to do with him, on which his dutiful son offered him an asylum under condition that he should never enter the fort. A house was built for him outside the ramparts; and here the trader, Nicolas Denys, found him in 1635. It is Denys who tells the above story,[1] which he probably got from the younger La Tour, — and which, as he tells it, is inconsistent with the known character of its pretended hero, who was no model of loyalty to his king, being a chameleon whose principles took the color of his interests. Denys says, further, that the elder La Tour had been invested with the Order of the Garter, and that

---

[1] Denys, *Description géographique et historique.*

the same dignity was offered to his son; which is absurd. The truth is, that Sir William Alexander, thinking that the two La Tours might be useful to him, made them both baronets of Nova Scotia.[1]

Young La Tour, while begging Louis XIII. for a commission to command in Acadia, got from Sir William Alexander not only the title of baronet, but also a large grant of land at and near Cape Sable, to be held as a fief of the Scottish Crown.[2] Again, he got from the French King a grant of land on the river St. John, and, to make assurance doubly sure, got leave from Sir William Alexander to occupy it.[3] This he soon did, and built a fort near the mouth of the river, not far from the present city of St. John.

Meanwhile the French had made a lodgment on the rock of Quebec, and not many years after, all North America from Florida to the Arctic circle, and from Newfoundland to the springs of the St. Lawrence, was given by King Louis to the Company of New France, with Richelieu at its head.[4] Sir William Alexander, jealous of this powerful rivalry, caused a private expedition to be fitted out under the brothers Kirke. It succeeded, and the French settle-

---

[1] *Grant from Sir William Alexander to Sir Claude de St. Étienne (de la Tour), 30 Nov., 1029. Ibid. to Charles de St. Étienne, Esq., Seigneur de St. Denniscourt and Baigneux, 12 May, 1630.* (Hazard, *State Papers,* i. 204, 208.) The names of both father and son appear on the list of baronets of Nova Scotia.

[2] *Patent from Sir William Alexander to Claude and Charles de la Tour, 30 April, 1630.*

[3] Williamson, *History of Maine,* i. 246.

[4] See "Pioneers of France," ii. 258.

ments in Acadia and Canada were transferred by conquest to England. England soon gave them back by the treaty of St. Germain;[1] and Claude de Razilly, a Knight of Malta, was charged to take possession of them in the name of King Louis.[2] Full powers were given him over the restored domains, together with grants of Acadian lands for himself.[3]

Razilly reached Port Royal in August, 1632, with three hundred men, and the Scotch colony planted there by Alexander gave up the place in obedience to an order from the King of England. Unfortunately for Charles de la Tour, Razilly brought with him an officer destined to become La Tour's worst enemy. This was Charles de Menou d'Aunay Charnisay, a gentleman of birth and character, who acted as his commander's man of trust, and who, in Razilly's name, presently took possession of such other feeble English and Scotch settlements as had been begun by Alexander or the people of New England along the coasts of Nova Scotia and Maine. This placed the French Crown and the Company of New France in sole possession for a time of the region then called Acadia.

When Acadia was restored to France, La Tour's

---

[1] *Traité de St. Germain en Laye*, 29 *Mars*, 1632, *Article* 3. **For** reasons of the restitution, see "Pioneers of France," ii. 272.

[2] *Convention avec le Sieur de Razilly pour aller reçevoir la Restitution du Port Royal*, etc., 27 *Mars*, 1632. *Commission du Sieur de Razilly*, 10 *May*, 1632.

[3] *Concession de la rivière et baye Saincte Croix à M. de Razilly*, 29 *May*, 1632.

English title to his lands at Cape Sable became worthless. He hastened to Paris to fortify his position; and, suppressing his dallyings with England and Sir William Alexander, he succeeded not only in getting an extensive grant of lands at Cape Sable, but also the title of lieutenant-general for the King in Fort Loméron and its dependencies,[1] and commander at Cape Sable for the Company of New France.

Razilly, who represented the King in Acadia, died in 1635, and left his authority to D'Aunay Charnisay, his relative and second in command. D'Aunay made his headquarters at Port Royal; and nobody disputed his authority except La Tour, who pretended to be independent of him in virtue of his commission from the Crown and his grant from the Company. Hence rose dissensions that grew at last into war.

The two rivals differed widely in position and qualities. Charles de Menou, Seigneur d'Aunay Charnisay, came of an old and distinguished family of Touraine,[2] and he prided himself above all things on his character of *gentilhomme français.* Charles

---

[1] *Revocation de la Commission du Sieur Charles de Saint-Étienne, Sieur de la Tour,* 23 *Fév.,* 1641.

[2] The modern representative of this family, Comte Jules de Menou, is the author of a remarkable manuscript book, written from family papers and official documents, and entitled *L'Acadie colonisée par Charles de Menou d'Aunay Charnisay.* I have followed Comte de Menou's spelling of the name. It is often written D'Aulnay, and by New England writers D'Aulncy. The manuscript just mentioned is in my possession. Comte de Menou is also the author of a printed work called *Preuves de l'Histoire de la Maison de Menou.*

Saint-Étienne de la Tour was of less conspicuous lineage.[1] In fact, his father, Claude de la Tour, is said by his enemies to have been at one time so reduced in circumstances that he carried on the trade of a mason in Rue St. Germain at Paris. The son, however, is called *gentilhomme d'une naissance distinguée*, both in papers of the court and in a legal document drawn up in the interest of his children. As he came to Acadia when a boy he could have had little education, and both he and D'Aunay carried on trade, — which in France would have derogated from their claims as gentlemen, though in America the fur-trade was not held inconsistent with *noblesse*.

Of La Tour's little kingdom at Cape Sable, with its rocks, fogs, and breakers, its seal-haunted islets and iron-bound shores guarded by Fort Loméron, we have but dim and uncertain glimpses. After the death of Biencourt, La Tour is said to have roamed the woods with eighteen or twenty men, "living a vagabond life with no exercise of religion."[2] He himself admits that he was forced to live like the Indians, as did Biencourt before him.[3] Better times had come, and he was now commander of Fort

---

[1] The true surname of La Tour's family, which belonged to the neighborhood of Evreux, in Normandy, was Turgis. The designation of La Tour was probably derived from the name of some family estate, after a custom common in France under the old régime. The Turgis's arms were " d'or au chevron de sable, accompagné de trois palmes de même."

[2] Menou, *L'Acadie colonisée par Charles de Menou d'Aunay Charnisay.*

[3] *La Tour au Roy*, 25 *Juillet*, 1627.

Loméron, — or, as he called it, Fort La Tour, — with a few Frenchmen and abundance of Micmac Indians. His next neighbor was the adventurer Nicolas Denys, who with a view to the timber trade had settled himself with twelve men on a small river a few leagues distant. Here Razilly had once made him a visit, and was entertained under a tent of boughs with a sylvan feast of wild pigeons, brant, teal, woodcock, snipe, and larks, cheered by profuse white wine and claret, and followed by a dessert of wild raspberries.[1]

On the other side of the Acadian peninsula D'Aunay reigned at Port Royal like a feudal lord, which in fact he was. Denys, who did not like him, says that he wanted only to rule, and treated his settlers like slaves; but this, even if true at the time, did not always remain so. D'Aunay went to France in 1641, and brought out, at his own charge, twenty families to people his seigniory.[2] He had already brought out a wife, having espoused Jeanne Molin (or Motin), daughter of the Seigneur de Courcelles. What with old settlers and new, about forty families were gathered at Port Royal and on the river Annapolis, and over these D'Aunay ruled like a feudal Robinson Crusoe.[3] He gave each colonist a farm charged with a perpetual rent of one sou an arpent, or French acre. The houses of the settlers

---

[1] Denys, *Description géographique et historique.*
[2] Rameau, *Une Colonie féodale en Amérique,* i. 93 (ed. 1889).
[3] *Ibid.,* i. 96, 97.

were log cabins, and the manor-house of their lord was a larger building of the same kind. The most pressing need was of defence, and D'Aunay lost no time in repairing and reconstructing the old fort on the point between Allen's River and the Annapolis. He helped his tenants at their work; and his confessor describes him as returning to his rough manor-house on a wet day, drenched with rain and bespattered with mud, but in perfect good humor, after helping some of the inhabitants to mark out a field. The confessor declares that during the eleven months of his acquaintance with him he never heard him speak ill of anybody whatever, a statement which must probably be taken with allowance. Yet this proud scion of a noble stock seems to have given himself with good grace to the rough labors of the frontiersman; while Father Ignace, the Capuchin friar, praises him for the merit, transcendent in clerical eyes, of constant attendance at mass and frequent confession.[1]

With his neighbors, the Micmac Indians, he was on the best of terms. He supplied their needs, and they brought him the furs that enabled him in some measure to bear the heavy charges of an establishment that could not for many years be self-supporting. In a single year the Indians are said to have brought three thousand moose-skins to Port Royal, besides beaver and other valuable furs. Yet, from a commercial point of view, D'Aunay did not

---

[1] *Lettre du Père Ignace de Paris, Capucin, 6 Aoust,* 1653.

prosper. He had sold or mortgaged his estates in France, borrowed large sums, built ships, bought cannon, levied soldiers, and brought over immigrants. He is reported to have had three hundred fighting men at his principal station, and sixty cannon mounted on his ships and forts; for besides Port Royal he had two or three smaller establishments.[1]

Port Royal was a scene for an artist, with its fort; its soldiers in breastplate and morion, armed with pike, halberd, or matchlock; its manor-house of logs, and its seminary of like construction; its twelve Capuchin friars, with cowled heads, sandalled feet, and the cord of Saint Francis; the birch canoes of Micmac and Abenaki Indians lying along the strand, and their feathered and painted owners lounging about the place or dozing around their wigwam fires. It was mediævalism married to primeval savagery. The friars were supported by a fund supplied by Richelieu, and their chief business was to convert the Indians into vassals of France, the Church, and the Chevalier d'Aunay. Hard by was a wooden chapel, where the seignior knelt in dutiful observance of every rite, and where, under a stone chiselled with his ancient scutcheon, one of his children lay buried. In the fort he had not forgotten to provide a dungeon for his enemies.

<hr>

[1] *Certificat à l'égard de M. d'Aunay Charnisay, signé Michel Boudrot, Lieutenant Général en l'Acadie, et autres, anciens habitans au pays, 5 Oct., 1687. Lettre du Roy de gouverneur et lieutenant général es costes de l'Acadie pour Charles de Menou, Sieur d'Aulnay Charnisay, Février, 1647.*

The worst of these was Charles de la Tour. Before the time of Razilly and his successor D'Aunay, La Tour had felt himself the chief man in Acadia; but now he was confronted by a rival higher in rank, superior in resources and court influence, proud, ambitious, and masterful.[1] He was bitterly jealous of D'Aunay; and, to strengthen himself against so formidable a neighbor, he got from the Company of New France the grant of a tract of land at the mouth of the river St. John, where he built a fort and called it after his own name, though it was better known as Fort St. Jean.[2] Thither he removed from his old post at Cape Sable, and Fort St. Jean now became his chief station. It confronted its rival, Port Royal, across the intervening Bay of Fundy.

Now began a bitter feud between the two chiefs, each claiming lands occupied by the other. The Court interposed to settle the dispute, but in its ignorance of Acadian geography its definitions were so obscure that the question was more embroiled than ever.[3]

---

[1] Besides succeeding to the authority of Razilly, D'Aunay had bought of his heirs their land claims in Acadia. *Arrêts du Conseil, 9 Mars,* 1642.

[2] *Concession de la Compagnie de la Nouvelle France à Charles de Saint-Étienne, Sieur de la Tour, Lieutenant Général de l'Acadie, du Fort de la Tour, dans la Rivière de St. Jean, du* 15 *Jan.,* 1635, in *Mémoires des Commissaires,* v. 113 (ed. 1756, 12mo).

[3] *Louis XIII. à d'Aunay,* 10 *Fév.,* 1638. This seems to be the occasion of Charlevoix's inexact assertion that Acadia was divided into three governments, under D'Aunay, La Tour, and Nicolas Denys, respectively. The title of Denys, such as it was, had no existence till 1654.

While the domestic feud of the rivals was gathering to a head, foreign heretics had fastened their clutches on various parts of the Atlantic coast which France and the Church claimed as their own. English heretics had made lodgment in Virginia, and Dutch heretics at the mouth of the Hudson; while other sectaries of the most malignant type had kennelled among the sands and pine-trees of Plymouth; and others still, slightly different, but equally venomous, had ensconced themselves on or near the small peninsula of Shawmut, at the head of La Grande Baye, or the Bay of Massachusetts. As it was not easy to dislodge them, the French dissembled for the present, yielded to the logic of events, and bided their time. But the interlopers soon began to swarm northward and invade the soil of Acadia, sacred to God and the King. Small parties from Plymouth built trading-houses at Machias and at what is now Castine, on the Penobscot. As they were competitors in trade, no less than foes of God and King Louis, and as they were too few to resist, both La Tour and D'Aunay resolved to expel them; and in 1633 La Tour attacked the Plymouth trading-house at Machias, killed two of the five men he found there, carried off the other three, and seized all the goods.[1] Two years later D'Aunay attacked the Plymouth trading-station at Penobscot, the Pentegoet of the French, and took it in the name of King Louis. That he might not appear in the part of a pirate, he set a

---

[1] Hubbard, *History of New England*, 103.

price on the goods of the traders, and then, having seized them, gave in return his promise to pay at some convenient time if the owners would come to him for the money.

He had called on La Tour to help him in this raid against Penobscot; but La Tour, unwilling to recognize his right to command, had refused, and had hoped that D'Aunay, becoming disgusted with his Acadian venture, which promised neither honor nor profit, would give it up, go back to France, and stay there.   About the year 1638 D'Aunay did in fact go to France, but not to stay; for in due time he reappeared, bringing with him his bride, Jeanne Motin, who had had the courage to share his fortunes, and whom he now installed at Port Royal, — a sure sign, as his rival thought, that he meant to make his home there.   Disappointed and angry, La Tour now lost patience, went to Port Royal, and tried to stir D'Aunay's soldiers to mutiny; then set on his Indian friends to attack a boat in which was one of D'Aunay's soldiers and a Capuchin friar, — the soldier being killed, though the friar escaped.[1]   This was the beginning of a quarrel waged partly at Port Royal and St. Jean, and partly before the admiralty court of Guienne and the royal council, partly with bullets and cannon-shot, and partly with edicts, decrees, and *procès verbaux*.   As D'Aunay had taken a wife, so too would La Tour; and he charged his agent Desjardins to bring him one from France.

<hr>

[1] Menou, *L'Acadie colonisée par Charles de Menou d'Aunay.*

The agent acquitted himself of his delicate mission, and shipped to Acadia one Marie Jacquelin, — daughter of a barber of Mans, if we may believe the questionable evidence of his rival. Be this as it may, Marie Jacquelin proved a prodigy of mettle and energy, espoused her husband's cause with passionate vehemence, and backed his quarrel like the intrepid Amazon she was. She joined La Tour at Fort St. Jean, and proved the most strenuous of allies.

About this time, D'Aunay heard that the English of Plymouth meant to try to recover Penobscot from his hands. On this he sent nine soldiers thither, with provisions and munitions. La Tour seized them on the way, carried them to Fort St. Jean, and, according to his enemies, treated them like slaves.

D'Aunay heard nothing of this till four months after, when, being told of it by Indians, he sailed in person to Penobscot with two small vessels, reinforced the place, and was on his way back to Port Royal when La Tour met him with two armed pinnaces. A fight took place, and one of D'Aunay's vessels was dismasted. He fought so well, however, that Captain Jamin, his enemy's chief officer, was killed; and the rest, including La Tour, his new wife, and his agent Desjardins, were forced to surrender, and were carried prisoners to Port Royal.

At the request of the Capuchin friars D'Aunay set them all at liberty, after compelling La Tour to sign a promise to keep the peace in future.[1] Both parties

---

[1] Menou, *L'Acadie colonisée par Charles de Menou d'Aunay.*

now laid their cases before the French courts, and, whether from the justice of his cause or from superior influence, D'Aunay prevailed. La Tour's commission was revoked, and he was ordered to report himself in France to receive the King's commands. Trusting to his remoteness from the seat of power, and knowing that the King was often ill served and worse informed, he did not obey, but remained in Acadia exercising his authority as before. D'Aunay's father, from his house in Rue St. Germain, watched over his son's interests, and took care that La Tour's conduct should not be unknown at court. A decree was thereupon issued directing D'Aunay to seize his rival's forts in the name of the King, and place them in charge of trusty persons. The order was precise; but D'Aunay had not at the time force enough to execute it, and the frugal King sent him only six soldiers. Hence he could only show the royal order to La Tour, and offer him a passage to France in one of his vessels if he had the discretion to obey. La Tour refused, on which D'Aunay returned to France to report his rival's contumacy. At about the same time La Tour's French agent sent him a vessel with succors. The King ordered it to be seized; but the order came too late, for the vessel had already sailed from Rochelle bound to Fort St. Jean.

When D'Aunay reported the audacious conduct of his enemy, the royal council ordered that the offender should be brought prisoner to France;[1] and D'Aunay,

---

[1] *Arrêt du Conseil*, 21 *Fér.*, 1642.

as the King's lieutenant-general in Acadia, was again required to execute the decree.[1] La Tour was now in the position of a rebel, and all legality was on the side of his enemy, who represented royalty itself.

D'Aunay sailed at once for Acadia, and in August, 1642, anchored at the mouth of the St. John, before La Tour's fort, and sent three gentlemen in a boat to read to its owner the decree of the council and the order of the King. La Tour snatched the papers, crushed them between his hands, abused the envoys roundly, put them and their four sailors into prison, and kept them there above a year.[2]

His position was now desperate, for he had placed himself in open revolt. Alarmed for the consequences, he turned for help to the heretics of Boston. True Catholics detested them as foes of God and man; but La Tour was neither true Catholic nor true Protestant, and would join hands with anybody who could serve his turn. Twice before he had made advances to the Boston malignants, and sent to them first one Rochet, and then one Lestang, with proposals of trade and alliance. The envoys were treated with courtesy, but could get no promise of active aid.[3]

La Tour's agent, Desjardins, had sent him from Rochelle a ship, called the "St. Clement," manned

---

[1] Menou, *L'Acadie colonisée.*

[2] Menou, *L'Acadie colonisée.* Moreau, *Histoire de l'Acadie*, 169, 170.

[3] Hubbard, *History of New England*, chap. liv. Winthrop, ii. 42, 88.

by a hundred and forty Huguenots, laden with stores and munitions, and commanded by Captain Mouron. In due time La Tour at his Fort St. Jean heard that the "St. Clement" lay off the mouth of the river, unable to get in because D'Aunay blockaded the entrance with two armed ships and a pinnace. On this he resolved to appeal in person to the heretics. He ran the blockade in a small boat under cover of night, and, accompanied by his wife, boarded the "St. Clement" and sailed for Boston.[1]

[1] Menou, *L'Acadie colonisée.*

CHAPTER II.

1643-1645.

LA TOUR AND THE PURITANS.

La Tour at Boston: his Meeting with Winthrop. — Boston in 1643. — Training Day. — An Alarm. — La Tour's Bargain. — Doubts and Disputes. — The Allies sail. — La Tour and Endicott. — D'Aunay's Overture to the Puritans. — Marie's Mission.

On the twelfth of June, 1643, the people of the infant town of Boston saw with some misgiving a French ship entering their harbor. It chanced that the wife of Captain Edward Gibbons, with her children, was on her way in a boat to a farm belonging to her husband on an island in the harbor. One of La Tour's party, who had before made a visit to Boston, and had been the guest of Gibbons, recognized his former hostess; and he, with La Tour and a few sailors, cast off from the ship and went to speak to her in a boat that was towed at the stern of the "St. Clement." Mrs. Gibbons, seeing herself chased by a crew of outlandish foreigners, took refuge on the island where Fort Winthrop was afterwards built, which was then known as the "Governor's Garden," as it had an orchard, a vineyard, and "many other conveniences."[1] The islands in the harbor, most of which were at that time well wooded, seem to have been favorite places of cultivation, as sheep and cattle were there safe from those pests of the mainland, the wolves. La Tour, no doubt to the dismay of Mrs. Gibbons and her children, landed after them, and was presently met by the governor himself, who, with his wife, two sons, and a daughter-in-law, had apparently rowed over to their garden for the unwonted recreation of an afternoon's outing.[2] La Tour made himself known to the governor, and, after mutual civilities, told him that a ship bringing supplies from France had been stopped by his enemy, D'Aunay, and that he had come to ask for help to raise the blockade and bring her to his fort. Winthrop replied that, before answering, he must consult the magistrates. As Mrs. Gibbons and her children were anxious to get home, the governor sent them to town in his own boat, promising to follow with his party in that of La Tour, who had placed it at his disposal. Meanwhile, the people of Boston had heard of what was taking place, and were in some anxiety, since, in a truly British distrust of all Frenchmen, they feared lest their governor might be kidnapped and held for ransom. Some of them accordingly took arms, and came in three boats to the rescue. In fact, remarks Winthrop, "if La Tour had been ill-minded towards us, he had such an

---

[1] Wood, *New England's Prospect*, part i., chap. x.
[2] Winthrop, ii. 127.

La Tour and Winthrop.

opportunity as we hope neither he nor any other shall ever have the like again."[1] The castle, or fort, which was on another island hard by, was defenceless, its feeble garrison having been lately withdrawn, and its cannon might easily have been turned on the town.

Boston, now in its thirteenth year, was a straggling village, with houses principally of boards or logs, gathered about a plain wooden meeting-house which formed the heart or vital organ of the place. The rough peninsula on which the infant settlement stood was almost void of trees, and was crowned by a hill split into three summits, — whence the name of Tremont, or Trimount, still retained by a street of the present city. Beyond the narrow neck of the peninsula were several smaller villages with outlying farms; but the mainland was for the most part a primeval forest, possessed by its original owners, — wolves, bears, and rattlesnakes. These last undesirable neighbors made their favorite haunt on a high rocky hill, called Rattlesnake Hill, not far inland, where, down to the present generation, they were often seen, and where good specimens may occasionally be found to this day.[2]

Far worse than wolves or rattlesnakes were the Pequot Indians, — a warlike race who had boasted

---

[1] Winthrop, ii. 127.

[2] Blue Hill in Milton. "Up into the country is a high hill which is called rattlesnake hill, where there is great store of these poysonous creatures." (Wood, *New England's Prospect.*) "They [the wolves] be the greatest inconveniency the country hath." (*Ibid.*)

that they would wipe the whites from the face of the earth, but who, by hard marching and fighting, had lately been brought to reason.

Worse than wolves, rattlesnakes, and Indians together were the theological quarrels that threatened to kill the colony in its infancy. Children are taught that the Puritans came to New England in search of religious liberty. The liberty they sought was for themselves alone. It was the liberty to worship in their own way, and to prevent all others from doing the like. They imagined that they held a monopoly of religious truth, and were bound in conscience to defend it against all comers. Their mission was to build up a western Canaan, ruled by the law of God; to keep it pure from error, and, if need were, purge it of heresy by persecution, — to which ends they set up one of the most detestable theocracies on record. Church and State were joined in one. Church-members alone had the right to vote. There was no choice but to remain politically a cipher, or embrace, or pretend to embrace, the extremest dogmas of Calvin. Never was such a premium offered to cant and hypocrisy; yet in the early days hypocrisy was rare, so intense and pervading was the faith of the founders of New England.

It was in the churches themselves, the appointed sentinels and defenders of orthodoxy, that heresy lifted its head and threatened the State with disruption. Where minds different in complexion and character were continually busied with subtle questions of theology, unity of opinion could not be long maintained; and innovation found a champion in one Mrs. Hutchinson, a woman of great controversial ability and inexhaustible fluency of tongue. Persons of a mystical turn of mind, or a natural inclination to contrariety, were drawn to her preachings; and the church of Boston, with three or four exceptions, went over to her in a body. "Sanctification," "justification," "revelations," the "covenant of grace," and the "covenant of works," mixed in furious battle with all the subtleties, sophistries, and venom of theological war; while the ghastly spectre of Antinomianism hovered over the fray, carrying terror to the souls of the faithful. The embers of the strife still burned hot when La Tour appeared to bring another firebrand.

As a "papist" or "idolater," though a mild one, he was sorely prejudiced in Puritan eyes, while his plundering of the Plymouth trading-house some years before, and killing two of its five tenants, did not tend to produce impressions in his favor; but it being explained that all five were drunk, and had begun the fray by firing on the French, the ire against him cooled a little. Landing with Winthrop, he was received under the hospitable roof of Captain Gibbons, whose wife had recovered from her fright at his approach. He went to church on Sunday, and the gravity of his demeanor gave great satisfaction, — a solemn carriage being of itself a virtue in Puritan eyes. Hence he was well treated, and his men were permitted to come ashore daily in small numbers.

The stated training-day of the Boston militia fell in the next week, and La Tour asked leave to exercise his soldiers with the rest. This was granted; and, escorted by the Boston trained band, about forty of them marched to the muster-field, which was probably the Common, — a large tract of pasture-land in which was a marshy pool, the former home of a colony of frogs, perhaps not quite exterminated by the sticks and stones of Puritan boys. This pool, cleaned, paved, and curbed with granite, preserves to this day the memory of its ancient inhabitants, and is still the Frog Pond, though bereft of frogs.

The Boston trained band, in steel caps and buff coats, went through its exercise; and the visitors, we are told, expressed high approval. When the drill was finished, the Boston officers invited La Tour's officers to dine, while his rank and file were entertained in like manner by the Puritan soldiers. There were more exercises in the afternoon, and this time it was the turn of the French, who, says Winthrop, "were very expert in all their postures and motions." A certain "judicious minister," in dread of popish conspiracies, was troubled in spirit at this martial display, and prophesied that "store of blood would be spilled in Boston," — a prediction that was not fulfilled, although an incident took place which startled some of the spectators. The Frenchmen suddenly made a sham charge, sword in hand, which the women took for a real one. The alarm was soon over; and as this demonstration ended the performance, La Tour asked leave of the governor to withdraw his men to their ship. The leave being granted, they fired a salute and marched to the wharf where their boat lay, escorted, as before, by the Boston trained band. During the whole of La Tour's visit he and Winthrop went amicably to church together every Sunday, — the governor being attended, on these and all other occasions while the strangers were in town, by a guard of honor of musketeers and halberd men. La Tour and his chief officers had their lodging and meals in the houses of the principal townsmen, and all seemed harmony and good-will.

La Tour, meanwhile, had laid his request before the magistrates, and produced among other papers the commission to Mouron, captain of his ship, dated in the last April, and signed and sealed by the Vice-Admiral of France, authorizing Mouron to bring supplies to La Tour, whom the paper styled Lieutenant-General for the King in Acadia; La Tour also showed a letter, genuine or forged, from the agent of the Company of New France, addressed to him as lieutenant-general, and warning him to beware of D'Aunay: from all which the Boston magistrates inferred that their petitioner was on good terms with the French government,[1] notwithstanding a letter

---

[1] Count Jules de Menou, in his remarkable manuscript book now before me, expresses his belief that the commission of the Vice-Admiral was genuine, but that the letter of the agent of the Company was a fabrication.

sent them by D'Aunay the year before, assuring them that La Tour was a proclaimed rebel, which in fact he was. Throughout this affair one is perplexed by the French official papers, whose entanglements and contradictions in regard to the Acadian rivals are past unravelling.

La Tour asked only for such help as would enable him to bring his own ship to his own fort; and, as his papers seemed to prove that he was a recognized officer of his King, Winthrop and the magistrates thought that they might permit him to hire such ships and men as were disposed to join him.

La Tour had tried to pass himself as a Protestant; but his professions were distrusted, notwithstanding the patience with which he had listened to the long-winded sermons of the Reverend John Cotton. As to his wife, however, there appears to have been but one opinion. She was approved as a sound Protestant "of excellent virtues;" and her denunciations of D'Aunay no doubt fortified the prejudice which was already strong against him for his seizure of the Plymouth trading-house at Penobscot, and for his aggressive and masterful character, which made him an inconvenient neighbor.

With the permission of the governor and the approval of most of the magistrates, La Tour now made a bargain with his host, Captain Gibbons, and a merchant named Thomas Hawkins. They agreed to furnish him with four vessels; to arm each of these with from four to fourteen small cannon, and man them with a certain number of sailors, La Tour himself completing the crews with Englishmen hired at his own charge. Hawkins was to command the whole. The four vessels were to escort La Tour and his ship, the "St. Clement," to the mouth of the St. John, in spite of D'Aunay and all other opponents. The agreement ran for two months; and La Tour was to pay £250 sterling a month for the use of the four ships, and mortgage to Gibbons and Hawkins his fort and all his Acadian property as security. Winthrop would give no commissions to Hawkins or any others engaged in the expedition, and they were all forbidden to fight except in self-defence; but the agreement contained the significant clause that all plunder was to be equally divided according to rule in such enterprises. Hence it seems clear that the contractors had an eye to booty; yet no means were used to hold them to their good behavior.

Now rose a brisk dispute, and the conduct of Winthrop was sharply criticised. Letters poured in upon him concerning "great dangers," "sin upon the conscience," and the like. He himself was clearly in doubt as to the course he was taking, and he soon called another meeting of magistrates, in which the inevitable clergy were invited to join; and they all fell to discussing the matter anew. As every man of them had studied the Bible daily from childhood up, texts were the chief weapons of the debate. Doubts were advanced as to whether Christians could lawfully help idolaters, and Jehoshaphat, Ahab, and

Josias were brought forward as cases in point. Then Solomon was cited to the effect that "he that meddleth with the strife that belongs not to him takes a dog by the ear;" to which it was answered that the quarrel did belong to us, seeing that Providence now offered us the means to weaken our enemy, D'Aunay, without much expense or trouble to ourselves. Besides, we ought to help a neighbor in distress, seeing that Joshua helped the Gibeonites, and Jehoshaphat helped Jehoram against Moab with the approval of Elisha. The opposing party argued that "by aiding papists we advance and strengthen popery;" to which it was replied that the opposite effect might follow, since the grateful papist, touched by our charity, might be won to the true faith and turned from his idols.

Then the debate continued on the more worldly grounds of expediency and statecraft, and at last Winthrop's action was approved by the majority. Still, there were many doubters, and the governor was severely blamed. John Endicott wrote to him that La Tour was not to be trusted, and that he and D'Aunay had better be left to fight it out between them, since if we help the former to put down his enemy he will be a bad neighbor to us.

Presently came a joint letter from several chief men of the colony,— Saltonstall, Bradstreet, Nathaniel Ward, John Norton, and others, — saying in substance: We fear international law has been ill observed; the merits of the case are not clear; we

are not called upon in charity to help **La Tour** (see
2 Chronicles xix. 2, and Proverbs xxvi. 17); this
quarrel is for England and France, and not for us; if
D'Aunay is not completely put down, we shall have
endless trouble; and "he that loses his life in an
unnecessary quarrel dies the devil's martyr."

This letter, known as the "Ipswich letter," touched
Winthrop to the quick.   He thought that it trenched
on his official dignity, and the asperity of his answer
betrays his sensitiveness.   He calls the remonstrance
"an act of an exorbitant nature," and says that it
"blows a trumpet to division and dissension."   "If
my neighbor is in trouble," he goes on to say, "I
must help him."   He maintains that "there is great
difference between giving permission to hire to guard
or transport, and giving commission to fight," and he
adds the usual Bible text, "The fear of man bringeth
a snare; but whoso putteth his trust in the Lord
shall be safe."[1]

In spite of Winthrop's reply, the Ipswich letter
had great effect; and he and the Boston magistrates
were much blamed, especially in the country towns.
The governor was too candid not to admit that he
had been in fault, though he limits his self-accusation
to three points: first, that he had given La Tour an
answer too hastily; next, that he had not sufficiently

---

[1] Winthrop's *Answer to the Ipswich Letter about La Tour* (no date),
in *Hutchinson Papers*, 122.   Bradstreet writes to him on the 21st of
June, "Our ayding of Latour was very grievous to many hereabouts,
the design being feared to be unwarrantable by dyvers."

consulted the elders or ministers; and lastly, that he had not opened the discussion with prayer.

The upshot was that La Tour and his allies sailed on the fourteenth of July. D'Aunay's three vessels fled before them to Port Royal. La Tour tried to persuade his Puritan friends to join him in an attack; but Hawkins, the English commander, would give no order to that effect, on which about thirty of the Boston men volunteered for the adventure. D'Aunay's followers had ensconced themselves in a fortified mill, whence they were driven with some loss. After burning the mill and robbing a pinnace loaded with furs, the Puritans returned home, having broken their orders and compromised their colony.

In the next summer, La Tour, expecting a serious attack from D'Aunay, — who had lately been to France, and was said to be on his way back with large reinforcements, — turned again to Massachusetts for help. The governor this time was John Endicott, of Salem. To Salem the suppliant repaired; and as Endicott spoke French, the conference was easy. The rugged bigot had before expressed his disapproval of "having anything to do with these idolatrous French;" but, according to Hubbard, he was so moved with compassion at the woful tale of his visitor that he called a meeting of magistrates and ministers to consider if anything could be done for him. The magistrates had by this time learned caution, and the meeting would do nothing but write a letter to D'Aunay, demanding satisfaction for his seizure of Penobscot and other aggressions, and declaring that the men who escorted La Tour to his fort in the last summer had no commission from Massachusetts, yet that if they had wronged him he should have justice, though if he seized any New England trading vessels they would hold him answerable. In short, La Tour's petition was not granted.

D'Aunay, when in France, had pursued his litigation against his rival, and the royal council had ordered that the contumacious La Tour should be seized, his goods confiscated, and he himself brought home a prisoner; which decree D'Aunay was empowered to execute, if he could. He had returned to Acadia the accredited agent of the royal will. It was reported at Boston that a Biscayan pirate had sunk his ship on the way; but the wish was father to the thought, and the report proved false. D'Aunay arrived safely, and was justly incensed at the support given by the Puritans in the last year to his enemy. But he too had strong reasons for wishing to be on good terms with his heretic neighbors. King Louis, moreover, had charged him not to offend them, since, when they helped La Tour, they had done so in the belief that he was commissioned as lieutenant-general for the King, and therefore they should be held blameless.

Hence D'Aunay made overtures of peace and friendship to the Boston Puritans. Early in October,

1644, they were visited by one Monsieur Marie, "supposed," says the chronicle, "to be a friar, but habited like a gentleman." He was probably one of the Capuchins who formed an important part of D'Aunay's establishment at Port Royal. The governor and magistrates received him with due consideration; and along with credentials from D'Aunay he showed them papers under the great seal of France, wherein the decree of the royal council was set forth in full, La Tour condemned as a rebel and traitor, and orders given to arrest both him and his wife. Henceforth there was no room to doubt which of the rival chiefs had the King and the law on his side. The envoy, while complaining of the aid given to La Tour, offered terms of peace to the governor and magistrates, — who replied to his complaints with their usual subterfuge, that they had given no commission to those who had aided La Tour, declaring at the same time that they could make no treaty without the concurrence of the commissioners of the United Colonies. They then desired Marie to set down his proposals in writing; on which he went to the house of one Mr. Fowle, where he lodged, and drew up in French his plan for a treaty, adding the proposal that the Bostonians should join D'Aunay against La Tour. Then he came back to the place of meeting and discussed the subject for half a day, — sometimes in Latin with the magistrates, and sometimes in French with the governor, that old soldier being probably ill versed in the classic

tongues. In vain they all urged that D'Aunay
should come to terms with La Tour. Marie replied,
that if La Tour would give himself up his life would
be spared, but that if he were caught he would lose
his head as a traitor; adding that his wife was worse
than he, being the mainspring of his rebellion.
Endicott and the magistrates refused active alliance;
but the talk ended in a provisional treaty of peace,
duly drawn up in Latin, Marie keeping one copy and
the governor the other. The agreement needed rati-
fication by the commissioners of the United Colonies
on one part, and by D'Aunay on the other. What
is most curious in the affair is the attitude of Massachusetts, which from first to last figures as an independent State, with no reference to the King under
whose charter it was building up its theocratic
republic, and consulting none but the infant confederacy of the New England colonies, of which it was
itself the head. As the commissioners of the confederacy were not then in session, Endicott and the
magistrates took the matter provisionally into their
own hands.

Marie had made good despatch, for he reached
Boston on a Friday and left it on the next Tuesday,
having finished his business in about three days, or
rather two, as one of the three was "the Sabbath."
He expressed surprise and gratification at the attention and courtesy with which he had been treated.
His hosts supplied him with horses, and some of
them accompanied him to Salem, where he had left

his vessel, and whence he sailed for Port Royal, well pleased.

Just before he came to Boston, that town had received a visit from Madame de la Tour, who, soon after her husband's successful negotiation with Winthrop in the past year, had sailed for France in the ship "St. Clement." She had labored strenuously in La Tour's cause; but the influence of D'Aunay's partisans was far too strong, and, being charged with complicity in her husband's misconduct, she was forbidden to leave France on pain of death. She set the royal command at naught, escaped to England, took passage in a ship bound for America, and after long delay landed at Boston. The English shipmaster had bargained to carry her to her husband at Fort St. Jean; but he broke his bond, and was sentenced by the Massachusetts courts to pay her £2,000 as damages. She was permitted to hire three armed vessels then lying in the harbor, to convey her to Fort St. Jean, where she arrived safely and rejoined La Tour.

Meanwhile, D'Aunay was hovering off the coast, armed with the final and conclusive decree of the royal council, which placed both husband and wife under the ban, and enjoined him to execute its sentence. But a resort to force was costly and of doubtful result, and D'Aunay resolved again to try the effect of persuasion. Approaching the mouth of the St. John, he sent to the fort two boats, commanded by his lieutenant, who carried letters from his chief, promising to La Tour's men pardon for their past conduct and payment of all wages due them if they would return to their duty. An adherent of D'Aunay declares that they received these advances with insults and curses. It was a little before this time that Madame de la Tour arrived from Boston. The same writer says that she fell into a transport of fury, "behaved like one possessed with a devil," and heaped contempt on the Catholic faith in the presence of her husband, who approved everything she did; and he further affirms that she so berated and reviled the Récollet friars in the fort that they refused to stay, and set out for Port Royal in the depth of winter, taking with them eight soldiers of the fort who were too good Catholics to remain in such a nest of heresy and rebellion. They were permitted to go, and were provided with an old pinnace and two barrels of Indian corn, with which, unfortunately for La Tour, they safely reached their destination.

On her arrival from Boston, Madame de la Tour had given her husband a piece of politic advice. Her enemies say that she had some time before renounced her faith to gain the favor of the Puritans; but there is reason to believe that she had been a Huguenot from the first. She now advised La Tour to go to Boston, declare himself a Protestant, ask for a minister to preach to his men, and promise that if the Bostonians would help him to master D'Aunay and conquer Acadia, he would share the conquest with them. La Tour admired the sagacious counsels of his wife, and sailed for Boston to put them in practice just before the friars and the eight deserters sailed for Port Royal, thus leaving their departure unopposed.

At Port Royal both friars and deserters found a warm welcome. D'Aunay paid the eight soldiers their long arrears of wages, and lodged the friars in the seminary with his Capuchins. Then he questioned them, and was well rewarded. They told him that La Tour had gone to Boston, leaving his wife with only forty-five men to defend the fort. Here was a golden opportunity. D'Aunay called his officers to council. All were of one mind. He mustered every man about Port Royal and embarked them in the armed ship of three hundred tons that had brought him from France; he then crossed the Bay of Fundy with all his force, anchored in a small harbor a league from Fort St. Jean, and sent the Récollet Père André to try to seduce more of La Tour's men, — an attempt which proved a failure. D'Aunay lay two months at his anchorage, during which time another ship and a pinnace joined him from Port Royal. Then he resolved to make an attack. Meanwhile, La Tour had persuaded a Boston merchant to send one Grafton to Fort St. Jean in a small vessel loaded with provisions, and bringing also a letter to Madame de la Tour containing a promise from her husband that he would join her in a month. When the Boston vessel appeared at the mouth of the St. John, D'Aunay seized it, placed Grafton and the few men with him on an island, and finally supplied them with a leaky sail-boat to make their way home as they best could.

D'Aunay now landed two cannon to batter Fort St. Jean on the land side; and on the seventeenth of April, having brought his largest ship within pistol-shot of the water rampart, he summoned the garrison to surrender.[1] They answered with a volley of cannon-shot, then hung out a red flag, and, according to D'Aunay's reporter, shouted "a thousand insults and blasphemies"![2] Towards evening a breach was made in the wall, and D'Aunay ordered a general assault. Animated by their intrepid mistress, the defenders fought with desperation, and killed or wounded many of the assailants, not without severe loss on their own side. Numbers prevailed at last;

---

[1] The site of Fort St. Jean, or Fort La Tour, has been matter of question. At Carleton, opposite the present city of St. John, are the remains of an earthen fort, by some supposed to be that of La Tour, but which is no doubt of later date, as the place was occupied by a succession of forts down to the Seven Years' War. On the other hand, it has been assumed that Fort La Tour was at Jemsec, which is about seventy miles up the river. Now, in the second mortgage deed of Fort La Tour to Major Gibbons, May 10, 1645, the fort is described as "*situé près de l'embouchure de la rivière de St. Jean.*" Moreover, there is a cataract just above the mouth of the river, which, though submerged at high tide, cannot be passed by heavy ships at any time; and as D'Aunay brought his largest ship of war to within pistol-shot of the fort, it must have been below the cataract. Mr. W. F. Ganong, after careful examination, is convinced that Fort La Tour was at Portland Point, on the east side of the St. John, at its mouth. See his paper on the subject in *Transactions of the Royal Society of Canada,* 1891.

[2] *Procès Verbal d'André Certain,* in Appendix A.

all resistance was overcome; the survivors of the garrison were made prisoners, and the fort was pillaged. Madame de la Tour, her maid, and another woman, who were all of their sex in the place, were among the captives, also Madame de la Tour's son, a mere child. D'Aunay pardoned some of his prisoners, but hanged the greater part, "to serve as an example to posterity," says his reporter. Nicolas Denys declares that he compelled Madame de la Tour to witness the execution with a halter about her neck; but the more trustworthy accounts say nothing of this alleged outrage. On the next day, the eighteenth of April, the bodies of the dead were decently buried, an inventory was made of the contents of the fort, and D'Aunay set his men to repair it for his own use. These labors occupied three weeks or more, during a part of which Madame de la Tour was left at liberty, till, being detected in an attempt to correspond with her husband by means of an Indian, she was put into confinement; on which, according to D'Aunay's reporter, "she fell ill with spite and rage," and died within three weeks, — after, as he tells us, renouncing her heresy in the chapel of the fort.

CHAPTER III.

1645–1710.

THE VICTOR VANQUISHED.

D'Aunay's Envoys to the Puritans: their Reception at Boston. — Winthrop and his "Papist" Guests. — Reconciliation. — Treaty. — Behavior of La Tour. — Royal Favors to D'Aunay: his Hopes; his Death; his Character. — Conduct of the Court towards him. — Intrigues of La Tour. — Madame D'Aunay. — La Tour marries her. — Children of D'Aunay. — Descendants of La Tour.

HAVING triumphed over his rival, D'Aunay was left free to settle his accounts with the Massachusetts Puritans, who had offended him anew by sending provisions to Fort St. Jean, having always insisted that they were free to trade with either party. They, on their side, were no less indignant with him for his seizure of Grafton's vessel and harsh treatment of him and his men.

After some preliminary negotiation and some rather sharp correspondence, D'Aunay, in September, 1646, sent a pinnace to Boston, bearing his former envoy, Marie, accompanied by his own secretary and by one Monsieur Louis.

It was Sunday, the Puritan Sabbath, when the three envoys arrived; and the pious inhabitants were preparing for the afternoon sermon. Marie and his two colleagues were met at the wharf by two militia officers, and conducted through the silent and dreary streets to the house of Captain, now Major, Gibbons, who seems to have taken upon himself in an especial manner the office of entertaining strangers of consequence.

All was done with much civility, but no ceremony; for the Lord's Day must be kept inviolate. Winthrop, who had again been chosen governor, now sent an officer, with a guard of musketeers, to invite the envoys to his own house. Here he regaled them with wine and sweetmeats, and then informed them of "our manner that all men either come to our publick meetings, or keep themselves quiet in their houses."[1] He then laid before them such books in Latin and French as he had, and told them that they were free to walk in his garden. Though the diversion offered was no doubt of the dullest, — since the literary resources of the colony then included little besides arid theology, and the walk in the garden promised but moderate delights among the bitter pot-herbs provided against days of fasting, — the victims resigned themselves with good grace, and, as the governor tells us, "gave no offence." Sunset came at last, and set the captives free.

On Monday both sides fell to business. The envoys showed their credentials; but, as the commissioners of the United Colonies were not yet in

____
[1] Winthrop, ii. 273, 275.

session, nothing conclusive could be done till Tuesday. Then, all being assembled, each party made its complaints of the conduct of the other, and a long discussion followed. Meals were provided for the three visitors at the "ordinary," or inn, where the magistrates dined during the sessions of the General Court. The governor, as their host, always sat with them at the board, and strained his Latin to do honor to his guests. They, on their part, that courtesies should be evenly divided, went every morning at eight o'clock to the governor's house, whence he accompanied them to the place of meeting; and at night he, or some of the commissioners in his stead, attended them to their lodging at the house of Major Gibbons.

Serious questions were raised on both sides; but as both wanted peace, explanations were mutually made and accepted. The chief difficulty lay in the undeniable fact, that, in escorting La Tour to his fort in 1643, the Massachusetts volunteers had chased D'Aunay to Port Royal, killed some of his men, burned his mill, and robbed his pinnace, for which wrongs the envoys demanded heavy damages. It was true that the governor and magistrates had forbidden acts of aggression on the part of the volunteers; but on the other hand they had had reason to believe that their prohibition would be disregarded, and had taken no measures to enforce it. The envoys clearly had good ground of complaint; and here, says Winthrop, "they did stick two days." At last they yielded so far as to declare that what D'Aunay wanted was not so much compensation in money as satisfaction to his honor by an acknowledgment of their fault on the part of the Massachusetts authorities; and they further declared that he would accept a moderate present in token of such acknowledgment. The difficulty now was to find such a present. The representatives of Massachusetts presently bethought themselves of a "very fair new sedan" which the Viceroy of Mexico had sent to his sister, and which had been captured in the West Indies by one Captain Cromwell, a corsair, who gave it to "our governor." Winthrop, to whom it was entirely useless, gladly parted with it in such a cause; and the sedan, being graciously accepted, ended the discussion.[1] The treaty was signed in duplicate by the commissioners of the United Colonies and the envoys of D'Aunay, and peace was at last concluded.

The conference had been conducted with much courtesy on both sides. One small cloud appeared, but soon passed away. The French envoys displayed the *fleur-de-lys* at the masthead of their pinnace as she lay in the harbor. The townsmen were incensed; and Monsieur Marie was told that to fly foreign colors in Boston harbor was not according to custom. He insisted for a time, but at length ordered the offending flag to be lowered.

On the twenty-eighth of September the envoys bade

______

[1] Winthrop, ii. 274.

farewell to Winthrop, who had accompanied them to their pinnace with a guard of honor. Five cannon saluted them from Boston, five from "the Castle," and three from Charlestown. A supply of mutton and a keg of sherry were sent on board their vessel; and then, after firing an answering salute from their swivels, they stood down the bay till their sails disappeared among the islands.

La Tour had now no more to hope from his late supporters. He had lost his fort, and, what was worse, he had lost his indomitable wife. Throughout the winter that followed his disaster he had been entertained by Samuel Maverick, at his house on Noddle's Island. In the spring he begged hard for further help; and, as he begged in vain, he sailed for Newfoundland to make the same petition to Sir David Kirke, who then governed that island. Kirke refused, but lent him a pinnace and sent him back to Boston. Here some merchants had the good nature or folly to intrust him with goods for the Indian trade, to the amount of four hundred pounds. Thus equipped, he sailed for Acadia in Kirke's pinnace, manned with his own followers and five New England men. On reaching Cape Sable, he conspired with the master of the pinnace and his own men to seize the vessel and set the New England sailors ashore, — which was done, La Tour, it is said, shooting one of them in the face with a pistol. It was winter, and the outcasts roamed along the shore for a fortnight, half frozen and half starved, till they were met by Micmac Indians, who gave them food and a boat, — in which, by rare good fortune, they reached Boston, where their story convinced the most infatuated that they had harbored a knave. "Whereby," solemnly observes the pious but much mortified Winthrop, who had been La Tour's best friend, "it appeared (as the Scripture saith) that there is no confidence in an unfaithful or carnal man."[1]

When the capture of Fort St. Jean was known at court the young King was well pleased, and promised to send D'Aunay the gift of a ship;[2] but he forgot to keep his word, and requited his faithful subject with the less costly reward of praises and honors. After a preamble reciting his merits, and especially his "care, courage, and valor" in "taking, by our express order, and reducing again under our authority the fort on the St. John which La Tour had rebelliously occupied with the aid of foreign sectaries," the King confirms D'Aunay's authority in Acadia, and extends it on paper from the St. Lawrence to Virginia, — empowering him to keep for himself such parts of this broad domain as he might want, and grant out the rest to others, who were to hold of him as vassals. He could build forts and cities, at his own expense; command by land and sea; make war or peace within the limits of his grant; appoint officers of government, justice, and police; and, in short, exercise sovereign power, with the simple

---

[1] Winthrop, ii. 266.

[2] *Le Roy à M. d'Aunay Charnisay*, 28 *Sept.*, 1645.

reservation of homage to the King, and a tenth part
of all gold, silver, and copper to the royal treasury.
A full monopoly of the fur-trade throughout his
dominion was conferred on him; and any infringe-
ment of it was to be punished by confiscation of ships
and goods, and thirty thousand livres of damages.
On his part he was enjoined to "establish the name,
power, and authority of the King; subject the nations
to his rule, and teach them the knowledge of the
true God and the light of the Christian faith."[1]
Acadia, in short, was made an hereditary fief; and
D'Aunay and his heirs became lords of a domain as
large as a European kingdom.

D'Aunay had spent his substance in the task of
civilizing a wilderness.[2] The King had not helped
him; and though he belonged to a caste which held
commerce in contempt, he must be a fur-trader or a
bankrupt. La Tour's Fort St. Jean was a better
trading-station than Port Royal, and it had wofully
abridged D'Aunay's profits. Hence an ignoble com-
petition in beaver-skins had greatly embittered their
quarrel. All this was over; Fort St. Jean, the best
trading-stand in Acadia, was now in its conqueror's
hands; and his monopoly was no longer a mere name,
but a reality.

[1] *Lettre du Roy de Gouverneur et Lieutenant Général es costes de
l'Acadie pour Charles de Menou d'Aulnay Charnisay, Février, 1647.
Lettre de la Reyne régente au même, 13 Avril, 1647.*

[2] His heirs estimated his outlays for the colony at 800,000 livres.
*Mémoire des filles du feu Seigneur d'Aulnay Charnisay, 1686. Placet
de Joseph de Menou d'Aunay Charnisay, fils ainé du feu Charles de
Menou d'Aunay Charnisay, 1658.*

Everything promised a thriving trade and a growing colony, when the scene was suddenly changed. On the twenty-fourth of May, 1650, a dark and stormy day, D'Aunay and his valet were in a birch canoe in the basin of Port Royal, not far from the mouth of the Annapolis. Perhaps neither master nor man was skilled in the management of the treacherous craft that bore them. The canoe overset. D'Aunay and the valet clung to it and got astride of it, one at each end. There they sat, sunk to the shoulders, the canoe though under water having buoyancy enough to keep them from sinking farther. So they remained an hour and a half; and at the end of that time D'Aunay was dead, not from drowning but from cold, for the water still retained the chill of winter. The valet remained alive; and in this condition they were found by Indians and brought to the north shore of the Annapolis, whither Father Ignace, the Superior of the Capuchins, went to find the body of his patron, brought it to the fort, and buried it in the chapel, in presence of his wife and all the soldiers and inhabitants.[1]

The Father Superior highly praises the dead chief, and is astonished that the earth does not gape and devour the slanderers who say that he died in desperation, as one abandoned of God. He admits that in former times cavillers might have found wherewith to accuse him, but declares that before his death he had amended all his faults. This is the testimony

---

[1] *Lettre du Rev. P. Ignace, Capucin, 6 Aoust, 1653.*

of a Capuchin, whose fraternity he had always favored. The Récollets, on the other hand, whose patron was La Tour, complained that D'Aunay had ill-used them, and demanded redress.[1]   He seems to have been a favorable example of his class; loyal to his faith and his King, tempering pride with courtesy, and generally true to his cherished ideal of the *gentilhomme Français*. In his qualities, as in his birth, he was far above his rival; and his death was the ruin of the only French colony in Acadia that deserved the name.

At the news of his enemy's fate a new hope possessed La Tour. He still had agents in France interested to serve him; while the father of D'Aunay, who acted as his attorney, was feeble with age, and his children were too young to defend their interests.

There is an extraordinary document bearing date February, 1651, or less than a year after D'Aunay's death. It is a complete reversal of the decree of 1647 in his favor. La Tour suddenly appears as the favorite of royalty, and all the graces before lavished on his enemy are now heaped upon him. The lately proscribed "rebel and traitor" is confirmed as governor and lieutenant-general in New France. His services to God and the King are rehearsed "as of our certain knowledge," and he is praised with the same emphasis used towards D'Aunay in the decree

---

[1] Papers to this effect are among the many pieces cited in the *Arrêt du Conseil d'État à l'égard du Seigneur de la Tour, 6 Mars,* 1644.

of 1647, and almost in the same words. The paper goes on to say that he, La Tour, would have converted the Indians and conquered Acadia for the King if D'Aunay had not prevented him.[1]

Unless this document is a fabrication in the interest of La Tour, as there is some reason to believe, it suggests strange reflections on colonial administration during the minority of Louis XIV. Genuine or not, La Tour profited by it, and after a visit to France, which proved a successful and fruitful one, he returned to Acadia with revived hopes. The widow of D'Aunay had eight children, all minors; and their grandfather, the octogenarian René de Menou, had been appointed their guardian. He sent an incompetent and faithless person to Port Royal to fulfil the wardship of which he was no longer capable.

The unfortunate widow and her children needed better help. D'Aunay had employed as his agent one Le Borgne, a merchant of Rochelle, who now succeeded in getting the old man under his influence, and induced him to sign an acknowledgment, said to be false, that D'Aunay's heirs owed him 260,000

---

[1] *Confirmation de Gouverneur et Lieutenant Général pour le Roy de la Nouvelle France, à la Coste de l'Acadie, au Sr. Charles de St. Étienne, Chevalier de la Tour,* 27 *Fév.,* 1651. A copy of this strange paper is before me. Comte de Menou, and after him, his follower Moreau, doubt the genuineness of the document, which, however, is alluded to without suspicion in the legal paper entitled *Mémoire* in re *Charles de St. Étienne, Seigneur de la Tour* (fils) *et ses frères et sœurs,* 1700. This *Mémoire* is in the interest of the heirs of La Tour, and is to be judged accordingly.

livres.[1] Le Borgne next came to Port Royal to push
his schemes; and here he inveigled or frightened the
widow into signing a paper to the effect that she and
her children owed him 205,286 livres. It was fortunate for his unscrupulous plans that he had to do
with the soft and tractable Madame d'Aunay, and
not with the high-spirited and intelligent Amazon
Madame La Tour. Le Borgne now seized on Port
Royal as security for the alleged debts; while La
Tour on his return from his visit to France induced
the perplexed and helpless widow to restore to him
Fort St. Jean, conquered by her late husband.
Madame d'Aunay, beset with insidious enemies, saw
herself and her children in danger of total ruin. She
applied to the Duc de Vendôme, grand-master, chief,
and superintendent of navigation, and offered to
share all her Acadian claims with him if he would
help her in her distress; but, from the first, Vendôme
looked more to his own interests than to hers. La
Tour was not satisfied with her concessions to him,
and perplexing questions rose between them touching
land claims and the fur-trade. To end these troubles
she took a desperate step, and on the twenty-fourth
of February, 1653, married her tormentor, the foe of
her late husband, who had now been dead not quite
three years.[2] Her chief thought seems to have been
for her children, whose rights are guarded, though

---

[1] *Mémoire* in re *Charles de St. Étienne* (fils de la Tour), etc.

[2] Rameau, i. 120. Menou and Moreau think that this marriage
took place two or three years later.

to little purpose, in the marriage contract. She and La Tour took up their abode at Fort St. Jean. Of the children of her first marriage four were boys and four were girls. They were ruined at last by the harpies leagued to plunder them, and sought refuge in France, where the boys were all killed in the wars of Louis XIV., and at least three of the girls became nuns.[1]

Now follow complicated disputes, without dignity or interest, and turning chiefly on the fur-trade. Le Borgne and his son, in virtue of their claims on the estate of D'Aunay, which were sustained by the French courts, got a lion's share of Acadia; a part fell also to La Tour and his children by his new wife, while Nicolas Denys kept a feeble hold on the shore of the Gulf of St. Lawrence as far north as Cape Rosiers.

War again broke out between France and England, and in 1654 Major Robert Sedgwick of Charlestown, Massachusetts, who had served in the civil war as a major-general of Cromwell, led a small New England force to Acadia under a commission from the Protector, captured Fort St. Jean, Port Royal, and all the other French stations, and conquered the colony for England. It was restored to France by the treaty of Breda, and captured again in 1690 by Sir William Phips. The treaty of Ryswick again restored it to France, till, in 1710, it was finally seized for England by General Nicholson.

---

[1] Menou, *L'Acadie colonisée.*

When, after Sedgwick's expedition, the English
were in possession of Acadia, La Tour, not for the
first time, tried to fortify his claims by a British title,
and, jointly with Thomas Temple and William
Crown, obtained a grant of the colony from Cromwell,
— though he soon after sold his share to his
copartner, Temple.   He seems to have died in 1666.[1]
Descendants of his were living in Acadia in 1830,
and some may probably still be found there.   As for
D'Aunay, no trace of his blood is left in the land
where he gave wealth and life for France and the
Church.

[1] Rameau, i. 122.

SECTION SECOND.

CANADA A MISSION.

CHAPTER IV.

1653–1658.

THE JESUITS AT ONONDAGA.

The Iroquois War. — Father Poncet: his Adventures. — Jesuit Boldness. — Le Moyne's Mission. — Chaumonot and Dablon. — Iroquois Ferocity. — The Mohawk Kidnappers. — Critical Position. — The Colony of Onondaga. — Speech of Chaumonot. — Omens of Destruction. — Device of the Jesuits. — The Medicine Feast. — The Escape.

In the summer of 1653 all Canada turned to fasting and penance, processions, vows, and supplications. The saints and the Virgin were beset with unceasing prayer. The wretched little colony was like some puny garrison, starving and sick, compassed with inveterate foes, supplies cut off, and succor hopeless.

At Montreal — the advance guard of the settlements, a sort of Castle Dangerous, held by about fifty Frenchmen, and said by a pious writer of the day to exist only by a continuous miracle — some two hundred Iroquois fell upon twenty-six Frenchmen. The Christians were outmatched, eight to one; but, says the chronicle, the Queen of Heaven was on their side, and the Son of Mary refuses nothing to his holy mother.[1]   Through her intercession, the Iroquois shot so wildly that at their first fire every bullet missed its mark, and they met with a bloody defeat. The palisaded settlement of Three Rivers, though in a position less exposed than that of Montreal, was in no less jeopardy. A noted war-chief of the Mohawk Iroquois had been captured here the year before, and put to death; and his tribe swarmed out, like a nest of angry hornets, to revenge him.   Not content with defeating and killing the commandant, Du Plessis Bochart, they encamped during the winter in the neighboring forest, watching for an opportunity to surprise the place.   Hunger drove them off, but they returned in the spring, infesting every field and pathway; till at length some six hundred of their warriors landed in secret and lay hidden in the depths of the woods, silently biding their time. Having failed, however, in an artifice designed to lure the French out of their defences, they showed themselves on all sides, plundering, burning, and destroying, up to the palisades of the fort.[2]

Of the three settlements which, with their feeble

---

[1] Le Mercier, *Relation*, 1653, 3.

[2] So bent were they on taking the place, that they brought their families, in order to make a permanent settlement. Marie de l'Incarnation, *Lettre du 6 Sept.*, 1653.

dependencies, then comprised the whole of Canada, Quebec was least exposed to Indian attacks, being partially covered by Montreal and Three Rivers. Nevertheless, there was no safety this year, even under the cannon of Fort St. Louis. At Cap Rouge, a few miles above, the Jesuit Poncet saw a poor woman who had a patch of corn beside her cabin, but could find nobody to harvest it. The father went to seek aid; met one Mathurin Franchetot, whom he persuaded to undertake the charitable task, and was returning with him, when they both fell into an ambuscade of Iroquois, who seized them and dragged them off. Thirty-two men embarked in canoes at Quebec to follow the retreating savages and rescue the prisoners. Pushing rapidly up the St. Lawrence, they approached Three Rivers, found it beset by the Mohawks, and bravely threw themselves into it, to the great joy of its defenders and discouragement of the assailants.

Meanwhile, the intercession of the Virgin wrought new marvels at Montreal, and a bright ray of hope beamed forth from the darkness and the storm to cheer the hearts of her votaries. It was on the twenty-sixth of June that sixty of the Onondaga Iroquois appeared in sight of the fort, shouting from a distance that they came on an errand of peace, and asking safe-conduct for some of their number. Guns, scalping-knives, tomahawks, were all laid aside; and, with a confidence truly astonishing, a deputation of chiefs, naked and defenceless, came into the midst of those

whom they had betrayed so often. The French had
a mind to seize them, and pay them in kind for past
treachery; but they refrained, seeing in this won-
drous change of heart the manifest hand of Heaven.
Nevertheless, it can be explained without a miracle.
The Iroquois, or at least the western nations of their
league, had just become involved in war with their
neighbors the Eries,[1] and "one war at a time" was
the sage maxim of their policy.

All was smiles and blandishment in the fort at
Montreal; presents were exchanged, and the deputies
departed, bearing home golden reports of the French.
An Oneida deputation soon followed; but the enraged
Mohawks still infested Montreal and beleaguered
Three Rivers, till one of their principal chiefs and
four of their best warriors were captured by a party
of Christian Hurons.   Then, seeing themselves
abandoned by the other nations of the league and
left to wage the war alone, they too made overtures
of peace.

A grand council was held at Quebec. Speeches
were made, and wampum-belts exchanged. The
Iroquois left some of their chief men as pledges of
sincerity, and two young soldiers offered themselves
as reciprocal pledges on the part of the French.
The war was over; at least Canada had found a
moment to take breath for the next struggle. The

---

[1] See "Jesuits in North America," ii. 264. The Iroquois, it will be
remembered, consisted of five "nations," or tribes, — the Mohawks,
Oneidas, Onondagas, Cayugas, and Senecas. For an account of
them, see the work just cited, Introduction.

fur-trade was restored again, with promise of plenty; for the beaver, profiting by the quarrels of their human foes, had of late greatly multiplied. It was a change from death to life; for Canada lived on the beaver, and robbed of this, her only sustenance, had been dying slowly since the strife began.[1]

"Yesterday," writes Father Le Mercier, "all was dejection and gloom; to-day, all is smiles and gayety. On Wednesday, massacre, burning, and pillage; on Thursday, gifts and visits, as among friends. If the Iroquois have their hidden designs, so too has God.

"On the day of the Visitation of the Holy Virgin, the chief, Aontarisati,[2] so regretted by the Iroquois, was taken prisoner by our Indians, instructed by our fathers, and baptized; and on the same day, being put to death, he ascended to heaven. I doubt not that he thanked the Virgin for his misfortune and the blessing that followed, and that he prayed to God for his countrymen.

"The people of Montreal made a solemn vow to celebrate publicly the *fête* of this mother of all blessings; whereupon the Iroquois came to ask for peace.

"It was on the day of the Assumption of this Queen of angels and of men that the Hurons took at

---

[1] According to Le Mercier, beaver to the value of from 200,000 to 300,000 livres was yearly brought down to the colony before the destruction of the Hurons (1649–50). Three years later, not one beaver-skin was brought to Montreal during a twelvemonth, and Three Rivers and Quebec had barely enough to pay for keeping the fortifications in repair.

[2] The chief whose death had so enraged the Mohawks.

Montreal that other famous Iroquois chief, whose capture caused the Mohawks to seek our alliance.

"On the day when the Church honors the Nativity of the Holy Virgin, the Iroquois granted Father Poncet his life; and he, or rather the Holy Virgin and the holy angels, labored so well in the work of peace, that on Saint Michael's Day it was resolved in a council of the elders that the father should be conducted to Quebec, and a lasting treaty made with the French."[1]

Happy as was this consummation, Father Poncet's path to it had been a thorny one. He has left us his own rueful story, written in obedience to the command of his superior. He and his companion in misery had been hurried through the forests, from Cap Rouge on the St. Lawrence to the Indian towns on the Mohawk. He tells us how he slept among dank weeds, dropping with the cold dew; how frightful colics assailed him as he waded waist-deep through a mountain stream; how one of his feet was blistered and one of his legs benumbed; how an Indian snatched away his reliquary and lost the precious contents. "I had," he says, "a picture of Saint Ignatius with our Lord bearing the cross, and another of Our Lady of Pity surrounded by the five wounds of her Son. They were my joy and my consolation; but I hid them in a bush, lest the Indians should laugh at them." He kept, however, a little image of the crown of thorns, in which he found great comfort,

____
[1] *Relation,* 1653, 18.

as well as in communion with his patron saints, Saint
Raphael, Saint Martha, and Saint Joseph.   On one
occasion he asked these celestial friends for something to soothe his thirst, and for a bowl of broth to
revive his strength.   Scarcely had he framed the
petition when an Indian gave him some wild plums;
and in the evening, as he lay fainting on the ground,
another brought him the coveted broth.   Weary and
forlorn, he reached at last the lower Mohawk town,
where, after being stripped, and with his companion
forced to run the gantlet, he was placed on a scaffold
of bark, surrounded by a crowd of grinning and
mocking savages.   As it began to rain, they took
him into one of their lodges, and amused themselves
by making him dance, sing, and perform various
fantastic tricks for their amusement.   He seems to
have done his best to please them; "but," adds the
chronicler, "I will say in passing, that as he did not
succeed to their liking in these buffooneries (*singeries*),
they would have put him to death if a young Huron
prisoner had not offered himself to sing, dance, and
make wry faces in place of the father, who had never
learned the trade."

Having sufficiently amused themselves, they left
him for a time in peace; when an old one-eyed Indian
approached, took his hands, examined them, selected
the left forefinger, and calling a child four or five
years old, gave him a knife, and told him to cut it
off, which the imp proceeded to do, his victim meanwhile singing the *Vexilla Regis*.   After this prelimi-

nary, they would have burned him, like Franchetot, his unfortunate companion, had not a squaw happily adopted him in place, as he says, of a deceased brother. He was installed at once in the lodge of his new relatives, where, bereft of every rag of Christian clothing, and attired in leggins, moccasins, and a greasy shirt, the astonished father saw himself transformed into an Iroquois. But his deliverance was at hand. A special agreement providing for it had formed a part of the treaty concluded at Quebec; and he now learned that he was to be restored to his countrymen. After a march of almost intolerable hardship, he saw himself once more among Christians, — Heaven, as he modestly thinks, having found him unworthy of martyrdom.

"At last," he writes, "we reached Montreal on the twenty-first of October, the nine weeks of my captivity being accomplished, in honor of Saint Michael and all the holy angels. On the sixth of November the Iroquois who conducted me made their presents to confirm the peace; and thus, on a Sunday evening, eighty-and-one days after my capture, — that is to say, nine times nine days, — this great business of the peace was happily concluded, the holy angels showing by this number nine, which is specially dedicated to them, the part they bore in this holy work."[1] This incessant supernaturalism is the key to the early history of New France.

[1] Poncet in *Relation*, 1653, 17. On Poncet's captivity see also *Morale Pratique des Jésuites*, vol. xxxiv. (4to) chap. xii.

Peace was made; but would peace endure?   There was little chance of it, and this for several reasons. First, the native fickleness of the Iroquois, who, astute and politic to a surprising degree, were in certain respects, like all savages, mere grown-up children.   Next, their total want of control over their fierce and capricious young warriors, any one of whom could break the peace with impunity whenever he saw fit; and, above all, the strong probability that the Iroquois had made peace in order, under cover of it, to butcher or kidnap the unhappy remnant of the Hurons who were living, under French protection, on the island of Orleans, immediately below Quebec.   I have already told the story of the destruction of this people and of the Jesuit missions established among them.[1]   The conquerors were eager to complete their bloody triumph by seizing upon the refugees of Orleans, killing the elders, and strengthening their own tribes by the adoption of the women, children, and youths.   The Mohawks and the Onondagas were competitors for the prize.   Each coveted the Huron colony, and each was jealous lest his rival should pounce upon it first.

When the Mohawks brought home Poncet, they covertly gave wampum-belts to the Huron chiefs, and invited them to remove to their villages.   It was the wolf's invitation to the lamb.   The Hurons, aghast with terror, went secretly to the Jesuits, and told them that demons had whispered in their ears an

---

[1] See "Jesuits in North America."

invitation to destruction. So helpless were both the Hurons and their French supporters, that they saw no recourse but dissimulation. The Hurons promised to go, and only sought excuses to gain time.

The Onondagas had a deeper plan. Their towns were already full of Huron captives, former converts of the Jesuits, cherishing their memory and constantly repeating their praises. Hence their tyrants conceived the idea that by planting at Onondaga a colony of Frenchmen under the direction of these beloved fathers, the Hurons of Orleans, disarmed of suspicion, might readily be led to join them. Other motives, as we shall see, tended to the same end, and the Onondaga deputies begged, or rather demanded, that a colony of Frenchmen should be sent among them.

Here was a dilemma. Was not this, like the Mohawk invitation to the Hurons, an invitation to butchery? On the other hand, to refuse would probably kindle the war afresh. The Jesuits had long nursed a project bold to temerity. Their great Huron mission was ruined; but might not another be built up among the authors of this ruin, and the Iroquois themselves, tamed by the power of the Faith, be annexed to the kingdoms of Heaven and of France? Thus would peace be restored to Canada, a barrier of fire opposed to the Dutch and English heretics, and the power of the Jesuits vastly increased. Yet the time was hardly ripe for such an attempt. Before thrusting a head into the tiger's jaws, it would be well to try the effect of thrusting in a hand. They resolved to compromise with the danger, and before risking a colony at Onondaga to send thither an envoy who could soothe the Indians, confirm them in pacific designs, and pave the way for more decisive steps. The choice fell on Father Simon Le Moyne.

The errand was mainly a political one; and this sagacious and able priest, versed in Indian languages and customs, was well suited to do it. "On the second day of the month of July, the festival of the Visitation of the Most Holy Virgin, ever favorable to our enterprises, Father Simon Le Moyne set out from Quebec for the country of the Onondaga Iroquois." In these words does Father Le Mercier chronicle the departure of his brother Jesuit. Scarcely was he gone when a band of Mohawks, under a redoubtable half-breed known as the Flemish Bastard, arrived at Quebec; and when they heard that the envoy was to go to the Onondagas without visiting their tribe, they took the imagined slight in high dudgeon, displaying such jealousy and ire that a letter was sent after Le Moyne, directing him to proceed to the Mohawk towns before his return. But he was already beyond reach, and the angry Mohawks were left to digest their wrath.

At Montreal, Le Moyne took a canoe, a young Frenchman, and two or three Indians, and began the tumultuous journey of the Upper St. Lawrence. Nature, or habit, had taught him to love the wilderness life. He and his companions had struggled all

day against the surges of La Chine, and were bivouacked at evening by the Lake of St. Louis, when
a cloud of mosquitoes fell upon them, followed by a
shower of warm rain. The father, stretched under
a tree, seems clearly to have enjoyed himself. "It
is a pleasure," he writes, "the sweetest and most
innocent imaginable, to have no other shelter than
trees planted by Nature since the creation of the
world." Sometimes, during their journey, this
primitive tent proved insufficient, and they would
build a bark hut or find a partial shelter under their
inverted canoe. Now they glided smoothly over the
sunny bosom of the calm and smiling river, and now
strained every nerve to fight their slow way against
the rapids, dragging their canoe upward in the
shallow water by the shore, as one leads an unwilling
horse by the bridle, or shouldering it and bearing it
through the forest to the smoother current above.
Game abounded; and they saw great herds of elk
quietly defiling between the water and the woods,
with little heed of men, who in that perilous region
found employment enough in hunting one another.

At the entrance of Lake Ontario they met a party
of Iroquois fishermen, who proved friendly, and
guided them on their way. Ascending the Onondaga,
they neared their destination; and now all misgivings
as to their reception at the Iroquois capital were dis-
pelled. The inhabitants came to meet them, bringing roasting ears of the young maize and bread made
of its pulp, than which they knew no luxury more

exquisite.   Their faces beamed welcome.   Le Moyne
was astonished.   "I never," he says, "saw the like
among Indians before."   They were flattered by his
visit, and, for the moment, were glad to see him.
They hoped for great advantages from the residence
of Frenchmen among them; and having the Erie war
on their hands, they wished for peace with Canada.
"One would call me brother," writes Le Moyne;
"another, uncle; another, cousin.   I never had so
many relations."

He was overjoyed to find that many of the Huron
converts, who had long been captives at Onondaga,
had not forgotten the teachings of their Jesuit
instructors.   Such influence as they had with their
conquerors was sure to be exerted in behalf of the
French.   Deputies of the Senecas, Cayugas, and
Oneidas at length arrived, and on the tenth of August
the criers passed through the town, summoning all
to hear the words of Onontio.   The naked dignitaries, sitting, squatting, or lying at full length,
thronged the smoky hall of council.   The father
knelt and prayed in a loud voice, invoking the aid of
Heaven, cursing the demons who are spirits of discord, and calling on the tutelar angels of the country
to open the ears of his listeners.   Then he opened
his packet of presents and began his speech.   "I was
full two hours," he says, "in making it, speaking in
the tone of a chief, and walking to and fro, after
their fashion, like an actor on a theatre."   Not only
did he imitate the prolonged accents of the Iroquois

orators, but he adopted and improved their figures of speech, and addressed them in turn by their respective tribes, bands, and families, calling their men of note by name, as if he had been born among them. They were delighted; and their ejaculations of approval — *hoh-hoh-hoh* — came thick and fast at every pause of his harangue. Especially were they pleased with the eighth, ninth, tenth, and eleventh presents, whereby the reverend speaker gave to the four upper nations of the league four hatchets to strike their new enemies, the Eries; while by another present he metaphorically daubed their faces with the war-paint. However it may have suited the character of a Christian priest to hound on these savage hordes to a war of extermination which they had themselves provoked, it is certain that, as a politician, Le Moyne did wisely; since in the war with the Eries lay the best hope of peace for the French.

The reply of the Indian orator was friendly to overflowing. He prayed his French brethren to choose a spot on the lake of Onondaga, where they might dwell in the country of the Iroquois, as they dwelt already in their hearts. Le Moyne promised, and made two presents to confirm the pledge. Then, his mission fulfilled, he set out on his return, attended by a troop of Indians. As he approached the lake, his escort showed him a large spring of water, possessed, as they told him, by a bad spirit. Le Moyne tasted it, then boiled a little of it, and produced a quantity of excellent salt. He had discovered the famous salt-springs of Onondaga.   Fishing and hunting, the party pursued their way till, at noon of the seventh of September, Le Moyne reached Montreal.[1]

When he reached Quebec, his tidings cheered for a while the anxious hearts of its tenants; but an unwonted incident soon told them how hollow was the ground beneath their feet.   Le Moyne, accompanied by two Onondagas and several Hurons and Algonquins, was returning to Montreal, when he and his companions were set upon by a war-party of Mohawks. The Hurons and Algonquins were killed.   One of the Onondagas shared their fate, and the other, with Le Moyne himself, was seized and bound fast.   The captive Onondaga, however, was so loud in his threats and denunciations that the Mohawks released both him and the Jesuit.[2]   Here was a foreshadowing of civil war, — Mohawk against Onondaga, Iroquois against Iroquois.   The quarrel was patched up, but fresh provocations were imminent.

The Mohawks took no part in the Erie war, and hence their hands were free to fight the French and the tribes allied with them.   Reckless of their promises, they began a series of butcheries, — fell upon the French at Isle aux Oies, killed a lay brother of the Jesuits at Sillery, and attacked Montreal. Here, being roughly handled, they came for a time

---

[1] *Journal du Père Le Moine, Relation*, 1654, chaps. vi. vii.

[2] Compare *Relation*, 1654, 33, and *Lettre de Marie de l'Incarnation*, 18 Oct., 1654.

to their senses, and offered terms, promising to spare the French, but declaring that they would still wage war against the Hurons and Algonquins. These were allies whom the French were pledged to protect; but so helpless was the colony that the insolent and humiliating proffer was accepted, and another peace ensued, as hollow as the last. The indefatigable Le Moyne was sent to the Mohawk towns to confirm it, "so far," says the chronicle, "as it is possible to confirm a peace made by infidels backed by heretics."[1] The Mohawks received him with great rejoicing; yet his life was not safe for a moment. A warrior, feigning madness, raved through the town with uplifted hatchet, howling for his blood; but the saints watched over him and balked the machinations of hell. He came off alive and returned to Montreal, spent with famine and fatigue.

Meanwhile a deputation of eighteen Onondaga chiefs arrived at Quebec. There was a grand council. The Onondagas demanded a colony of Frenchmen to dwell among them. Lauson, the governor, dared neither to consent nor to refuse. A middle course was chosen; and two Jesuits, Chaumonot and Dablon, were sent, like Le Moyne, partly to gain time, partly to reconnoitre, and partly to confirm the Onondagas in such good intentions as they might entertain. Chaumonot was a veteran of the Huron mission, who, miraculously as he himself supposed, had acquired a

---

[1] *Copie de Deux Lettres envoyées de la Nouvelle France au Père Procureur des Missions de la Compagnie de Jésus.*

great fluency in the Huron tongue, which is closely allied to that of the Iroquois.   Dablon, a new-comer, spoke, as yet, no Indian.

Their voyage up the St. Lawrence was enlivened by an extraordinary bear-hunt, and by the antics of one of their Indian attendants, who, having dreamed that he had swallowed a frog, roused the whole camp by the gymnastics with which he tried to rid himself of the intruder.   On approaching Onondaga, they were met by a chief who sang a song of welcome, a part of which he seasoned with touches of humor, — apostrophizing the fish in the river Onondaga, naming each sort, great or small, and calling on them in turn to come into the nets of the Frenchmen and sacrifice life cheerfully for their behoof.   Hereupon there was much laughter among the Indian auditors.   An unwonted cleanliness reigned in the town; the streets had been cleared of refuse, and the arched roofs of the long houses of bark were covered with red-skinned children staring at the entry of the "black robes."

Crowds followed behind, and all was jubilation. The dignitaries of the tribe met them on the way, and greeted them with a speech of welcome.   A feast of bear's meat awaited them; but, unhappily, it was Friday, and the fathers were forced to abstain.

"On Monday, the fifteenth of November, at nine in the morning, after having secretly sent to Paradise a dying infant by the waters of baptism, all the elders and the people having assembled, we opened

the council by public prayer." Thus writes Father
Dablon. His colleague, Chaumonot, a Frenchman
bred in Italy, now rose, with a long belt of wampum
in his hand, and proceeded to make so effective a
display of his rhetorical gifts that the Indians were
lost in admiration, and their orators put to the blush
by his improvements on their own metaphors. "If
he had spoken all day," said the delighted auditors,
"we should not have had enough of it." "The
Dutch," added others, "have neither brains nor
tongues; they never tell us about paradise and hell;
on the contrary, they lead us into bad ways."

On the next day the chiefs returned their answer.
The council opened with a song or chant, which was
divided into six parts, and which, according to
Dablon, was exceedingly well sung. The burden
of the fifth part was as follows: —

"Farewell war! farewell tomahawk! We have
been fools till now; henceforth we will be brothers,
— yes, we will be brothers."

Then came four presents, the third of which
enraptured the fathers. It was a belt of seven thousand beads of wampum. "But this," says Dablon,
"was as nothing to the words that accompanied it."
"It is the gift of the faith," said the orator. "It is
to tell you that we are believers; it is to beg you not
to tire of instructing us. Have patience, seeing that
we are so dull in learning prayer; push it into our
heads and our hearts." Then he led Chaumonot
into the midst of the assembly, clasped him in his

arms, tied the belt about his waist, and protested, with a suspicious redundancy of words, that as he clasped the father, so would he clasp the faith.

What had wrought this sudden change of heart? The eagerness of the Onondagas that the French should settle among them had, no doubt, a large share in it.   For the rest, the two Jesuits saw abundant signs of the fierce, uncertain nature of those with whom they were dealing.   Erie prisoners were brought in and tortured before their eyes, — one of them being a young stoic of about ten years, who endured his fate without a single outcry.   Huron women and children, taken in war and adopted by their captors, were killed on the slightest provocation, and sometimes from mere caprice.   For several days the whole town was in an uproar with the crazy follies of the " dream feast," [1] and one of the Fathers nearly lost his life in this Indian Bedlam.

One point was clear: the French must make a settlement at Onondaga, and that speedily, or, despite their professions of brotherhood, the Onondagas would make war.   Their attitude became menacing; from urgency they passed to threats; and the two priests felt that the critical posture of affairs must at once be reported at Quebec.   But here a difficulty arose.   It was the beaver-hunting season; and, eager as were the Indians for a French colony, not one of them would offer to conduct the Jesuits to Quebec in order to fetch one.   It was not until

---

[1] See " Jesuits in North America," i. 154.

nine masses had been said to Saint John the Baptist,
that a number of Indians consented to forego their
hunting, and escort Father Dablon home.[1] Chaumonot
remained at Onondaga, to watch his dangerous hosts
and soothe their rising jealousies.

It was the second of March when Dablon began his
journey. His constitution must have been of iron,
or he would have succumbed to the appalling hardships of the way. It was neither winter nor spring.
The lakes and streams were not yet open, but the
half-thawed ice gave way beneath the foot. One of
the Indians fell through and was drowned. Swamp
and forest were clogged with sodden snow, and
ceaseless rains drenched them as they toiled on,
knee-deep in slush. Happily, the St. Lawrence was
open. They found an old wooden canoe by the
shore, embarked, and reached Montreal after a journey of four weeks.

Dablon descended to Quebec. There was long
and anxious counsel in the chambers of Fort St.
Louis. The Jesuits had information that if the
demands of the Onondagas were rejected, they would
join the Mohawks to destroy Canada. But why
were they so eager for a colony of Frenchmen? Did
they want them as hostages, that they might attack
the Hurons and Algonquins without risk of French
interference; or would they massacre them, and then,
like tigers mad with the taste of blood, turn upon

---

[1] De Quen, *Relation*, 1656, 35. Chaumonot, in his Autobiography,
ascribes the miracle to the intercession of the deceased Brébeuf.

the helpless settlements of the St. Lawrence? An abyss yawned on either hand.   Lauson, the governor, was in an agony of indecision; but at length he declared for the lesser and remoter peril, and gave his voice for the colony. The Jesuits were of the same mind, though it was they, and not he, who must bear the brunt of danger. "The blood of the martyrs is the seed of the Church," said one of them; "and if we die by the fires of the Iroquois, we shall have won eternal life by snatching souls from the fires of hell."

Preparation was begun at once. The expense fell on the Jesuits, and the outfit is said to have cost them seven thousand livres, — a heavy sum for Canada at that day. A pious gentleman, Zachary Du Puys, major of the fort of Quebec, joined the expedition with ten soldiers; and between thirty and forty other Frenchmen also enrolled themselves, impelled by devotion or destitution. Four Jesuits, — Le Mercier, the superior, with Dablon, Ménard, and Frémin, — besides two lay brothers of the order, formed, as it were, the pivot of the enterprise. The governor made them the grant of a hundred square leagues of land in the heart of the Iroquois country, — a preposterous act, which, had the Iroquois known it, would have rekindled the war; but Lauson had a mania for land-grants, and was himself the proprietor of vast domains which he could have occupied only at the cost of his scalp.

Embarked in two large boats and followed by

twelve canoes filled with Hurons, Onondagas, and a
few Senecas lately arrived, they set out on the seventeenth of May "to attack the demons," as Le Mercier
writes, "in their very stronghold." With shouts,
tears, and benedictions, priests, soldiers, and inhabitants waved farewell from the strand. They passed
the bare steeps of Cape Diamond and the mission-
house nestled beneath the heights of Sillery, and
vanished from the anxious eyes that watched the
last gleam of their receding oars.[1]

Meanwhile three hundred Mohawk warriors had
taken the war-path, bent on killing or kidnapping
the Hurons of Orleans. When they heard of the
departure of the colonists for Onondaga, their rage
was unbounded; for not only were they full of jealousy towards their Onondaga confederates, but they
had hitherto derived great profit from the control
which their local position gave them over the traffic
between this tribe and the Dutch of the Hudson, —
upon whom the Onondagas, in common with all the
upper Iroquois, had been dependent for their guns,
hatchets, scalping-knives, beads, blankets, and
brandy. These supplies would now be furnished by
the French, and the Mohawk speculators saw their
occupation gone. Nevertheless, they had just made
peace with the French, and for the moment were not
quite in the mood to break it. To wreak their spite,
they took a middle course, — crouched in ambush

<hr>

[1] Marie de l'Incarnation, *Lettres*, 1656. Le Mercier, *Relation*,
1657, chap. iv. Chaulmer, *Nouveau Monde*, ii. 265, 322, 319.

among the bushes at Point St. Croix, ten or twelve leagues above Quebec, allowed the boats bearing the French to pass unmolested, and fired a volley at the canoes in the rear, filled with Onondagas, Senecas, and Hurons. Then they fell upon them with a yell, and, after wounding a lay brother of the Jesuits who was among them, bound and flogged such of the Indians as they could seize. The astonished Onondagas protested and threatened; whereupon the Mohawks feigned great surprise, declared that they had mistaken them for Hurons, called them brothers, and suffered the whole party to escape without further injury.[1]

The three hundred marauders now paddled their large canoes of elm-bark stealthily down the current, passed Quebec undiscovered in the dark night of the nineteenth of May, landed in early morning on the island of Orleans, and ambushed themselves to surprise the Hurons as they came to labor in their cornfields. They were tolerably successful, — killed six, and captured more than eighty, the rest taking refuge in their fort, where the Mohawks dared not attack them.

At noon, the French on the rock of Quebec saw forty canoes approaching from the island of Orleans, and defiling, with insolent parade, in front of the town, all crowded with the Mohawks and their prisoners, among whom were a great number of Huron

---

[1] Compare Marie de l'Incarnation, *Lettre* 14 *Août*, 1656, Le Jeune, *Relation*, 1657, 9.

girls. Their captors, as they passed, forced them to sing and dance. The Hurons were the allies, or rather the wards, of the French, who were in every way pledged to protect them. Yet the cannon of Fort St. Louis were silent, and the crowd stood gaping in bewilderment and fright. Had an attack been made, nothing but a complete success and the capture of many prisoners to serve as hostages could have prevented the enraged Mohawks from taking their revenge on the Onondaga colonists. The emergency demanded a prompt and clear-sighted soldier. The governor, Lauson, was a gray-haired civilian, who, however enterprising as a speculator in wild lands, was in no way matched to the desperate crisis of the hour. Some of the Mohawks landed above and below the town, and plundered the houses from which the scared inhabitants had fled. Not a soldier stirred and not a gun was fired. The French, bullied by a horde of naked savages, became an object of contempt to their own allies.

The Mohawks carried their prisoners home, burned six of them, and adopted or rather enslaved the rest.[1]

Meanwhile the Onondaga colonists pursued their perilous way. At Montreal they exchanged their heavy boats for canoes, and resumed their journey with a flotilla of twenty of these sylvan vessels. A few days after, the Indians of the party had the satisfaction of pillaging a small band of Mohawk hunters,

[1] See authorities just cited, and Perrot, *Mœurs des Sauvages*, 106.

in vicarious reprisal for their own wrongs. On the twenty-sixth of June, as they neared Lake Ontario, they heard a loud and lamentable voice from the edge of the forest; whereupon, having beaten their drum to show that they were Frenchmen, they beheld a spectral figure, lean and covered with scars, which proved to be a pious Huron,— one Joachim Ondakout, captured by the Mohawks in their descent on the island of Orleans, five or six weeks before. They had carried him to their village and begun to torture him; after which they tied him fast and lay down to sleep, thinking to resume their pleasure on the morrow. His cuts and burns being only on the surface, he had the good fortune to free himself from his bonds, and, naked as he was, to escape to the woods. He held his course northwestward, through regions even now a wilderness, gathered wild strawberries to sustain life, and in fifteen days reached the St. Lawrence, nearly dead with exhaustion. The Frenchmen gave him food and a canoe, and the living skeleton paddled with a light heart for Quebec.

The colonists themselves soon began to suffer from hunger. Their fishing failed on Lake Ontario, and they were forced to content themselves with cranberries of the last year, gathered in the meadows. Of their Indians, all but five deserted them. The Father Superior fell ill, and when they reached the mouth of the Oswego many of the starving Frenchmen had completely lost heart. Weary and faint, they dragged their canoes up the rapids, when suddenly they were cheered by the sight of a stranger canoe swiftly descending the current. The Onondagas, aware of their approach, had sent it to meet them, laden with Indian corn and fresh salmon. Two more canoes followed, freighted like the first; and now all was abundance till they reached their journey's end, the Lake of Onondaga. It lay before them in the July sun, a glittering mirror, framed in forest verdure.

They knew that Chaumonot with a crowd of Indians was awaiting them at a spot on the margin of the water, which he and Dablon had chosen as the site of their settlement. Landing on the strand, they fired, to give notice of their approach, five small cannon which they had brought in their canoes. Waves, woods, and hills resounded with the thunder of their miniature artillery. Then re-embarking, they advanced in order, four canoes abreast, towards the destined spot. In front floated their banner of white silk, embroidered in large letters with the name of Jesus. Here were Du Puys and his soldiers, with the picturesque uniforms and quaint weapons of their time; Le Mercier and his Jesuits in robes of black; hunters and bush-rangers; Indians painted and feathered for a festal day. As they neared the place where a spring bubbling from the hillside is still known as the "Jesuits' Well," they saw the edge of the forest dark with the muster of savages whose yells of welcome answered the salvo of their guns. Happily for them, a flood of summer rain saved them from the harangues of the Onondaga orators, and forced white men and red alike to seek such shelter as they could find. Their hosts, with hospitable intent, would fain have sung and danced all night; but the Frenchmen pleaded fatigue, and the courteous savages, squatting around their tents, chanted in monotonous tones to lull them to sleep. In the morning they woke refreshed, sang *Te Deum*, reared an altar, and, with a solemn mass, took possession of the country in the name of Jesus.[1]

Three things, which they saw or heard of in their new home, excited their astonishment. The first was the vast flight of wild pigeons which in spring darkened the air around the Lake of Onondaga; the second was the salt springs of Salina; the third was the rattlesnakes, which Le Mercier describes with excellent precision, — adding that, as he learns from the Indians, their tails are good for toothache and their flesh for fever. These reptiles, for reasons best known to themselves, haunted the neighborhood of the salt-springs, but did not intrude their presence into the abode of the French.

On the seventeenth of July, Le Mercier and Chaumonot, escorted by a file of soldiers, set out for Onondaga, scarcely five leagues distant. They followed the Indian trail, under the leafy arches of the woods, by hill and hollow, still swamp and gurgling brook, till through the opening foliage they saw the Iroquois capital, compassed with cornfields and girt with its rugged palisade. As the Jesuits, like black spectres,

---

[1] Le Mercier, *Relation*, 1657, 14.

issued from the shadows of the forest, followed by
the plumed soldiers with shouldered arquebuses, the
red-skinned population swarmed out like bees, and
they defiled to the town through gazing and admiring
throngs.   All conspired to welcome them. Feast
followed feast throughout the afternoon, till, what
with harangues and songs, bear's meat, beaver-tails,
and venison, beans, corn, and grease, they were
wellnigh killed with kindness.   "If, after this, they
murder us," writes Le Mercier, "it will be from
fickleness, not premeditated treachery." But the
Jesuits, it seems, had not sounded the depths of
Iroquois dissimulation.[1]

There was one exception to the real or pretended
joy.   Some Mohawks were in the town, and their
orator was insolent and sarcastic; but the ready
tongue of Chaumonot turned the laugh against him
and put him to shame.

Here burned the council-fire of the Iroquois, and
at this very time the deputies of the five tribes were
assembling. The session opened on the twenty-fourth.
In the great council-house, on the earthen floor and the
broad platforms, beneath the smoke-begrimed concave
of the bark roof, stood, sat, or squatted the wisdom
and valor of the confederacy, — Mohawks, Oneidas,

---

[1] The Jesuits were afterwards told by Hurons, captive among
the Mohawks and the Onondagas, that, from the first, it was
intended to massacre the French as soon as their presence had
attracted the remnant of the Hurons of Orleans into the power of
the Onondagas. *Lettre du P. Ragueneau au R. P. Provincial*, 31
Août, 1658.

Onondagas, Cayugas, and Senecas; sachems, counsellors, orators, warriors fresh from Erie victories; tall, stalwart figures, limbed like Grecian statues.

The pressing business of the council over, it was Chaumonot's turn to speak. But, first, all the Frenchmen, kneeling in a row, with clasped hands, sang the *Veni Creator*, amid the silent admiration of the auditors. Then Chaumonot rose, with an immense wampum-belt in his hand, and said:

"It is not trade that brings us here. Do you think that your beaver-skins can pay us for all our toils and dangers? Keep them, if you like; or, if any fall into our hands, we shall use them only for your service. We seek not the things that perish. It is for the Faith that we have left our homes to live in your hovels of bark, and eat food which the beasts of our country would scarcely touch. We are the messengers whom God has sent to tell you that his Son became a man for the love of you; that this man, the Son of God, is the prince and master of men; that he has prepared in heaven eternal joys for those who obey him, and kindled the fires of hell for those who will not receive his word. If you reject it, whoever you are, — Onondaga, Seneca, Mohawk, Cayuga, or Oneida, — know that Jesus Christ, who inspires my heart and my voice, will plunge you one day into hell. Avert this ruin; be not the authors of your own destruction; accept the truth; listen to the voice of the Omnipotent."

Such, in brief, was the pith of the father's exhorta-

tion. As he spoke Indian like a native, and as his
voice and gestures answered to his words, we may
believe what Le Mercier tells us, that his hearers
listened with mingled wonder, admiration, and terror.
The work was well begun. The Jesuits struck while
the iron was hot; built a small chapel for the mass,
installed themselves in the town, and preached and
catechised from morning till night.

The Frenchmen at the lake were not idle. The
chosen site of their settlement was the crown of a
hill commanding a broad view of waters and forests.
The axemen fell to their work, and a ghastly wound
soon gaped in the green bosom of the woodland.
Here, among the stumps and prostrate trees of the
unsightly clearing, the blacksmith built his forge,
saw and hammer plied their trade; palisades were
shaped and beams squared, in spite of heat, mosquitoes, and fever. At one time twenty men were ill,
and lay gasping under a wretched shed of bark; but
they all recovered, and the work went on, till at
length a capacious house, large enough to hold the
whole colony, rose above the ruin of the forest. A
palisade was set around it, and the Mission of Saint
Mary of Gannentaa [1] was begun.

France and the Faith were intrenched on the Lake
of Onondaga. How long would they remain there?
The future alone could tell. The mission, it must

---

[1] *Gannentaa* or *Ganuntaah* is still the Iroquois name for Lake
Onondaga. According to Morgan, it means "Material for Council-
Fire."

not be forgotten, had a double scope, — half ecclesiastical, half political. The Jesuits had essayed a fearful task, — to convert the Iroquois to God and to the King, thwart the Dutch heretics of the Hudson, save souls from hell, avert ruin from Canada, and thus raise their order to a place of honor and influence both hard-earned and well-earned. The mission at Lake Onondaga was but a base of operations. Long before they were lodged and fortified here, Chaumonot and Ménard set out for the Cayugas, whence the former proceeded to the Senecas, the most numerous and powerful of the five confederate nations; and in the following spring another mission was begun among the Oneidas. Their reception was not unfriendly; but such was the reticence and dissimulation of these inscrutable savages, that it was impossible to foretell results. The women proved, as might be expected, far more impressible than the men; and in them the fathers placed great hope, since in this, the most savage people of the continent, women held a degree of political influence never perhaps equalled in any civilized nation.[1]

---

[1] Women, among the Iroquois, had a council of their own, which, according to Lafitau, who knew this people well, had the initiative in discussion, subjects presented by them being settled in the council of chiefs and elders. In this latter council the women had an orator, often of their own sex, to represent them. The matrons had a leading voice in determining the succession of chiefs. There were also female chiefs, one of whom, with her attendants, came to Quebec with an embassy in 1655 (Marie de l'Incarnation). In the torture of prisoners, great deference was

But while infants were baptized and squaws converted, the crosses of the mission were many and
great. The devil bestirred himself with more than
his ordinary activity; "for," as one of the fathers
writes, "when in sundry nations of the earth men
are rising up in strife against us [the Jesuits], then
how much more the demons, on whom we continually
wage war!" It was these infernal sprites, as the
priests believed, who engendered suspicions and
calumnies in the dark and superstitious minds of the
Iroquois, and prompted them in dreams to destroy
the apostles of the Faith. Whether the foe was of
earth or hell, the Jesuits were like those who tread
the lava-crust that palpitates with the throes of the
coming eruption, while the molten death beneath
their feet glares white-hot through a thousand
crevices. Yet, with a sublime enthusiasm and a
glorious constancy, they toiled and they hoped,
though the skies around were black with portent.

In the year in which the colony at Onondaga was
begun, the Mohawks murdered the Jesuit Garreau
on his way up the Ottawa. In the following spring,
a hundred Mohawk warriors came to Quebec to carry

paid to the judgment of the women, who, says Champlain, were
thought more skilful and subtle than the men.

The learned Lafitau, whose book appeared in 1724, dwells at
length on the resemblance of the Iroquois to the ancient Lycians,
among whom, according to Grecian writers, women were in the
ascendant. "Gynecocracy, or the rule of women," continues
Lafitau, "which was the foundation of the Lycian government,
was probably common in early times to nearly all the barbarous
people of Greece." *Mœurs des Sauvages,* i. 460 (ed. in 4to).

more of the Hurons into slavery, — though the remnant of that unhappy people, since the catastrophe of the last year, had sought safety in a palisaded camp within the limits of the French town, and immediately under the ramparts of Fort St. Louis. Here, one might think, they would have been safe; but Charny, son and successor of Lauson, seems to have been even more imbecile than his father, and listened meekly to the threats of the insolent strangers who told him that unless he abandoned the Hurons to their mercy, both they and the French should feel the weight of Mohawk tomahawks. They demanded, further, that the French should give them boats to carry their prisoners; but, as there were none at hand, this last humiliation was spared. The Mohawks were forced to make canoes, in which they carried off as many as possible of their victims.

When the Onondagas learned this last exploit of their rivals, their jealousy knew no bounds, and a troop of them descended to Quebec to claim their share in the human plunder. Deserted by the French, the despairing Hurons abandoned themselves to their fate; and about fifty of those whom the Mohawks had left obeyed the behest of their tyrants, and embarked for Onondaga. They reached Montreal in July, and thence proceeded towards their destination in company with the Onondaga warriors. The Jesuit Ragueneau, bound also for Onondaga, joined them. Five leagues above Montreal, the warriors left him behind; but he found an old canoe on the bank, in which, after abandoning most of his baggage, he contrived to follow with two or three Frenchmen who were with him. There was a rumor that a hundred Mohawk warriors were lying in wait among the Thousand Islands to plunder the Onondagas of their Huron prisoners. It proved a false report. A speedier catastrophe awaited these unfortunates.

Towards evening on the third of August, after the party had landed to encamp, an Onondaga chief made advances to a Christian Huron girl, as he had already done at every encampment since leaving Montreal. Being repulsed for the fourth time, he split her head with his tomahawk. It was the beginning of a massacre. The Onondagas rose upon their prisoners, killed seven men, all Christians, before the eyes of the horrified Jesuit, and plundered the rest of all they had. When Ragueneau protested, they told him with insolent mockery that they were acting by direction of the governor and the superior of the Jesuits. The priest himself was secretly warned that he was to be killed during the night; and he was surprised in the morning to find himself alive.[1] On reaching Onondaga, some of the Christian captives were burned, including several women and their infant children.[2]

The confederacy was a hornet's nest, buzzing with

---

[1] *Lettre de Ragueneau au R. P. Provincial,* 9 *Août,* 1657 (*Rel.,* 1657).

[2] *Ibid.,* 21 *Août,* 1658 (*Rel.,* 1658).

preparation, and fast pouring out its wrathful swarms. The indomitable Le Moyne had gone again to the Mohawks, whence he wrote that two hundred of them had taken the war-path against the Algonquins of Canada; and, a little later, that all were gone but women, children, and old men. A great war-party of twelve hundred Iroquois from all the five cantons was to advance into Canada in the direction of the Ottawa. The settlements on the St. Lawrence were infested with prowling warriors, who killed the Indian allies of the French, and plundered the French themselves, whom they treated with an insufferable insolence; for they felt themselves masters of the situation, and knew that the Onondaga colony was in their power. Near Montreal they killed three Frenchmen. "They approach like foxes," writes a Jesuit, "attack like lions, and disappear like birds." Charny, fortunately, had resigned the government in despair in order to turn priest, and the brave soldier d'Ailleboust had taken his place. He caused twelve of the Iroquois to be seized and held as hostages. This seemed to increase their fury. An embassy came to Quebec and demanded the release of the hostages, but were met with a sharp reproof and a flat refusal.

At the mission on Lake Onondaga the crisis was drawing near. The unbridled young warriors, whose capricious lawlessness often set at naught the monitions of their crafty elders, killed wantonly at various times thirteen Christian Hurons, captives at

Onondaga.   Ominous reports reached the ears of the colonists.   They heard of a secret council at which their death was decreed.   Again, they heard that they were to be surprised and captured, that the Iroquois in force were then to descend upon Canada, lay waste the outlying settlements, and torture them, the colonists, in sight of their countrymen, by which they hoped to extort what terms they pleased.   At length a dying Onondaga, recently converted and baptized, confirmed the rumors, and revealed the whole plot.

It was to take effect before the spring opened; but the hostages in the hands of d'Ailleboust embarrassed the conspirators and caused delay.   Messengers were sent in haste to call in the priests from the detached missions; and all the colonists, fifty-three in number, were soon gathered at their fortified house on the lake.   Their situation was frightful.   Fate hung over them by a hair, and escape seemed hopeless.   Of Du Puys's ten soldiers, nine wished to desert; but the attempt would have been fatal.   A throng of Onondaga warriors were day and night on the watch, bivouacked around the house.   Some of them had built their huts of bark before the gate, and here, with calm, impassive faces, they lounged and smoked their pipes; or, wrapped in their blankets, strolled about the yards and outhouses, attentive to all that passed.   Their behavior was very friendly.   The Jesuits, themselves adepts in dissimulation, were amazed at the depth of their duplicity; for the conviction had been forced upon them that some of the chiefs had nursed their treachery from the first. In this extremity Du Puys and the Jesuits showed an admirable coolness, and among them devised a plan of escape, critical and full of doubt, but not devoid of hope.

First, they must provide means of transportation; next, they must contrive to use them undiscovered. They had eight canoes, all of which combined would not hold half their company. Over the mission-house was a large loft or garret, and here the carpenters were secretly set at work to construct two large and light flat-boats, each capable of carrying fifteen men. The task was soon finished. The most difficult part of their plan remained.

There was a beastly superstition prevalent among the Hurons, the Iroquois, and other tribes. It consisted of a "medicine" or mystic feast, in which it was essential that the guests should devour everything set before them, however inordinate in quantity, unless absolved from duty by the person in whose behalf the solemnity was ordained, — he, on his part, taking no share in the banquet. So grave was the obligation, and so strenuously did the guests fulfil it, that even their ostrich digestion was sometimes ruined past redemption by the excess of this benevolent gluttony. These *festins à manger tout* had been frequently denounced as diabolical by the Jesuits, during their mission among the Hurons; but now, with a pliancy of conscience as excusable in this case as in any other, they resolved to set aside their scruples, although, judged from their point of view, they were exceedingly well founded.

Among the French was a young man who had been adopted by an Iroquois chief, and who spoke the language fluently. He now told his Indian father that it had been revealed to him in a dream that he would soon die unless the spirits were appeased by one of these magic feasts. Dreams were the oracles of the Iroquois, and woe to those who slighted them. A day was named for the sacred festivity. The fathers killed their hogs to meet the occasion, and, that nothing might be wanting, they ransacked their stores for all that might give piquancy to the entertainment. It took place in the evening of the twentieth of March, apparently in a large enclosure outside the palisade surrounding the mission-house. Here, while blazing fires or glaring pine-knots shed their glow on the wild assemblage, Frenchmen and Iroquois joined in the dance, or vied with each other in games of agility and skill. The politic fathers offered prizes to the winners, and the Indians entered with zest into the sport, the better, perhaps, to hide their treachery and hoodwink their intended victims; for they little suspected that a subtlety, deeper this time than their own, was at work to countermine them. Here too were the French musicians, and drum, trumpet, and cymbal lent their clangor to the din of shouts and laughter. Thus the evening wore on, till at length the serious labors of the feast began.

The kettles were brought in, and their steaming contents ladled into the wooden bowls which each provident guest had brought with him. Seated gravely in a ring, they fell to their work. It was a point of high conscience not to flinch from duty on these solemn occasions; and though they might burn the young man to-morrow, they would gorge themselves like vultures in his behoof to-day.

Meantime, while the musicians strained their lungs and their arms to drown all other sounds, a band of anxious Frenchmen, in the darkness of the cloudy night, with cautious tread and bated breath, carried the boats from the rear of the mission-house down to the border of the lake. It was near eleven o'clock. The miserable guests were choking with repletion. They prayed the young Frenchman to dispense them from further surfeit. "Will you suffer me to die?" he asked, in piteous tones. They bent to their task again; but Nature soon reached her utmost limit, and they sat helpless as a conventicle of gorged turkey-buzzards, without the power possessed by those unseemly birds to rid themselves of the burden. "That will do," said the young man; "you have eaten enough: my life is saved. Now you can sleep till we come in the morning to waken you for prayers."[1] And one of his companions played soft airs on a violin to lull them to repose. Soon all were asleep, or in a lethargy akin to sleep. The few remaining Frenchmen now silently withdrew and

---

[1] *Lettre de Marie de l'Incarnation à son fils*, 4 *Oct.*, 1658.

cautiously descended to the shore, where their comrades, already embarked, lay on their oars anxiously awaiting them.   Snow was falling fast as they pushed out upon the murky waters.   The ice of the winter had broken up, but recent frosts had glazed the surface with a thin crust.   The two boats led the way, and the canoes followed in their wake, while men in the bows of the foremost boat broke the ice with clubs as they advanced.   They reached the outlet and rowed swiftly down the dark current of the Oswego.   When day broke, Lake Onondaga was far behind, and around them was the leafless, lifeless forest.

When the Indians woke in the morning, dull and stupefied from their nightmare slumbers, they were astonished at the silence that reigned in the mission-house.   They looked through the palisade.   Nothing was stirring but a bevy of hens clucking and scratching in the snow, and one or two dogs imprisoned in the house and barking to be set free.   The Indians waited for some time, then climbed the palisade, burst in the doors, and found the house empty.   Their amazement was unbounded.   How, without canoes, could the French have escaped by water?   And how else could they escape?   The snow which had fallen during the night completely hid their footsteps.   A superstitious awe seized the Iroquois.   They thought that the "black-robes" and their flock had flown off through the air.

Meanwhile the fugitives pushed their flight with

the energy of terror, passed in safety the rapids of the
Oswego, crossed Lake Ontario, and descended the
St. Lawrence with the loss of three men drowned
in the rapids. On the third of April they reached
Montreal, and on the twenty-third arrived at Quebec.
They had saved their lives; but the mission of Onon-
daga was a miserable failure.[1]

[1] On the Onondaga mission, the authorities are Marie de
l'Incarnation, *Lettres Historiques*, and *Relations des Jésuites*, 1657
and 1658, where the story is told at length, accompanied with
several interesting letters and journals. Chaumonot, in his *Auto-
biographie*, speaks only of the Seneca mission, and refers to the
Relations for the rest. Dollier de Casson, in his *Histoire du Montréal*, mentions the arrival of the fugitives at that place, the sight
of which, he adds complacently, cured them of their fright. The
Journal des Supérieurs des Jésuites chronicles with its usual brevity
the ruin of the mission and the return of the party to Quebec.

The contemporary Jesuits, in their account, say nothing of the
superstitious character of the feast. It is Marie de l'Incarnation
who lets out the secret. The later Jesuit Charlevoix, much to his
credit, repeats the story without reserve.

Since the above chapter was written, the remarkable narratives
of Pierre Esprit Radisson have been rescued from the obscurity
where they have lain for more than two centuries. Radisson, a
native of St. Malo, was a member of the colony at Onondaga; but
having passed into the service of England, he wrote in a language
which, for want of a fitter name, may be called English. He does
not say that the feast was of the kind known as *festin à manger tout*,
though he asserts that one of the priests pretended to have broken
his arm, and that the Indians believed that the "feasting was to be
done for the safe recovery of the father's health." Like the other
writers, he says that the feasters gorged themselves like wolves and
became completely helpless, "making strange kinds of faces that
turned their eyes up and downe," till, when almost bursting, they
were forced to cry *Skenon*, which according to Radisson means
"enough." Radisson adds that it was proposed that the French,
"being three and fifty in number, while the Iroquois were
but 100 beasts not able to budge," should fall upon the impotent

savages and kill them all, but that the Jesuits would not consent. His account of the embarkation and escape of the colonists agrees with that of the other writers.   See *Second Voyage made in the Upper Country of the Iroquoits*, in *Publications of the Prince Society*, 1885.

The Sulpitian Allet, in the *Morale Pratique des Jésuites*, says that the French placed effigies of soldiers in the fort to deceive the Indians.

CHAPTER V.

1642–1661.

THE HOLY WARS OF MONTREAL.

Dauversière. — Mance and Bourgeoys. — Miracle. — A Pious Defaulter. — Jesuit and Sulpitian. — Montreal in 1659. — The Hospital Nuns. — The Nuns and the Iroquois. — More Miracles. — The Murdered Priests. — Brigeac and Closse. — Soldiers of the Holy Family.

On the second of July, 1659, the ship "St. André" lay in the harbor of Rochelle, crowded with passengers for Canada. She had served two years as a hospital for marines, and was infected with a contagious fever. Including the crew, some two hundred persons were on board, more than half of whom were bound for Montreal. Most of these were sturdy laborers, artisans, peasants, and soldiers, together with a troop of young women, their present or future partners; a portion of the company set down on the old record as "sixty virtuous men and thirty-two pious girls." There were two priests also, Vignal and Le Maître, both destined to a speedy death at the hands of the Iroquois. But the most conspicuous among these passengers for Montreal were two groups of women in the habit of nuns, under the direction of Marguerite

Marguerite de Bourgeoys.

Bourgeoys and Jeanne Mance. Marguerite Bourgeoys, whose kind, womanly face bespoke her fitness for the task, was foundress of the school for female children at Montreal; her companion, a tall, austere figure, worn with suffering and care, was directress of the hospital. Both had returned to France for aid, and were now on their way back, each with three recruits, — three being the mystic number, as a type of the Holy Family, to whose worship they were especially devoted.

Amid the bustle of departure, the shouts of sailors, the rattling of cordage, the flapping of sails, the tears and the embracings, an elderly man, with heavy plebeian features, sallow with disease, and in a sober, half-clerical dress, approached Mademoiselle Mance and her three nuns, and, turning his eyes to heaven, spread his hands over them in benediction. It was Le Royer de la Dauversière, founder of the sister-hood of St. Joseph, to which the three nuns belonged. "Now, O Lord," he exclaimed, with the look of one whose mission on earth is fulfilled, "permit thou thy servant to depart in peace!"

Sister Maillet, who had charge of the meagre treasury of the community, thought that something more than a blessing was due from him, and asked where she should apply for payment of the interest of the twenty thousand livres which Mademoiselle Mance had placed in his hands for investment. Dauversière changed countenance, and replied with a troubled voice: "My daughter, God will provide for you. Place your trust in Him."[1] He was bank-rupt, and had used the money of the sisterhood to pay a debt of his own, leaving the nuns penniless.

I have related in another place[2] how an association of devotees, inspired, as they supposed, from heaven, had undertaken to found a religious colony at Montreal in honor of the Holy Family. The essentials of the proposed establishment were to be a semi-nary of priests dedicated to the Virgin, a hospital to Saint Joseph, and a school to the Infant Jesus; while a settlement was to be formed around them simply for their defence and maintenance. This pious pur-pose had in part been accomplished. It was seven-teen years since Mademoiselle Mance had begun her labors in honor of Saint Joseph. Marguerite Bourgeoys had entered upon hers more recently; yet even then the attempt was premature, for she found no white children to teach. In time, however, this want was supplied, and she opened her school in a stable, which answered to the stable of Bethlehem, lodging with her pupils in the loft, and instructing them in Roman Catholic Christianity, with such rudiments of mundane knowledge as she and her advisers thought fit to impart.

Mademoiselle Mance found no lack of hospital work, for blood and blows were rife at Montreal, where the woods were full of Iroquois, and not a

---

1 Faillon, *Vie de M'lle Mance*, i. 172. This volume is illustrated with a portrait of Dauversière.

2 *The Jesuits in North America.*

Le Royer de la Dauversière.

OBIIT 6 NOV 1659
AET 63

moment was without its peril. Though years began
to tell upon her, she toiled patiently at her dreary
task, till, in the winter of 1657, she fell on the ice
of the St. Lawrence, broke her right arm, and dis-
located the wrist. Bouchard, the surgeon of Montreal,
set the broken bones, but did not discover the dis-
location. The arm in consequence became totally
useless, and her health wasted away under incessant
and violent pain. Maisonneuve, the civil and military chief of the settlement, advised her to go to
France for assistance in the work to which she was
no longer equal; and Marguerite Bourgeoys, whose
pupils, white and red, had greatly multiplied, resolved
to go with her for a similar object. They set out
in September, 1658, landed at Rochelle, and went
thence to Paris. Here they repaired to the seminary
of St. Sulpice; for the priests of this community
were joined with them in the work at Montreal, of
which they were afterwards to become the feudal
proprietors.

Now ensued a wonderful event, if we may trust
the evidence of sundry devout persons. Olier, the
founder of St. Sulpice, had lately died, and the two
pilgrims would fain pay their homage to his heart,
which the priests of his community kept as a precious
relic, enclosed in a leaden box. The box was
brought, when the thought inspired Mademoiselle
Mance to try its miraculous efficacy and invoke the
intercession of the departed founder. She did so,
touching her disabled arm gently with the leaden

casket. Instantly a grateful warmth pervaded the shrivelled limb, and from that hour its use was restored. It is true that the Jesuits ventured to doubt the Sulpitian miracle, and even to ridicule it; but the Sulpitians will show to this day the attestation of Mademoiselle Mance herself, written with the fingers once paralyzed and powerless.[1] Nevertheless, the cure was not so thorough as to permit her again to take charge of her patients.

Her next care was to visit Madame de Bullion, a devout lady of great wealth, who was usually designated at Montreal as "the unknown benefactress," because, though her charities were the mainstay of the feeble colony, and though the source from which they proceeded was well known, she affected, in the interest of humility, the greatest secrecy, and required those who profited by her gifts to pretend ignorance whence they came. Overflowing with zeal for the pious enterprise, she received her visitor with enthusiasm, lent an open ear to her recital, responded graciously to her appeal for aid, and paid over to her the sum, munificent at that day, of twenty-two thousand francs. Thus far successful, Mademoiselle Mance repaired to the town of La Flèche to visit Le Royer de la Dauversière.

It was this wretched fanatic who, through visions and revelations, had first conceived the plan of a

---

[1] For an account of this miracle, written in perfect good faith and supported by various attestations, see Faillon, *Vie de M'lle Mance*, chap. iv.

hospital in honor of Saint Joseph at Montreal.[1] He had found in Mademoiselle Mance a zealous and efficient pioneer; but the execution of his scheme required a community of hospital nuns, and therefore he had labored for the last eighteen years to form one at La Flèche, meaning to despatch its members in due time to Canada. The time at length was come. Three of the nuns were chosen, — Sisters Brésoles, Macé, and Maillet, — and sent under the escort of certain pious gentlemen to Rochelle. Their exit from La Flèche was not without its difficulties. Dauversière was in ill odor, not only from the multiplicity of his debts, but because, in his character of agent of the association of Montreal, he had at various times sent thither those whom his biographer describes as "the most virtuous girls to be found at La Flèche," intoxicating them with religious excitement, and shipping them for the New World against the will of their parents. It was noised through the town that he had kidnapped and sold them; and now the report spread abroad that he was about to crown his iniquity by luring away three young nuns. A mob gathered at the convent gate, and the escort were forced to draw their swords to open a way for the terrified sisters.

Of the twenty-two thousand francs which she had received, Mademoiselle Mance kept two thousand for immediate needs, and confided the rest to the hands of Dauversière, who, hard pressed by his creditors,

---

[1] See "The Jesuits in North America."

used it to pay one of his debts; and then, to his horror, found himself unable to replace it. Racked by the gout and tormented by remorse, he betook himself to his bed in a state of body and mind truly pitiable. One of the miracles, so frequent in the early annals of Montreal, was vouchsafed in answer to his prayer, and he was enabled to journey to Rochelle and bid farewell to his nuns. It was but a brief respite; he returned home to become the prey of a host of maladies, and to die at last a lingering and painful death.

While Mademoiselle Mance was gaining recruits in La F⸺e, Marguerite Bourgeoys was no less successful in ⸺r native town of Troyes; and she rejoined her co⸺panions at Rochelle, accompanied by Sisters Châtel⸺ Crolo, and Raisin, her destined assistants in the school at Montreal. Meanwhile, the Sulpitians and others interested in the pious enterprise, had spared no effort to gather men to strengthen the colony, and young women to serve as their wives; and all were now mustered at Rochelle, waiting for embarkation. Their waiting was a long one. Laval, bishop at Quebec, was allied to the Jesuits, and looked on the colonists of Montreal with more than coldness. Sulpitian writers say that his agents used every effort to discourage them, and that certain persons at Rochelle told the master of the ship in which the emigrants were to sail that they were not to be trusted to pay their passage-money. Hereupon ensued a delay of more than two months before means could be found to quiet the scruples of the prudent commander. At length the anchor was weighed, and the dreary voyage begun.

The woe-begone company, crowded in the filthy and infected ship, were tossed for two months more on the relentless sea, buffeted by repeated storms and wasted by a contagious fever, which attacked nearly all of them and reduced Mademoiselle Mance to extremity. Eight or ten died and were dropped overboard, after a prayer from the two priests. At length land hove in sight; the piny odors of the forest regaled their languid senses as they sailed up the broad estuary of the St. Lawrence and anchored under the rock of Quebec.

High aloft, on the brink of the cliff, they saw the *fleur-de-lis* waving above the fort of St. Louis, and, beyond, the cross on the tower of the cathedral traced against the sky, the houses of the merchants on the strand below, and boats and canoes drawn up along the bank. The bishop and the Jesuits greeted them as co-workers in a holy cause, with an unction not wholly sincere. Though a unit against heresy, the pious founders of New France were far from unity among themselves. To the thinking of the Jesuits, Montreal was a government within a government, a wheel within a wheel. This rival Sulpitian settlement was in their eyes an element of disorganization adverse to the disciplined harmony of the Canadian Church, which they would fain have seen, with its focus at Quebec, radiating light unrefracted to the uttermost parts of the colony. That is to say, they wished to control it unchecked, through their ally the bishop.

The emigrants, then, were received with a studious courtesy, which veiled but thinly a stiff and persistent opposition. The bishop and the Jesuits were especially anxious to prevent the La Flèche nuns from establishing themselves at Montreal, where they would form a separate community under Sulpitian influence; and in place of the newly arrived sisters they wished to substitute nuns from the Hôtel Dieu of Quebec, who would be under their own control. That which most strikes the non-Catholic reader throughout this affair is the constant reticence and dissimulation practised, not only between Jesuits and Montrealists, but among the Montrealists themselves. Their self-devotion, great as it was, was fairly matched by their disingenuousness.[1]

All difficulties being overcome, the Montrealists embarked in boats and ascended the St. Lawrence, leaving Quebec infected with the contagion they had brought. The journey now made in a single night cost them fifteen days of hardship and danger. At length they reached their new home. The little settlement lay before them, still gasping betwixt life and death, in a puny, precarious infancy. Some

[1] See, for example, chapter iv. of Faillon's Life of Mademoiselle Mance. The evidence is unanswerable, the writer being the partisan and admirer of most of those whose *pieuse tromperie*, to use the expression of Dollier de Casson, he describes in apparent unconsciousness that anybody will see reason to cavil at it.

forty small, compact houses were ranged parallel to
the river, chiefly along the line of what is now St.
Paul's Street.   On the left there was a fort, and on
a rising ground at the right a massive windmill of
stone, enclosed with a wall or palisade pierced for
musketry, and answering the purpose of a redoubt
or block-house.[1]   Fields studded with charred and
blackened stumps, between which crops were growing, stretched away to the edges of the bordering
forest; and the green, shaggy back of the mountain
towered over all.

There were at this time a hundred and sixty men
at Montreal, about fifty of whom had families, or at
least wives.   They greeted the new-comers with a
welcome which, this time, was as sincere as it was
warm, and bestirred themselves with alacrity to provide them with shelter for the winter.   As for the
three nuns from La Flèche, a chamber was hastily
made for them over two low rooms which had served
as Mademoiselle Mance's hospital.   This chamber
was twenty-five feet square, with four cells for the
nuns, and a closet for stores and clothing, which for
the present was empty, as they had landed in such
destitution that they were forced to sell all their
scanty equipment to gain the bare necessaries of
existence.   Little could be hoped from the colonists,
who were scarcely less destitute than they.   Such
was their poverty, — thanks to Dauversière's breach

---

[1] *Lettre du Vicomte d'Argenson, Gouverneur du Canada, 4 Août,*
1659, MS.

of trust, — that when their clothes were worn out, they were unable to replace them, and were forced to patch them with such material as came to hand. Maisonneuve the governor, and the pious Madame d'Ailleboust, being once on a visit to the hospital, amused themselves with trying to guess of what stuff the habits of the nuns had originally been made, and were unable to agree on the point in question.[1]

Their chamber, which they occupied for many years, being hastily built of ill-seasoned planks, let in the piercing cold of the Canadian winter through countless cracks and chinks; and the driving snow sifted through in such quantities that they were sometimes obliged, the morning after a storm, to remove it with shovels. Their food would freeze on the table before them, and their coarse brown bread had to be thawed on the hearth before they could cut it. These women had been nurtured in ease, if not in luxury. One of them, Judith de Brésoles, had in her youth, by advice of her confessor, run away from parents who were devoted to her, and immured herself in a convent, leaving them in agonies of doubt as to her fate. She now acted as superior of the little community. One of her nuns records of her that she had a fervent devotion for the Infant Jesus; and that, along with many more spiritual graces, he inspired her with so transcendent a skill in cookery, that "with a small piece of lean pork and a few herbs

<hr>

[1] *Annales des Hospitalières de Villemarie, par la Sœur Morin,* — a contemporary record, from which Faillon gives long extracts.

she could make soup of a marvellous relish."[1]　Sister Macé was charged with the care of the pigs and hens, to whose wants she attended in person, though she too had been delicately bred.　In course of time, the sisterhood was increased by additions from without, — though more than twenty girls who entered the hospital as novices recoiled from the hardship, and took husbands in the colony.　Among a few who took the vows, Sister Jumeau should not pass unnoticed.　Such was her humility that, though of a good family and unable to divest herself of the marks of good breeding, she pretended to be the daughter of a poor peasant, and persisted in repeating the pious falsehood till the merchant Le Ber told her flatly that he did not believe her.

The sisters had great need of a man to do the heavy work of the house and garden, but found no means of hiring one, when an incident, in which they saw a special providence, excellently supplied the want.　There was a poor colonist named Jouaneaux, to whom a piece of land had been given at some distance from the settlement.　Had he built a cabin upon it, his scalp would soon have paid the forfeit; but, being bold and hardy, he devised a plan by which he might hope to sleep in safety without abandoning the farm which was his only possession.　Among the stumps of his clearing there was one hol-

---

[1] "C'était par son recours à l'Enfant Jésus qu'elle trouvait tous ces secrets et d'autres semblables," writes in our own day the excellent annalist, Faillon.

low with age.   Under this he dug a sort of cave, the entrance of which was a small hole carefully hidden by brushwood.   The hollow stump was easily converted into a chimney; and by creeping into his burrow at night, or when he saw signs of danger, he escaped for some time the notice of the Iroquois.   But though he could dispense with a house, he needed a barn for his hay and corn; and while he was building one, he fell from the ridge of the roof and was seriously hurt. He was carried to the Hôtel Dieu, where the nuns showed him every attention, until, after a long confinement, he at last recovered.   Being of a grateful nature and enthusiastically devout, he was so touched by the kindness of his benefactors, and so moved by the spectacle of their piety, that he conceived the wish of devoting his life to their service.   To this end a contract was drawn up, by which he pledged himself to work for them as long as strength remained; and they, on their part, agreed to maintain him in sickness or old age.

This stout-hearted retainer proved invaluable; though had a guard of soldiers been added, it would have been no more than the case demanded.   Montreal was not palisaded, and at first the hospital was as much exposed as the rest.   The Iroquois would skulk at night among the houses, like wolves in a camp of sleeping travellers on the prairies; though the human foe was, of the two, incomparably the bolder, fiercer, and more bloodthirsty.   More than once one of these prowling savages was known to

have crouched all night in a rank growth of wild
mustard in the garden of the nuns, vainly hoping
that one of them would come out within reach of his
tomahawk.   During summer, a month rarely passed
without a fight, sometimes within sight of their
windows.   A burst of yells from the ambushed
marksmen, followed by a clatter of musketry, would
announce the opening of the fray, and promise the
nuns an addition to their list of patients.   On these
occasions they bore themselves according to their
several natures.   Sister Morin, who had joined their
number three years after their arrival, relates that
Sister Brésoles and she used to run to the belfry
and ring the tocsin to call the inhabitants together.
"From our high station," she writes, "we could
sometimes see the combat, which terrified us extremely,
so that we came down again as soon as we could,
trembling with fright, and thinking that our last
hour was come.   When the tocsin sounded, my
Sister Maillet would become faint with excess of
fear; and my Sister Macé, as long as the alarm continued, would remain speechless, in a state pitiable to
see.   They would both get into a corner of the rood-
loft, before the Holy Sacrament, so as to be prepared
for death, or else go into their cells.   As soon as I
heard that the Iroquois were gone, I went to tell
them, which comforted them and seemed to restore
them to life.   My Sister Brésoles was stronger and
more courageous; her terror, which she could not
help, did not prevent her from attending the sick

and receiving the dead and wounded who were brought in."

The priests of St. Sulpice, who had assumed the entire spiritual charge of the settlement, and who were soon to assume its entire temporal charge also, had for some years no other lodging than a room at the hospital, adjoining those of the patients. They caused the building to be fortified with palisades, and the houses of some of the chief inhabitants were placed near it, for mutual defence. They also built two fortified houses, called Ste. Marie and St. Gabriel, at the two extremities of the settlement, and lodged in them a considerable number of armed men, whom they employed in clearing and cultivating the surrounding lands, the property of their community. All other outlying houses were also pierced with loopholes, and fortified as well as the slender means of their owners would permit. The laborers always carried their guns to the field, and often had need to use them. A few incidents will show the state of Montreal and the character of its tenants.

In the autumn of 1657 there was a truce with the Iroquois, under cover of which three or four of them came to the settlement. Nicolas Godé and Jean Saint-Père were on the roof of their house, laying thatch, when one of the visitors aimed his arquebuse at Saint-Père, and brought him to the ground like a wild turkey from a tree. Now ensued a prodigy; for the assassins, having cut off his head and carried it home to their village, were amazed to hear it speak

to them in good Iroquois, scold them for their per-
fidy, and threaten them with the vengeance of
Heaven; and they continued to hear its voice of
admonition even after scalping it and throwing away
the skull.[1]   This story, circulated at Montreal on the
alleged authority of the Indians themselves, found believers among the most intelligent men of the colony.

Another miracle, which occurred several years
later, deserves to be recorded. Le Maître, one of
the two priests who had sailed from France with
Mademoiselle Mance and her nuns, being one day at
the fortified house of St. Gabriel, went out with the
laborers in order to watch while they were at their
work. In view of a possible enemy, he had girded
himself with an earthly sword; but seeing no sign of
danger, he presently took out his breviary, and, while
reciting his office with eyes bent on the page, walked
into an ambuscade of Iroquois, who rose before him
with a yell.

He shouted to the laborers, and, drawing his
sword, faced the whole savage crew, in order, probably, to give the men time to snatch their guns.
Afraid to approach, the Iroquois fired and killed
him; then rushed upon the working party, who
escaped into the house, after losing several of their
number. The victors cut off the head of the heroic
priest, and tied it in a white handkerchief which
they took from a pocket of his cassock. It is said
that on reaching their villages they were astonished

<hr>

[1] Dollier de Casson, *Histoire du Montréal*, 1657-1658.

to find the handkerchief without the slightest stain of blood, but stamped indelibly with the features of its late owner, so plainly marked that none who had known him could fail to recognize them.[1] This not very original miracle, though it found eager credence at Montreal, was received coolly, like other Montreal miracles, at Quebec; and Sulpitian writers complain that the bishop, in a long letter which he wrote to the Pope, made no mention of it whatever.

Le Maître, on the voyage to Canada, had been accompanied by another priest, Guillaume de Vignal, who met a fate more deplorable than that of his companion, though unattended by any recorded miracle. Le Maître had been killed in August. In the October following, Vignal went with thirteen men, in a flat-boat and several canoes, to Isle à la Pierre, nearly opposite Montreal, to get stone for the seminary which the priests had recently begun to build. With him was a pious and valiant gentleman named Claude de Brigeac, who, though but thirty years of age, had come as a soldier to Montreal, in the hope of dying in defence of the true Church, and thus reaping the reward of a martyr. Vignal and three or four men had scarcely landed when they were set upon by a large band of Iroquois who lay among the bushes waiting to receive them. The rest of the

---

[1] This story is told by Sister Morin, Marguerite Bourgeoys, and Dollier de Casson, on the authority of one Lavigne, then a prisoner among the Iroquois, who declared that he had seen the handkerchief in the hands of the returning warriors.

party, who were still in their boats, with a cowardice rare at Montreal, thought only of saving themselves. Claude de Brigeac alone leaped ashore and ran to aid his comrades. Vignal was soon mortally wounded. Brigeac shot the chief dead with his arquebuse, and then, pistol in hand, held the whole troop for an instant at bay; but his arm was shattered by a gunshot, and he was seized, along with Vignal, René Cuillérier, and Jacques Dufresne. Crossing to the main shore, immediately opposite Montreal, the Iroquois made, after their custom, a small fort of logs and branches, in which they ensconced themselves, and then began to dress the wounds of their prisoners. Seeing that Vignal was unable to make the journey to their villages, they killed him, divided his flesh, and roasted it for food.

Brigeac and his fellows in misfortune spent a woful night in this den of wolves; and in the morning their captors, having breakfasted on the remains of Vignal, took up their homeward march, dragging the Frenchmen with them. On reaching Oneida, Brigeac was tortured to death with the customary atrocities. Cuillérier, who was present, declared that they could wring from him no cry of pain, but that throughout he ceased not to pray for their conversion. The witness himself expected the same fate, but an old squaw happily adopted him, and thus saved his life. He eventually escaped to Albany, and returned to Canada by the circuitous but comparatively safe route of New York and Boston.

In the following winter, Montreal suffered an irreparable loss in the death of the brave Major Closse, a man whose intrepid coolness was never known to fail in the direst emergency. Going to the aid of a party of laborers attacked by the Iroquois, he was met by a crowd of savages, eager to kill or capture him. His servant ran off. He snapped a pistol at the foremost assailant, but it missed fire. His remaining pistol served him no better, and he was instantly shot down. "He died," writes Dollier de Casson, "like a brave soldier of Christ and the King." Some of his friends once remonstrating with him on the temerity with which he exposed his life, he replied: "Messieurs, I came here only to die in the service of God; and if I thought I could not die here, I would leave this country to fight the Turks, that I might not be deprived of such a glory."[1]

The fortified house of Ste. Marie, belonging to the priests of St. Sulpice, was the scene of several hot and bloody fights. Here, too, occurred the following nocturnal adventure. A man named Lavigne, who had lately returned from captivity among the Iroquois, chancing to rise at night and look out of the window, saw by the bright moonlight a number of naked warriors stealthily gliding round a corner and crouching near the door, in order to kill the first Frenchman who should go out in the morning. He silently woke his comrades; and, having the rest of the night for consultation, they arranged their plan

[1] Dollier de Casson, *Histoire du Montréal*, 1661. 1662.

so well that some of them, sallying from the rear of the house, came cautiously round upon the Iroquois, placed them between two fires, and captured them all.

The summer of 1661 was marked by a series of calamities scarcely paralleled even in the annals of this disastrous epoch. Early in February, thirteen colonists were surprised and captured; next came a fight between a large band of laborers and two hundred and sixty Iroquois; in the following month, ten more Frenchmen were killed or taken; and thenceforth, till winter closed, the settlement had scarcely a breathing space. "These hobgoblins," writes the author of the *Relation* of this year, "sometimes appeared at the edge of the woods, assailing us with abuse; sometimes they glided stealthily into the midst of the fields, to surprise the men at work; sometimes they approached the houses, harassing us without ceasing, and, like importunate harpies or birds of prey, swooping down on us whenever they could take us unawares."[1]

Speaking of the disasters of this year, the soldier-priest, Dollier de Casson, writes: "God, who afflicts the body only for the good of the soul, made a marvellous use of these calamities and terrors to hold the people firm in their duty towards Heaven. Vice was then almost unknown here, and in the midst of war religion flourished on all sides in a manner very different from what we now see in time of peace."[2]

---

[1] Le Jeune, *Relation*, 1661, p. 3 (ed. 1858).
[2] *Histoire du Montréal*, 1660, 1661.

The war was, in fact, a war of religion. The small redoubts of logs, scattered about the skirts of the settlement to serve as points of defence in case of attack, bore the names of saints, to whose care they were commended. There was one placed under a higher protection, and called the "Redoubt of the Infant Jesus." Chomedey de Maisonneuve, the pious and valiant governor of Montreal, to whom its successful defence is largely due, resolved, in view of the increasing fury and persistency of the Iroquois attacks, to form among the inhabitants a military fraternity, to be called "Soldiers of the Holy Family of Jesus, Mary, and Joseph;" and to this end he issued a proclamation, of which the following is the characteristic beginning: —

"We, Paul de Chomedey, governor of the island of Montreal and lands thereon dependent, on information given us from divers quarters that the Iroquois have formed the design of seizing upon this settlement by surprise or force, have thought it our duty, seeing that this island is the property of the Holy Virgin,[1] to invite and exhort those zealous for her service to unite together by squads, each of seven persons; and after choosing a corporal by a plurality of voices, to report themselves to us for enrolment in our garrison, and, in this capacity, to obey our orders, to the end that the country may be saved."

[1] This is no figure of speech. The Associates of Montreal, after receiving a grant of the island from Jean de Lauson, placed it under the protection of the Virgin, and formally declared her to be the proprietor of it from that day forth forever.

Twenty squads, numbering in all one hundred and forty men, whose names, appended to the proclamation, may still be seen on the ancient records of Montreal, answered the appeal and enrolled themselves in the holy cause.

The whole settlement was in a state of religious exaltation. As the Iroquois were regarded as actual myrmidons of Satan in his malign warfare against Mary and her divine Son, those who died in fighting them were held to merit the reward of martyrs, assured of a seat in paradise.

And now it remains to record one of the most heroic feats of arms ever achieved on this continent. That it may be rated as it merits, it will be well to glance for a moment at the condition of Canada, under the portentous cloud of war which constantly overshadowed it.[1]

---

[1] In all that relates to Montreal, I cannot be sufficiently grateful to the Abbé Faillon, the indefatigable, patient, conscientious chronicler of its early history ; an ardent and prejudiced Sulpitian, a priest who three centuries ago would have passed for credulous, and, withal, a kind-hearted and estimable man. His numerous books on his favorite theme, with the vast and heterogeneous mass of facts which they embody, are invaluable, provided their partisan character be well kept in mind. His recent death leaves his principal work unfinished. His *Histoire de la Colonie Française en Canada* — it might more fitly be called *Histoire du Montréal* — is unhappily little more than half complete.

CHAPTER VI.

1660, 1661.

THE HEROES OF THE LONG SAUT.

Canada had writhed for twenty years, with little respite, under the scourge of Iroquois war. During a great part of this dark period the entire French population was less than three thousand. What, then, saved them from destruction? In the first place, the settlements were grouped around three fortified posts, — Quebec, Three Rivers, and Montreal, — which in time of danger gave asylum to the fugitive inhabitants. Again, their assailants were continually distracted by other wars, and never, except at a few spasmodic intervals, were fully in earnest to destroy the French colony. Canada was indispensable to them. The four upper nations of the league soon became dependent on her for supplies; and all the nations alike appear, at a very early period, to have conceived the policy on which they afterwards distinctly acted, of balancing the rival settlements of the Hudson and the St. Lawrence, the one against the other. They would torture, but not kill. It was but rarely that, in fits of fury, they struck their hatchets at the brain; and thus the bleeding and gasping colony lingered on in torment.

The seneschal of New France, son of the governor Lauson, was surprised and killed on the island of Orleans, along with seven companions. About the same time, the same fate befell the son of Godefroy, one of the chief inhabitants of Quebec. Outside the fortifications there was no safety for a moment. A universal terror seized the people. A comet appeared above Quebec, and they saw in it a herald of destruction. Their excited imaginations turned natural phenomena into portents and prodigies. A blazing canoe sailed across the sky; confused cries and lamentations were heard in the air; and a voice of thunder sounded from mid-heaven.[1] The Jesuits despaired for their scattered and persecuted flocks. "Everywhere," writes their superior, "we see infants to be saved for heaven, sick and dying to be baptized, adults to be instructed; but everywhere we see the Iroquois. They haunt us like persecuting goblins. They kill our new-made Christians in our arms. If they meet us on the river, they kill us. If they find us in the huts of our Indians, they burn us and them together."[2]   And he appeals urgently for troops

[1] Marie de l'Incarnation, *Lettre, Septembre,* 1661.
[2] *Relation,* 1660 (anonymous), 3.

to destroy them, as a holy work inspired by God, and needful for his service.

Canada was still a mission, and the influence of the Church was paramount and pervading. At Quebec, as at Montreal, the war with the Iroquois was regarded as a war with the hosts of Satan. Of the settlers' cabins scattered along the shores above and below Quebec, many were provided with small iron cannon, made probably by blacksmiths in the colony; but they had also other protectors. In each was an image of the Virgin or some patron saint; and every morning the pious settler knelt before the shrine to beg the protection of a celestial hand in his perilous labors of the forest or the farm.

When, in the summer of 1658, the young Vicomte d'Argenson came to assume the thankless task of governing the colony, the Iroquois war was at its height. On the day after his arrival, he was washing his hands before seating himself at dinner in the hall of the Château St. Louis, when cries of alarm were heard, and he was told that the Iroquois were close at hand. In fact, they were so near that their war-whoops and the screams of their victims could plainly be heard. Argenson left his guests, and, with such a following as he could muster at the moment, hastened to the rescue; but the assailants were too nimble for him. The forests, which grew at that time around Quebec, favored them both in attack and in retreat. After a year or two of experience, he wrote urgently to the court for troops. He adds that, what with the demands of the harvest and the unmilitary character of many of the settlers, the colony could not furnish more than a hundred men for offensive operations. A vigorous, aggressive war, he insists, is absolutely necessary, and this not only to save the colony, but to save the only true faith; "for," to borrow his own words, "it is this colony alone which has the honor to be in the communion of the Holy Church. Everywhere else reigns the doctrine of England or Holland, to which I can give no other name, because there are as many creeds as there are subjects who embrace them. They do not care in the least whether the Iroquois and the other savages of this country have or have not a knowledge of the true God, or else they are so malicious as to inject the venom of their errors into souls incapable of distinguishing the truth of the gospel from the falsehoods of heresy; and hence it is plain that religion has its sole support in the French colony, and that, if this colony is in danger, religion is equally in danger."[1]

Among the most interesting memorials of the time are two letters written by François Hertel, a youth of eighteen, captured at Three Rivers, and carried to the Mohawk towns in the summer of 1661. He belonged to one of the best families of Canada, and was the favorite child of his mother, to whom the second of the two letters is addressed. The first is to the Jesuit Le Moyne, who had gone to Onondaga,

---

[1] *Papiers d'Argenson; Mémoire sur le sujet de la guerre des Iroquois*, 1659 (1660 ?). *MS.*

in July of that year, to effect the release of French prisoners in accordance with the terms of a truce.[1] Both letters were written on birch-bark: —

My Reverend Father, — The very day when you left Three Rivers I was captured, at about three in the afternoon, by four Iroquois of the Mohawk tribe. I would not have been taken alive, if, to my sorrow, I had not feared that I was not in a fit state to die. If you came here, my Father, I could have the happiness of confessing to you ; and I do not think they would do you any harm ; and I think that I could return home with you. I pray you to pity my poor mother, who is in great trouble. You know, my Father, how fond she is of me. I have heard from a Frenchman, who was taken at Three Rivers on the 1st of August, that she is well, and comforts herself with the hope that I shall see you. There are three of us Frenchmen alive here. I commend myself to your good prayers, and particularly to the Holy Sacrifice of the Mass. I pray you, my Father, to say a mass for me. I pray you give my dutiful love to my poor mother, and console her, if it pleases you.

My Father, I beg your blessing on the hand that writes to you, which has one of the fingers burned in the bowl of an Indian pipe, to satisfy the Majesty of God which I have offended. The thumb of the other hand is cut off ; but do not tell my mother of it.

My Father, I pray you to honor me with a word from your hand in reply, and tell me if you shall come here before winter.

Your most humble and most obedient servant,

François Hertel.

[1] Journal des Jésuites, 300.

The following is the letter to his mother, sent probably, with the other, to the charge of Le Moyne: —

My most dear and honored Mother, — I know very well that my capture must have distressed you very much. I ask you to forgive my disobedience. It is my sins that have placed me where I am. I owe my life to your prayers, and those of M. de Saint-Quentin, and of my sisters. I hope to see you again before winter. I pray you to tell the good brethren of Notre Dame to pray to God and the Holy Virgin for me, my dear mother, and for you and all my sisters.

Your poor

Fanchon.

This, no doubt, was the name by which she had called him familiarly when a child. And who was this "Fanchon," this devout and tender son of a fond mother? New England can answer to her cost. When, twenty-nine years later, a band of French and Indians issued from the forest and fell upon the fort and settlement of Salmon Falls, it was François Hertel who led the attack; and when the retiring victors were hard pressed by an overwhelming force, it was he who, sword in hand, held the pursuers in check at the bridge of Wooster River, and covered the retreat of his men. He was ennobled for his services, and died at the age of eighty, the founder of one of the most distinguished families of Canada.[1]

---

[1] His letters of nobility, dated 1716, will be found in Daniel's *Histoire des Grandes Familles Françaises du Canada*, 404.

To the New England of old he was the abhorred chief of Popish malignants and murdering savages. The New England of to-day will be more just to the brave defender of his country and his faith.

In May, 1660, a party of French Algonquins captured a Wolf, or Mohegan, Indian, naturalized among the Iroquois, brought him to Quebec, and burned him there with their usual atrocity of torture. A modern Catholic writer says that the Jesuits could not save him; but this is not so. Their influence over the consciences of the colonists was at that time unbounded, and their direct political power was very great. A protest on their part, and that of the newly arrived bishop, who was in their interest, could not have failed of effect. The truth was, they did not care to prevent the torture of prisoners of war, — not solely out of that spirit of compliance with the savage humor of Indian allies which stains so often the pages of French American history, but also, and perhaps chiefly, from motives purely religious. Torture, in their eyes, seems to have been a blessing in disguise. They thought it good for the soul, and in case of obduracy the surest way of salvation. "We have very rarely indeed," writes one of them, "seen the burning of an Iroquois without feeling sure that he was on the path to paradise; and we never knew one of them to be surely on the path to paradise without seeing him pass through this fiery punishment."[1] So they let the Wolf burn; but

----

[1] *Relation*, 1660, 31.

first, having instructed him after their fashion, they
baptized him, and his savage soul flew to heaven out
of the fire. "Is it not," pursues the same writer, "a
marvel to see a wolf changed at one stroke into a
lamb, and enter into the fold of Christ, which he
came to ravage?"

Before he died, he requited their spiritual cares
with a startling secret. He told them that eight
hundred Iroquois warriors were encamped below
Montreal; that four hundred more, who had wintered
on the Ottawa, were on the point of joining them;
and that the united force would swoop upon Quebec,
kill the governor, lay waste the town, and then
attack Three Rivers and Montreal.[1] This time, at
least, the Iroquois were in deadly earnest. Quebec
was wild with terror. The Ursulines and the nuns
of the Hôtel Dieu took refuge in the strong and extensive building which the Jesuits had just finished,
opposite the Parish Church. Its walls and palisades
made it easy of defence; and in its yards and court
were lodged the terrified Hurons, as well as the
fugitive inhabitants of the neighboring settlements.
Others found asylum in the fort, and others in the
convent of the Ursulines, which, in place of nuns,
was occupied by twenty-four soldiers, who fortified
it with redoubts, and barricaded the doors and
windows. Similar measures of defence were taken
at the Hôtel Dieu, and the streets of the Lower
Town were strongly barricaded. Everybody was in

---

[1] Marie de l'Incarnation, *Lettre*, 25 *Juin*, 1660.

arms, and the *Qui vive* of the sentries and patrols resounded all night.[1]

Several days passed, and no Iroquois appeared. The refugees took heart, and began to return to their deserted farms and dwellings. Among the rest was a family consisting of an old woman, her daughter, her son-in-law, and four small children, living near St. Anne, some twenty miles below Quebec. On reaching home, the old woman and the man went to their work in the fields, while the mother and children remained in the house. Here they were pounced upon and captured by eight renegade Hurons, Iroquois by adoption, who placed them in their large canoe, and paddled up the river with their prize. It was Saturday, a day dedicated to the Virgin; and the captive mother prayed to her for aid, "feeling," writes a Jesuit, "a full conviction that, in passing before Quebec on a Saturday, she would be delivered by the power of this Queen of Heaven." In fact, as the marauders and their captives glided in the darkness of night by Point Levi, under the shadow of the shore, they were greeted with a volley of musketry from the bushes, and a band of French and Algonquins dashed into the water to seize them. Five of the eight were taken, and the rest shot or drowned. The governor had heard of the descent at St. Anne, and despatched a

---

[1] On this alarm at Quebec compare Marie de l'Incarnation, 25 Juin, 1660; *Relation*, 1660, 5; Juchereau, *Histoire de l'Hôtel-Dieu de Québec*, 125, and *Journal des Jésuites*, 282.

party to lie in ambush for the authors of it. The Jesuits, it is needless to say, saw a miracle in the result. The Virgin had answered the prayer of her votary, — "though it is true," observes the father who records the marvel, "that, in the volley, she received a mortal wound." The same shot struck the infant in her arms. The prisoners were taken to Quebec, where four of them were tortured with even more ferocity than had been shown in the case of the unfortunate Wolf.[1] Being questioned, they confirmed his story, and expressed great surprise that the Iroquois had not come, adding that they must have stopped to attack Montreal or Three Rivers. Again all was terror, and again days passed and no enemy appeared. Had the dying converts, so charitably despatched to heaven through fire, sought an unhallowed consolation in scaring the abettors of their torture with a lie? Not at all. Bating a slight exaggeration, they had told the truth. Where, then, were the Iroquois? As one small point of

---

[1] The torturers were Christian Algonquins, converts of the Jesuits. Chaumonot, who was present to give spiritual aid to the sufferers, describes the scene with horrible minuteness. "I could not," he says, "deliver them from their torments." Perhaps not: but it is certain that the Jesuits as a body, with or without the bishop, could have prevented the atrocity, had they seen fit. They sometimes taught their converts to pray for their enemies. It would have been well had they taught them not to torture them. I can recall but one instance in which they did so. The prayers for enemies were always for a spiritual, not a temporal good. The fathers held the body in slight account, and cared little what happened to it.

steel disarms the lightning of its terrors, so did the heroism of a few intrepid youths divert this storm of war, and save Canada from a possible ruin.

In the preceding April, before the designs of the Iroquois were known, a young officer named Daulac, commandant of the garrison of Montreal, asked leave of Maisonneuve, the governor, to lead a party of volunteers against the enemy. His plan was bold to desperation. It was known that Iroquois warriors in great numbers had wintered among the forests of the Ottawa. Daulac proposed to waylay them on their descent of the river, and fight them without regard to disparity of force. The settlers of Montreal had hitherto acted solely on the defensive, for their numbers had been too small for aggressive war. Of late their strength had been somewhat increased, and Maisonneuve, judging that a display of enterprise and boldness might act as a check on the audacity of the enemy, at length gave his consent.

Adam Daulac, or Dollard, Sieur des Ormeaux, was a young man of good family, who had come to the colony three years before, at the age of twenty-two. He had held some military command in France, though in what rank does not appear. It was said that he had been involved in some affair which made him anxious to wipe out the memory of the past by a noteworthy exploit; and he had been busy for some time among the young men of Montreal, inviting them to join him in the enterprise he meditated. Sixteen of them caught his spirit, struck hands with him, and pledged their word. They bound themselves by oath to accept no quarter; and, having gained Maisonneuve's consent, they made their wills, confessed, and received the sacraments. As they knelt for the last time before the altar in the chapel of the Hôtel Dieu, that sturdy little population of pious Indian-fighters gazed on them with enthusiasm, not unmixed with an envy which had in it nothing ignoble. Some of the chief men of Montreal, with the brave Charles Le Moyne at their head, begged them to wait till the spring sowing was over, that they might join them; but Daulac refused. He was jealous of the glory and the danger, and he wished to command, which he could not have done had Le Moyne been present.

The spirit of the enterprise was purely mediæval. The enthusiasm of honor, the enthusiasm of adventure, and the enthusiasm of faith were its motive forces. Daulac was a knight of the early crusades among the forests and savages of the New World. Yet the incidents of this exotic heroism are definite and clear as a tale of yesterday. The names, ages, and occupations of the seventeen young men may still be read on the ancient register of the parish of Montreal; and the notarial acts of that year, preserved in the records of the city, contain minute accounts of such property as each of them possessed. The three eldest were of twenty-eight, thirty, and thirty-one years respectively. The age of the rest varied from twenty-one to twenty-seven. They were of various callings, — soldiers, armorers, locksmiths, lime-burners, or settlers without trades. The greater number had come to the colony as part of the reinforcement brought by Maisonneuve in 1653.

After a solemn farewell, they embarked in several canoes well supplied with arms and ammunition. They were very indifferent canoe-men; and it is said that they lost a week in vain attempts to pass the swift current of St. Anne, at the head of the island of Montreal. At length they were more successful, and entering the mouth of the Ottawa, crossed the Lake of Two Mountains, and slowly advanced against the current.

Meanwhile, forty warriors of that remnant of the Hurons who, in spite of Iroquois persecutions, still lingered at Quebec, had set out on a war-party, led by the brave and wily Etienne Annahotaha, their most noted chief. They stopped by the way at Three Rivers, where they found a band of Christian Algonquins under a chief named Mituvemeg. Annahotaha challenged him to a trial of courage, and it was agreed that they should meet at Montreal, where they were likely to find a speedy opportunity of putting their mettle to the test. Thither, accordingly, they repaired, the Algonquin with three followers, and the Huron with thirty-nine.

It was not long before they learned the departure of Daulac and his companions. "For," observes the honest Dollier de Casson, "the principal fault of our Frenchmen is to talk too much." The wish seized them to share the adventure, and to that end the

Huron chief asked the governor for a letter to Daulac, to serve as credentials. Maisonneuve hesitated. His faith in Huron valor was not great, and he feared the proposed alliance. Nevertheless, he at length yielded so far as to give Annahotaha a letter, in which Daulac was told to accept or reject the proffered reinforcement as he should see fit. The Hurons and Algonquins now embarked, and paddled in pursuit of the seventeen Frenchmen.

They meanwhile had passed with difficulty the swift current at Carillon, and about the first of May reached the foot of the more formidable rapid called the Long Saut, where a tumult of waters, foaming among ledges and bowlders, barred the onward way. It was needless to go farther. The Iroquois were sure to pass the Saut, and could be fought here as well as elsewhere. Just below the rapid, where the forests sloped gently to the shore, among the bushes and stumps of the rough clearing made in constructing it, stood a palisade fort, the work of an Algonquin war-party in the past autumn. It was a mere enclosure of trunks of small trees planted in a circle, and was already ruinous. Such as it was, the Frenchmen took possession of it. Their first care, one would think, should have been to repair and strengthen it; but this they seem not to have done, — possibly, in the exaltation of their minds, they scorned such precaution. They made their fires, and slung their kettles on the neighboring shore; and here they were soon joined by the Hurons and

Algonquins. Daulac, it seems, made no objection to their company, and they all bivouacked together. Morning and noon and night they prayed in three different tongues; and when at sunset the long reach of forests on the farther shore basked peacefully in the level rays, the rapids joined their hoarse music to the notes of their evening hymn.

In a day or two their scouts came in with tidings that two Iroquois canoes were coming down the Saut. Daulac had time to set his men in ambush among the bushes at a point where he thought the strangers likely to land. He judged aright. The canoes, bearing five Iroquois, approached, and were met by a volley fired with such precipitation that one or more of them escaped the shot, fled into the forest, and told their mischance to their main body, two hundred in number, on the river above. A fleet of canoes suddenly appeared, bounding down the rapids, filled with warriors eager for revenge. The allies had barely time to escape to their fort, leaving their kettles still slung over the fires. The Iroquois made a hasty and desultory attack, and were quickly repulsed. They next opened a parley, hoping, no doubt, to gain some advantage by surprise. Failing in this, they set themselves, after their custom on such occasions, to building a rude fort of their own in the neighboring forest.

This gave the French a breathing-time, and they used it for strengthening their defences. Being provided with tools, they planted a row of stakes within their palisade, to form a double fence, and filled the intervening space with earth and stones to the height of a man, leaving some twenty loop-holes, at each of which three marksmen were stationed. Their work was still unfinished when the Iroquois were upon them again. They had broken to pieces the birch canoes of the French and their allies, and, kindling the bark, rushed up to pile it blazing against the palisade; but so brisk and steady a fire met them that they recoiled, and at last gave way. They came on again, and again were driven back, leaving many of their number on the ground, — among them the principal chief of the Senecas. Some of the French dashed out, and, covered by the fire of their comrades, hacked off his head, and stuck it on the palisade, while the Iroquois howled in a frenzy of helpless rage. They tried another attack, and were beaten off a third time.

This dashed their spirits, and they sent a canoe to call to their aid five hundred of their warriors who were mustered near the mouth of the Richelieu. These were the allies whom, but for this untoward check, they were on their way to join for a combined attack on Quebec, Three Rivers, and Montreal. It was maddening to see their grand project thwarted by a few French and Indians ensconced in a paltry redoubt, scarcely better than a cattle-pen; but they were forced to digest the affront as best they might.

Meanwhile, crouched behind trees and logs, they beset the fort, harassing its defenders day and night with a spattering fire and a constant menace of attack. Thus five days passed. Hunger, thirst, and want of sleep wrought fatally on the strength of the French and their allies, who, pent up together in their narrow prison, fought and prayed by turns. Deprived as they were of water, they could not swallow the crushed Indian corn, or "hominy," which was their only food. Some of them, under cover of a brisk fire, ran down to the river and filled such small vessels as they had; but this pittance only tantalized their thirst. They dug a hole in the fort, and were rewarded at last by a little muddy water oozing through the clay.

Among the assailants were a number of Hurons, adopted by the Iroquois and fighting on their side. These renegades now shouted to their countrymen in the fort, telling them that a fresh army was close at hand; that they would soon be attacked by seven or eight hundred warriors; and that their only hope was in joining the Iroquois, who would receive them as friends. Annahotaha's followers, half dead with thirst and famine, listened to their seducers, took the bait, and, one, two, or three at a time, climbed the palisade and ran over to the enemy, amid the hootings and execrations of those whom they deserted. Their chief stood firm; and when he saw his nephew, La Mouche, join the other fugitives, he fired his pistol at him in a rage. The four Algonquins, who had no mercy to hope for, stood fast, with the courage of despair.

On the fifth day an uproar of unearthly yells from seven hundred savage throats, mingled with a clattering salute of musketry, told the Frenchmen that the expected reinforcement had come; and soon, in the forest and on the clearing, a crowd of warriors mustered for the attack. Knowing from the Huron deserters the weakness of their enemy, they had no doubt of an easy victory. They advanced cautiously, as was usual with the Iroquois before their blood was up, screeching, leaping from side to side, and firing as they came on; but the French were at their posts, and every loophole darted its tongue of fire. Besides muskets, they had heavy musketoons of large calibre, which, scattering scraps of lead and iron among the throng of savages, often maimed several of them at one discharge. The Iroquois, astonished at the persistent vigor of the defence, fell back discomfited. The fire of the French, who were themselves completely under cover, had told upon them with deadly effect. Three days more wore away in a series of futile attacks, made with little concert or vigor; and during all this time Daulac and his men, reeling with exhaustion, fought and prayed as before, sure of a martyr's reward.

The uncertain, vacillating temper common to all Indians now began to declare itself. Some of the Iroquois were for going home. Others revolted at the thought, and declared that it would be an eternal disgrace to lose so many men at the hands of so paltry an enemy, and yet fail to take revenge. It was resolved to make a general assault, and volunteers were called for to lead the attack. After the custom on such occasions, bundles of small sticks were thrown upon the ground, and those picked them up who dared, thus accepting the gage of battle, and enrolling themselves in the forlorn hope. No precaution was neglected. Large and heavy shields four or five feet high were made by lashing together three split logs with the aid of cross-bars. Covering themselves with these mantelets, the chosen band advanced, followed by the motley throng of warriors. In spite of a brisk fire, they reached the palisade, and, crouching below the range of shot, hewed furiously with their hatchets to cut their way through. The rest followed close, and swarmed like angry hornets around the little fort, hacking and tearing to get in.

Daulac had crammed a large musketoon with powder, and plugged up the muzzle. Lighting the fuse inserted in it, he tried to throw it over the barrier, to burst like a grenade among the crowd of savages without; but it struck the ragged top of one of the palisades, fell back among the Frenchmen and exploded, killing and wounding several of them, and nearly blinding others. In the confusion that followed, the Iroquois got possession of the loopholes, and, thrusting in their guns, fired on those within. In a moment more they had torn a breach in the palisade; but, nerved with the energy of desperation, Daulac and his followers sprang to defend it.

Another breach was made, and then another.   Daulac was struck dead, but the survivors kept up the fight. With a sword or a hatchet in one hand and a knife in the other, they threw themselves against the throng of enemies, striking and stabbing with the fury of madmen; till the Iroquois, despairing of taking them alive, fired volley after volley and shot them down.   All was over, and a burst of triumphant yells proclaimed the dear-bought victory.

Searching the pile of corpses, the victors found four Frenchmen still breathing.   Three had scarcely a spark of life, and, as no time was to be lost, they burned them on the spot.   The fourth, less fortunate, seemed likely to survive, and they reserved him for future torments.   As for the Huron deserters, their cowardice profited them little.   The Iroquois, regardless of their promises, fell upon them, burned some at once, and carried the rest to their villages for a similar fate.   Five of the number had the good fortune to escape; and it was from them, aided by admissions made long afterwards by the Iroquois themselves, that the French of Canada derived all their knowledge of this glorious disaster.[1]

---

[1] When the fugitive Hurons reached Montreal, they were unwilling to confess their desertion of the French, and declared that they and some others of their people, to the number of fourteen, had stood by them to the last.   This was the story told by one of them to the Jesuit Chaumonot, and by him communicated in a letter to his friends at Quebec.   The substance of this letter is given by Marie de l'Incarnation, in her letter to her son of June 25, 1660.   The Jesuit *Relation* of this year gives another long account of the affair, also derived from the Huron deserters, who this time

To the colony it proved a salvation.   The Iroquois had had fighting enough.   If seventeen Frenchmen, four Algonquins, and one Huron, behind a picket fence, could hold seven hundred warriors at bay so long, what might they expect from many such, fight-

only pretended that ten of their number remained with the French. They afterwards admitted that all had deserted but Annahotaha, as appears from the account drawn up by Dollier de Casson, in his *Histoire du Montréal*.   Another contemporary, Belmont, who heard the story from an Iroquois, makes the same statement.   All these writers, though two of them were not friendly to Montreal, agree that Daulac and his followers saved Canada from a disastrous invasion.   The governor, Argenson, in a letter written on the fourth of July following, and in his *Mémoire sur le sujet de la guerre des Iroquois*, expresses the same conviction.   Before me is an extract, copied from the *Petit Registre de la Cure de Montréal*, giving the names and ages of Daulac's men.

Radisson, the famous *voyageur*, says that, on his way down the Ottawa from Lake Superior, he passed the Long Saut eight days after the destruction of Daulac and his party; and he gives an account of the fight that answers on the whole to those of the other writers.   He adds, however, that the Hurons remained outside the fort, which was too small to hold them, and that only the seventeen Frenchmen and four Algonquins — or twenty-one in all — were under cover.   He also says that the reinforcement which joined the two hundred Iroquois who began the attack consisted of "five hundred and fifty Iroquoits of the lower nation [Mohawks] and fifty Orijonot" (Oneidas?), — making with the original assailants eight hundred in all.   (*Publications of the Prince Society*, 1885, 233.)   Radisson, whose narratives were not written till some years after the events that they record, forgets the date of the fight at the Long Saut, which would appear from him to have happened three years after it really took place.

Abbé Faillon took extreme pains to collect the evidence touching Daulac's heroism, and, though Radisson's writings were unknown to him, his narrative should be consulted by those interested in the subject.   See his anonymous *Histoire de la Colonie Française au Canada*, ii. chap. xv.

ing behind walls of stone? For that year they thought no more of capturing Quebec and Montreal, but went home dejected and amazed, to howl over their losses, and nurse their dashed courage for a day of vengeance.

CHAPTER VII.

1657-1668.

THE DISPUTED BISHOPRIC.

Canada, gasping under the Iroquois tomahawk, might, one would suppose, have thought her cup of tribulation full, and, sated with inevitable woe, have sought consolation from the wrath without in a holy calm within. Not so, however; for while the heathen raged at the door, discord rioted at the hearthstone. Her domestic quarrels were wonderful in number, diversity, and bitterness. There was the standing quarrel of Montreal and Quebec, the quarrels of priests with one another, of priests with the governor, and of the governor with the intendant, besides ceaseless wranglings of rival traders and rival peculators.

Some of these disputes were local and of no special significance; while others are very interesting, because, on a remote and obscure theatre, they represent, sometimes in striking forms, the contending passions, and principles of a most important epoch of history. To begin with one which even to this day has left a root of bitterness behind it.

The association of pious enthusiasts who had founded Montreal [1] was reduced in 1657 to a remnant of five or six persons, whose ebbing zeal and over-taxed purses were no longer equal to the devout but arduous enterprise. They begged the priests of the Seminary of St. Sulpice to take it off their hands. The priests consented; and, though the conveyance of the island of Montreal to these its new proprietors did not take effect till some years later, four of the Sulpitian fathers — Queylus, Souart, Galinée, and Allet — came out to the colony and took it in charge. Thus far Canada had had no bishop, and the Sulpitians now aspired to give it one from their own brotherhood. Many years before, when the Récollets had a foothold in the colony, they too, or at least some of them, had cherished the hope of giving Canada a bishop of their own. As for the Jesuits, who for nearly thirty years had of themselves consti-tuted the Canadian church, they had been content thus far to dispense with a bishop; for having no rivals in the field, they had felt no need of episcopal support.

The Sulpitians put forward Queylus as their candi-date for the new bishopric. The assembly of French

---

[1] See "Jesuits in North America," ii. chap. xxii.

clergy approved, and Cardinal Mazarin himself seemed to sanction, the nomination. The Jesuits saw that their time of action was come. It was they who had borne the heat and burden of the day, the toils, privations, and martyrdoms, while as yet the Sulpitians had done nothing and endured nothing. If any body of ecclesiastics was to have the nomination of a bishop, it clearly belonged to them, the Jesuits. Their might, too, matched their right. They were strong at court; Mazarin withdrew his assent, and the Jesuits were invited to name a bishop to their liking.

Meanwhile the Sulpitians, despairing of the bishopric, had sought their solace elsewhere. Ships bound for Canada had usually sailed from ports within the jurisdiction of the Archbishop of Rouen, and the departing missionaries had received their ecclesiastical powers from him, till he had learned to regard Canada as an outlying section of his diocese. Not unwilling to assert his claims, he now made Queylus his vicar-general for all Canada, thus clothing him with episcopal powers, and placing him over the heads of the Jesuits. Queylus, in effect though not in name a bishop, left his companion Souart in the spiritual charge of Montreal, came down to Quebec, announced his new dignity, and assumed the curacy of the parish. The Jesuits received him at first with their usual urbanity, an exercise of self-control rendered more easy by their knowledge that one more potent than Queylus would soon arrive to supplant him.[1]

The vicar of the Archbishop of Rouen was a man of many virtues, devoted to good works, as he understood them; rich, for the Sulpitians were under no vow of poverty; generous in almsgiving, busy, indefatigable, overflowing with zeal, vivacious in temperament and excitable in temper, impatient of opposition, and, as it seems, incapable, like his destined rival, of seeing any way of doing good but his own. Though the Jesuits were outwardly courteous, their partisans would not listen to the new curé's sermons, or listened only to find fault; and germs of discord grew vigorously in the parish of Quebec. Prudence was not among the virtues of Queylus. He launched two sermons against the Jesuits, in which he likened himself to Christ and them to the Pharisees. "Who," he supposed them to say, "is this Jesus, so beloved of the people, who comes to cast discredit on us, who for thirty or forty years have governed church and state here, with none to dispute us?"[2] He denounced such of his

[1] A detailed account of the experiences of Queylus at Quebec, immediately after his arrival, as related by himself, will be found in a memoir by the Sulpitian Allet, in *Morale Pratique des Jésuites*, xxxiv. chap. xii. In chapter ten of the same volume the writer says that he visited Queylus at Mont St. Valérien, after his return from Canada. "Il me prit à part; nous nous promenâmes assez longtemps dans le jardin et il m'ouvrit son cœur sur la conduite des Jésuites dans le Canada et partout ailleurs. Messieurs de St. Sulpice savent bien ce qu'il m'en a pu dire, et je suis assuré qu'ils ne diront pas que je l'ai dû prendre pour des mensonges."

[2] *Journal des Jésuites, Octobre,* 1657.

hearers as came to pick flaws in his discourse, and told them it would be better for their souls if they lay in bed at home, sick of a "good quartan fever." His ire was greatly kindled by a letter of the Jesuit Pijart, which fell into his hands through a female adherent, the pious Madame d'Ailleboust, and in which that father declared that he, Queylus, was waging war on him and his brethren more savagely than the Iroquois.[1] "He was as crazy at sight of a Jesuit," writes an adverse biographer, "as a mad dog at sight of water."[2] He cooled, however, on being shown certain papers which proved that his position was neither so strong nor so secure as he had supposed; and the governor, Argenson, at length persuaded him to retire to Montreal.[3]

The queen-mother, Anne of Austria, always inclined to the Jesuits, had invited Father Le Jeune, who was then in France, to make choice of a bishop for Canada. It was not an easy task. No Jesuit was eligible, for the sage policy of Loyola had excluded members of the order from the bishopric. The signs of the times portended trouble for the Canadian church, and there was need of a bishop who would assert her claims and fight her battles. Such a man could not be made an instrument of the Jesuits; therefore there was double need that he should be one with them in sympathy and purpose.

---

[1] *Journal des Jésuites, Octobre,* 1657.

[2] Viger, *Notice Historique sur l'Abbé de Queylus.*

[3] *Papiers d'Argenson.*

They made a sagacious choice.   Le Jeune presented
to the queen-mother the name of François Xavier de
Laval-Montmorency, Abbé de Montigny.

Laval, for by this name he was thenceforth known,
belonged to one of the proudest families of Europe,
and, churchman as he was, there is much in his
career to remind us that in his veins ran the blood
of the stern Constable of France, Anne de Montmorency.   Nevertheless, his thoughts from childhood
had turned towards the Church, or, as his biographers
will have it, all his aspirations were heavenward.
He received the tonsure at the age of nine.   The
Jesuit Bagot confirmed and moulded his youthful
predilections; and at a later period he was one of a
band of young zealots formed under the auspices of
Bernières de Louvigni, royal treasurer at Caen, who,
though a layman, was reputed almost a saint.   It
was Bernières who had borne the chief part in the
pious fraud of the pretended marriage through which
Madame de la Peltrie escaped from her father's roof
to become foundress of the Ursulines of Quebec.[1]
He had since renounced the world, and dwelt at
Caen in a house attached to an Ursuline convent,
and known as the "Hermitage."   Here he lived like
a monk, in the midst of a community of young
priests and devotees, who looked to him as their
spiritual director, and whom he trained in the
maxims and practices of the most extravagant, or, as

----

[1] See "Jesuits in North America," i. chap. xiv.

his admirers say, the most sublime ultramontane piety.[1]

The conflict between the Jesuits and the Jansenists was then at its height. The Jansenist doctrines of election and salvation by grace, which sapped the power of the priesthood and impugned the authority of the Pope himself in his capacity of holder of the keys of heaven, were to the Jesuits an abomination; while the rigid morals of the Jansenists stood in stern contrast to the pliancy of Jesuit casuistry. Bernières and his disciples were zealous, not to say fanatical, partisans of the Jesuits. There is a long account of the "Hermitage" and its inmates from the pen of the famous Jansenist Nicole, — an opponent, it is true, but one whose qualities of mind and character give weight to his testimony.[2]

"In this famous Hermitage," says Nicole, "the late Sieur de Bernières brought up a number of young men, to whom he taught a sort of sublime and transcendental devotion called *passive prayer*, because in it the mind does not act at all, but merely receives the divine operation; and this devotion is the source of all those visions and revelations in which the Hermitage is so prolific." In short, he and his disciples were mystics of the most exalted type. Nicole pursues: "After having thus subtilized

[1] La Tour in his *Vie de Laval* gives his maxims at length.

[2] *Mémoire pour faire connoistre l'esprit et la conduite de la Compagnie établie en la ville de Caen, appellée l'Hermitage* (Bibliothèque Nationale. Imprimés. Partie Réservée). Written in 1660.

their minds, and almost sublimed them into vapor, he rendered them capable of detecting Jansenists under any disguise, insomuch that some of his followers said that they knew them by the scent, as dogs know their game; but the aforesaid Sieur de Bernières denied that they had so subtile a sense of smell, and said that the mark by which he detected Jansenists was their disapproval of his teachings or their opposition to the Jesuits."

The zealous band at the Hermitage was aided in its efforts to extirpate error by a sort of external association in the city of Caen, consisting of merchants, priests, officers, petty nobles, and others, all inspired and guided by Bernières. They met every week at the Hermitage, or at the houses of one another. Similar associations existed in other cities of France, besides a fraternity in the Rue St. Dominique at Paris, which was formed by the Jesuit Bagot, and seems to have been the parent, in a certain sense, of the others. They all acted together when any important object was in view.

Bernières and his disciples felt that God had chosen them not only to watch over doctrine and discipline in convents and in families, but also to supply the prevalent deficiency of zeal in bishops and other dignitaries of the Church. They kept, too, a constant eye on the humbler clergy, and whenever a new preacher appeared in Caen, two of their number were deputed to hear his sermon and report upon it. If he chanced to let fall a word concerning the grace of God, they denounced him for Jansenistic heresy. Such commotion was once raised in Caen by charges of sedition and Jansenism, brought by the Hermitage against priests and laymen hitherto without attaint, that the Bishop of Bayeux thought it necessary to interpose; but even he was forced to pause, daunted by the insinuations of Bernières that he was in secret sympathy with the obnoxious doctrines.

Thus the Hermitage and its affiliated societies constituted themselves a sort of inquisition in the interest of the Jesuits; "for what," asks Nicole, "might not be expected from persons of weak minds and atrabilious dispositions, dried up by constant fasts, vigils, and other austerities, besides meditations of three or four hours a day, and told continually that the Church is in imminent danger of ruin through the machinations of the Jansenists, who are represented to them as persons who wish to break up the foundations of the Christian faith and subvert the mystery of the Incarnation; who believe neither in transubstantiation, the invocation of saints, nor indulgences; who wish to abolish the sacrifice of the Mass and the sacrament of Penitence, oppose the worship of the Holy Virgin, deny free-will and substitute predestination in its place, and, in fine, conspire to overthrow the authority of the Supreme Pontiff?"

Among other anecdotes, Nicole tells the following: One of the young zealots of the Hermitage took it into his head that all Caen was full of Jansenists,

and that the curés of the place were in league with
them.   He inoculated four others with this notion,
and they resolved to warn the people of their danger.
They accordingly made the tour of the streets, without hats or collars, and with coats unbuttoned,
though it was a cold winter day, stopping every
moment to proclaim in a loud voice that all the curés,
excepting two, whom they named, were abettors of
the Jansenists.   A mob was soon following at their
heels, and there was great excitement.   The magistrates chanced to be in session, and hearing of the
disturbance, they sent constables to arrest the authors
of it.   Being brought to the bar of justice and questioned by the judge, they answered that they were
doing the work of God, and were ready to die in the
cause; that Caen was full of Jansenists, and that the
curés had declared in their favor, inasmuch as they
denied any knowledge of their existence.   Four of
the five were locked up for a few days, tried, and
sentenced to a fine of a hundred livres, with a
promise of further punishment should they again
disturb the peace.[1]

The fifth, being pronounced out of his wits by the
physicians, was sent home to his mother, at a village
near Argentan, where two or three of his fellow
zealots presently joined him.   Among them, they
persuaded his mother, who had hitherto been devoted

---

[1] Nicole is not the only authority for this story.   It is also told
by a very different writer.   See *Notice Historique de l'Abbaye de Ste.
Claire d'Argentan*, 124.

to household cares, to exchange them for a life of mystical devotion. "These three or four persons," says Nicole, "attracted others as imbecile as themselves." Among these recruits were a number of women, and several priests. After various acts of fanaticism, "two or three days before last Pentecost," proceeds the narrator, "they all set out, men and women, for Argentan. The priests had drawn the skirts of their cassocks over their heads, and tied them about their necks with twisted straw. Some of the women had their heads bare, and their hair streaming loose over their shoulders. They picked up filth on the road, and rubbed their faces with it; and the most zealous ate it, saying that it was necessary to mortify the taste. Some held stones in their hands, which they knocked together to draw the attention of the passers-by. They had a leader, whom they were bound to obey; and when this leader saw any mud-hole particularly deep and dirty, he commanded some of the party to roll themselves in it, which they did forthwith.[1]

"After this fashion, they entered the town of Argentan, and marched, two by two, through all the streets, crying with a loud voice that the Faith was perishing, and that whoever wished to save it must quit the country and go with them to Canada,

[1] These proceedings were probably intended to produce the result which was the constant object of the mystics of the Hermitage; namely, the "annihilation of self," with a view to a perfect union with God. To become despised of men was an important if not an essential step in this mystical suicide.

whither they were soon to repair. It is said that they still hold this purpose, and that their leaders declare it revealed to them that they will find a vessel ready at the first port to which Providence directs them. The reason why they choose Canada for an asylum is, that Monsieur de Montigny (Laval), Bishop of Petræa, who lived at the Hermitage a long time, where he was instructed in mystical theology by Monsieur de Bernières, exercises episcopal functions there; and that the Jesuits, who are their oracles, reign in that country."

This adventure, like the other, ended in a collision with the police. "The priests," adds Nicole, "were arrested, and are now waiting trial; and the rest were treated as mad, and sent back with shame and confusion to the places whence they had come."

Though these pranks took place after Laval had left the Hermitage, they serve to characterize the school in which he was formed; or, more justly speaking, to show its most extravagant side. That others did not share the views of the celebrated Jansenist, may be gathered from the following passage of the funeral oration pronounced over the body of Laval half a century later: —

"The humble abbé was next transported into the terrestrial paradise of Monsieur de Bernières. It is thus that I call, as it is fitting to call it, that famous Hermitage of Caen, where the seraphic author of the ' Christian Interior ' [Bernières] transformed into angels all those who had the happiness to be the companions of his solitude and of his spiritual exercises. It was there that, during four years, the fervent abbé drank the living and abounding waters of grace which have since flowed so benignly over this land of Canada. In this celestial abode his ordinary occupations were prayer, mortification, instruction of the poor, and spiritual readings or conferences; his recreations were to labor in the hospitals, wait upon the sick and poor, make their beds, dress their wounds, and aid them in their most repulsive needs."[1]

In truth, Laval's zeal was boundless, and the exploits of self-humiliation recorded of him were unspeakably revolting.[2] Bernières himself regarded him as a light by which to guide his own steps in ways of holiness. He made journeys on foot about the country, disguised, penniless, begging from door to door, and courting scorn and opprobrium, "in order," says his biographer, "that he might suffer for the love of God." Yet, though living at this time in a state of habitual religious exaltation, he was by nature no mere dreamer; and in whatever heights his spirit might wander, his feet were always planted on the solid earth. His flaming zeal had for its servants a hard, practical nature, perfectly fitted for the battle of life, a narrow intellect, a stiff and

---

[1] *Eloge funèbre de Messire François Xavier de Laval-Montmorency, par Messire de la Colombière, Vicaire Général.*

[2] See La Tour, *Vie de Laval*, liv. i. Some of them were closely akin to that of the fanatics mentioned above, who ate "immondices d'animaux" to mortify the taste.

persistent will, and, as his enemies thought, the love of domination native to his blood.

Two great parties divided the Catholics of France, — the Gallican or national party, and the ultramontane or papal party. The first, resting on the Scriptural injunction to give tribute to Cæsar, held that to the King, the Lord's anointed, belonged the temporal, and to the Church the spiritual power. It held also that the laws and customs of the Church of France could not be broken at the bidding of the Pope.[1] The ultramontane party, on the other hand, maintained that the Pope, Christ's vicegerent on earth, was supreme over earthly rulers, and should of right hold jurisdiction over the clergy of all Christendom, with powers of appointment and removal. Hence they claimed for him the right of nominating bishops in France. This had anciently been exercised by assemblies of the French clergy, but in the reign of Francis I. the King and the Pope had combined to wrest it from them by the Concordat of Bologna. Under this compact, which was still in force, the Pope appointed French bishops on the nomination of the King, — a plan which displeased the Gallicans, and did not satisfy the ultramontanes.

The Jesuits, then as now, were the most forcible exponents of ultramontane principles. The Church to rule the world; the Pope to rule the Church; the Jesuits to rule the Pope, — such was and is the

---

[1] See the famous *Quatre Articles* of 1682, in which the liberties of the Gallican Church are asserted.

simple programme of the Order of Jesus; and to it they have held fast, except on a few rare occasions of misunderstanding with the Vicegerent of Christ.[1] In the question of papal supremacy, as in most things else, Laval was of one mind with them.

Those versed in such histories will not be surprised to learn that when he received the royal nomination, humility would not permit him to accept it; nor that, being urged, he at length bowed in resignation, still protesting his unworthiness. Nevertheless, the royal nomination did not take effect. The ultramontanes outflanked both the King and the Gallicans, and by adroit strategy made the new prelate completely a creature of the papacy. Instead of appointing him Bishop of Quebec, in accordance with the royal initiative, the Pope made him his vicar apostolic for Canada, — thus evading the King's nomination, and affirming that Canada, a country of infidel savages, was excluded from the concordat, and under his (the Pope's) jurisdiction pure and simple. The Gallicans were enraged. The Archbishop of Rouen vainly opposed, and the parliaments of Rouen and of Paris vainly protested. The papal party prevailed. The King, or rather Mazarin, gave his consent, subject to certain conditions, the chief of which was an oath of allegiance; and Laval, grand vicar apostolic, decorated with the title of Bishop of Petræa, sailed

---

[1] For example, not long after this time, the Jesuits, having a dispute with Innocent XI., threw themselves into the party of opposition.

for his wilderness diocese in the spring of 1659.[1]
He was but thirty-six years of age, but even when a
boy he could scarcely have seemed young.

Queylus, for a time, seemed to accept the situation,
and tacitly admit the claim of Laval as his ecclesiastical superior; but, stimulated by a letter from the
Archbishop of Rouen, he soon threw himself into an
attitude of opposition,[2] in which the popularity which
his generosity to the poor had won for him gave him
an advantage very annoying to his adversary. The
quarrel, it will be seen, was three-sided, — Gallican
against ultramontane, Sulpitian against Jesuit,
Montreal against Quebec. To Montreal the recal-
citrant abbé, after a brief visit to Quebec, had again
retired; but even here, girt with his Sulpitian
brethren and compassed with partisans, the arm
of the vicar apostolic was long enough to reach
him.

By temperament and conviction Laval hated a
divided authority, and the very shadow of a schism
was an abomination in his sight. The young King,
who, though abundantly jealous of his royal power,
was forced to conciliate the papal party, had sent
instructions to Argenson, the governor, to support
Laval, and prevent divisions in the Canadian

---

[1] Compare La Tour, *Vie de Laval*, with the long statement in
Faillon, *Colonie Française*, ii. 315–335. Faillon gives various documents in full, including the royal letter of nomination and those
in which the King gives a reluctant consent to the appointment of
the vicar apostolic.

[2] *Journal des Jésuites, Septembre*, 1657.

Church.[1] These instructions served as the pretext of a procedure sufficiently summary. A squad of soldiers, commanded, it is said, by the governor himself, went up to Montreal, brought the indignant Queylus to Quebec, and shipped him thence for France.[2] By these means, writes Father Lalemant, order reigned for a season in the Church.

It was but for a season. Queylus was not a man to bide his defeat in tranquillity, nor were his brother Sulpitians disposed to silent acquiescence. Laval, on his part, was not a man of half measures. He had an agent in France, and partisans strong at court. Fearing, to borrow the words of a Catholic writer, that the return of Queylus to Canada would prove "injurious to the glory of God," he bestirred himself to prevent it. The young King, then at Aix, on his famous journey to the frontiers of Spain to marry the Infanta, was induced to write to Queylus, ordering him to remain in France.[3] Queylus, however, repaired to Rome; but even against this movement provision had been made: accusations of Jansenism had gone before him, and he met a cold welcome. Nevertheless, as he had powerful friends near the Pope, he succeeded in removing these adverse impressions, and even in obtaining certain bulls relating to the establishment

[1] *Lettre du Roi à d'Argenson,* 14 *Mai,* 1659.

[2] Belmont, *Histoire du Canada,* A.D. 1659. Memoir by Abbé d'Allet, in *Morale Pratique des Jésuites,* xxxiv. 725.

[3] *Lettre du Roi à Queylus,* 27 *Fév.,* 1660.

of the parish of Montreal, and favorable to the
Sulpitians. Provided with these, he set at nought
the King's letter, embarked under an assumed
name, and sailed to Quebec, where he made his
appearance on the third of August, 1661,[1] to the
extreme wrath of Laval.

A ferment ensued. Laval's partisans charged the
Sulpitians with Jansenism and opposition to the will
of the Pope. A preacher more zealous than the rest
denounced them as priests of Antichrist; and as to
the bulls in their favor, it was affirmed that Queylus
had obtained them by fraud from the Holy Father.
Laval at once issued a mandate forbidding him to
proceed to Montreal till ships should arrive with
instructions from the King.[2] At the same time he
demanded of the governor that he should interpose
the civil power to prevent Queylus from leaving
Quebec.[3] As Argenson, who wished to act as peace-
maker between the belligerent fathers, did not at
once take the sharp measures required of him, Laval
renewed his demand on the next day, — calling on
him, in the name of God and the King, to compel
Queylus to yield the obedience due to him, the vicar
apostolic.[4] At the same time he sent another to the
offending abbé, threatening to suspend him from
priestly functions if he persisted in his rebellion.[5]

<hr>

1 *Journal des Jésuites, Août,* 1661.
2 *Lettre de Laval à Queylus,* 4 *Août,* 1661.
3 *Lettre de Laval à d'Argenson, Ibid.*
4 *Ibid.,* 5 *Août,* 1661.
5 *Lettre de Laval à Queylus, Ibid.*

The incorrigible Queylus, who seems to have lived for some months in a simmer of continual indignation, set at nought the vicar apostolic as he had set at nought the King, took a boat that very night, and set out for Montreal under cover of darkness. Great was the ire of Laval when he heard the news in the morning. He despatched a letter after him, declaring him suspended *ipso facto*, if he did not instantly return and make his submission.[1] This letter, like the rest, failed of the desired effect; but the governor, who had received a second mandate from the King to support Laval and prevent a schism,[2] now reluctantly interposed the secular arm, and Queylus was again compelled to return to France.[3]

His expulsion was a Sulpitian defeat. Laval, always zealous for unity and centralization, had some time before taken steps to repress what he regarded as a tendency to independence at Montreal. In the preceding year he had written to the Pope: "There are some secular priests [Sulpitians] at Montreal, whom the Abbé de Queylus brought out with him in 1657, and I have named for the functions of curé the one among them whom I thought the least disobedient." The bulls which Queylus had obtained from Rome related to this very curacy, and greatly disturbed the mind of the vicar apostolic. He accordingly wrote again to the Pope: "I pray

<hr>

[1] *Lettre de Laval à Queylus, 6 Août, 1661.*

[2] *Lettre du Roi à d'Argenson, 13 Mai, 1660.*

[3] For the governor's attitude in this affair, consult the *Papiers d'Argenson,* containing his despatches.

your Holiness to let me know your will concerning the jurisdiction of the Archbishop of Rouen. M. l'Abbé de Queylus, who has come out this year as vicar of this archbishop, has tried to deceive us by surreptitious letters, and has obeyed neither our prayers nor our repeated commands to desist. But he has received orders from the King to return immediately to France, to render an account of his disobedience; and he has been compelled by the governor to conform to the will of his Majesty. What I now fear is that on his return to France, by using every kind of means, employing new artifices, and falsely representing our affairs, he may obtain from the Court of Rome powers which may disturb the peace of our Church; for the priests whom he brought with him from France, and who live at Montreal, are animated with the same spirit of disobedience and division; and I fear, with good reason, that all belonging to the Seminary of St. Sulpice, who may come hereafter to join them, will be of the same disposition. If what is said is true, that by means of fraudulent letters the right of patronage of the pretended parish of Montreal has been granted to the superior of this seminary, and the right of appointment to the Archbishop of Rouen, then is altar reared against altar in our Church of Canada; for the clergy of Montreal will always stand in opposition to me, the vicar apostolic, and to my successors." [1]

----

[1] *Lettre de Laval au Pape*, 22 *Oct.*, 1661. Printed by Faillon, from the original in the archives of the Propaganda.

These dismal forebodings were never realized. The Holy See annulled the obnoxious bulls; the Archbishop of Rouen renounced his claims, and Queylus found his position untenable. Seven years later, when Laval was on a visit to France, a reconciliation was brought about between them. The former vicar of the Archbishop of Rouen made his submission to the vicar of the Pope, and returned to Canada as a missionary. Laval's triumph was complete, to the joy of the Jesuits, — silent, if not idle, spectators of the tedious and complex quarrel.

CHAPTER VIII.

1659, 1660.

LAVAL AND ARGENSON.

François de Laval: his Position and Character. — Arrival of Argenson. — The Quarrel.

WE are touching delicate ground. To many excellent Catholics of our own day Laval is an object of veneration. The Catholic university of Quebec glories in bearing his name, and certain modern ecclesiastical writers rarely mention him in terms less reverent than "the virtuous prelate," or "the holy prelate." Nor are some of his contemporaries less emphatic in eulogy. Mother Juchereau de Saint-Denis, Superior of the Hôtel Dieu, wrote immediately after his death: "He began in his tenderest years the study of perfection, and we have reason to think that he reached it, since every virtue which Saint Paul demands in a bishop was seen and admired in him;" and on his first arrival in Canada, Mother Marie de l'Incarnation, Superior of the Ursulines, wrote to her son that the choice of such a prelate was not of man, but of God. "I will not," she adds, "say that he is a saint; but I may say with

truth that he lives like a saint and an apostle."
And she describes his austerity of life; how he had
but two servants, a gardener — whom he lent on
occasion to his needy neighbors — and a valet; how
he lived in a small hired house, saying that he would
not have one of his own if he could build it for only
five sous; and how, in his table, furniture, and bed,
he showed the spirit of poverty, even, as she thinks,
to excess. His servant, a lay brother named Houssart,
testified, after his death, that he slept on a hard
bed, and would not suffer it to be changed even
when it became full of fleas; and, what is more to
the purpose, that he gave fifteen hundred or two
thousand francs to the poor every year.[1] Houssart
also gives the following specimen of his austerities:
"I have seen him keep cooked meat five, six, seven,
or eight days in the heat of summer; and when it
was all mouldy and wormy he washed it in warm
water and ate it, and told me that it was very good."
The old servant was so impressed by these and other
proofs of his master's sanctity, that "I determined,"
he says, "to keep everything I could that had
belonged to his holy person, and after his death to
soak bits of linen in his blood when his body was
opened, and take a few bones and cartilages from his
breast, cut off his hair, and keep his clothes, and
such things, to serve as most precious relics."

---

[1] *Lettre du Frère Houssart, ancien serviteur de M'g'r de Laval* à
M. Tremblay, 1 *Sept.*, 1708. This letter is printed, though with one
or two important omissions, in the *Abeille*, vol. i. (Quebec, 1848.)

These pious cares were not in vain, for the relics proved greatly in demand.

Several portraits of Laval are extant. A drooping nose of portentous size; a well-formed forehead; a brow strongly arched; a bright, clear eye; scanty hair, half hidden by a black skullcap; thin lips, compressed and rigid, betraying a spirit not easy to move or convince; features of that indescribable cast which marks the priestly type, — such is Laval, as he looks grimly down on us from the dingy canvas of two centuries ago.

He is one of those concerning whom Protestants and Catholics, at least ultramontane Catholics, will never agree in judgment. The task of eulogizing him may safely be left to those of his own way of thinking. It is for us to regard him from the standpoint of secular history. And, first, let us credit him with sincerity. He believed firmly that the princes and rulers of this world ought to be subject to guidance and control at the hands of the Pope, the vicar of Christ on earth. But he himself was the Pope's vicar, and, so far as the bounds of Canada extended, the Holy Father had clothed him with his own authority. The glory of God demanded that this authority should suffer no abatement; and he, Laval, would be guilty before Heaven if he did not uphold the supremacy of the Church over the powers both of earth and of hell.

Of the faults which he owed to nature, the principal seems to have been an arbitrary and domineering temper. He was one of those who by nature lean always to the side of authority; and in the English Revolution he would inevitably have stood for the Stuarts; or, in the American Revolution, for the Crown. But being above all things a Catholic and a priest, he was drawn by a constitutional necessity to the ultramontane party, or the party of centralization. He fought lustily, in his way, against the natural man; and humility was the virtue to the culture of which he gave his chief attention; but soil and climate were not favorable. His life was one long assertion of the authority of the Church, and this authority was lodged in himself. In his stubborn fight for ecclesiastical ascendency, he was aided by the impulses of a nature that loved to rule, and could not endure to yield. His principles and his instinct of domination were acting in perfect unison, and his conscience was the handmaid of his fault. Austerities and mortifications, playing at beggar, sleeping in beds full of fleas, or performing prodigies of gratuitous dirtiness in hospitals, however fatal to self-respect, could avail little against influences working so powerfully and so insidiously to stimulate the most subtle of human vices. The history of the Roman Church is full of Lavals.

The Jesuits, adepts in human nature, had made a sagacious choice when they put forward this conscientious, zealous, dogged, and pugnacious priest to fight their battles. Nor were they ill pleased that, for the present, he was not Bishop of Canada,

but only vicar apostolic; for such being the case,
they could have him recalled if on trial they did not
like him, while an unacceptable bishop would be an
evil past remedy.

Canada was entering a state of transition. Hitherto
ecclesiastical influence had been all in all. The
Jesuits, by far the most educated and able body of
men in the colony, had controlled it, not alone in
things spiritual, but virtually in things temporal
also; and the governor may be said to have been
little else than a chief of police, under the direction
of the missionaries. The early governors were
themselves deeply imbued with the missionary spirit.
Champlain was earnest above all things for convert-
ing the Indians; Montmagny was half-monk, for he
was a Knight of Malta; d'Ailleboust was so insanely
pious that he lived with his wife like monk and nun.
A change was at hand. From a mission and a trading station, Canada was soon to become, in the true
sense, a colony; and civil government had begun to
assert itself on the banks of the St. Lawrence. The
epoch of the martyrs and apostles was passing away,
and the man of the sword and the man of the gown
— the soldier and the legist — were threatening to
supplant the paternal sway of priests; or, as Laval
might have said, the hosts of this world were
beleaguering the sanctuary, and he was called of
Heaven to defend it. His true antagonist, though
three thousand miles away, was the great minister
Colbert, as purely a statesman as the vicar apostolic

was purely a priest. Laval, no doubt, could see behind the statesman's back another adversary, — the Devil.

Argenson was governor when the crozier and the sword began to clash, which is merely another way of saying that he was governor when Laval arrived. He seems to have been a man of education, moderation, and sense, and he was also an earnest Catholic; but if Laval had his duties to God, so had Argenson his duties to the King, of whose authority he was the representative and guardian. If the first collisions seem trivial, they were no less the symptoms of a grave antagonism. Argenson could have purchased peace only by becoming an agent of the Church.

The vicar apostolic, or, as he was usually styled, the bishop, being, it may be remembered, titular Bishop of Petræa in Arabia, presently fell into a quarrel with the governor touching the relative position of their seats in church, — a point which, by the way, was a subject of contention for many years, and under several successive governors. This time the case was referred to the ex-governor, d'Ailleboust, and a temporary settlement took place.[1] A few weeks after, on the fête of Saint Francis Xavier, when the Jesuits were accustomed to ask the dignitaries of the colony to dine in their refectory after mass, a fresh difficulty arose, — Should the governor or the bishop have the higher seat at table? The

---

[1] Lalemant, in *Journal des Jésuites, Septembre,* 1659.

question defied solution; so the fathers invited neither of them.[1]

Again, on Christmas, at the midnight mass, the deacon offered incense to the bishop, and then, in obedience to an order from him, sent a subordinate to offer it to the governor, instead of offering it himself. Laval further insisted that the priests of the choir should receive · incense before the governor received it. Argenson resisted, and a bitter quarrel ensued.[2]

The late governor, d'Ailleboust, had been churchwarden *ex officio;*[3] and in this pious community the office was esteemed as an addition to his honors. Argenson had thus far held the same position; but Laval declared that he should hold it no longer. Argenson, to whom the bishop had not spoken on the subject, came soon after to a meeting of the wardens, and, being challenged, denied Laval's right to dismiss him. A dispute ensued, in which the bishop, according to his Jesuit friends, used language not very respectful to the representative of royalty.[4]

On occasion of the "solemn catechism," the bishop insisted that the children should salute him before saluting the governor. Argenson, hearing of this, declined to come. A compromise was contrived. It was agreed that when the rival dignitaries entered,

---

[1] Lalemant, in *Journal des Jésuites, Decembre,* 1659.

[2] *Ibid.; Lettre d'Argenson à MM. de la Compagnie de St. Sulpice.*

[3] *Livre des Délibérations de la Fabrique de Québec.*

[4] *Journal des Jésuites, Novembre,* 1660.

the children should be busied in some manual exercise which should prevent their saluting either. Nevertheless, two boys, "enticed and set on by their parents," saluted the governor first, to the great indignation of Laval. They were whipped on the next day for breach of orders.[1]

Next there was a sharp quarrel about a sentence pronounced by Laval against a heretic, to which the governor, good Catholic as he was, took exception.[2] Palm Sunday came, and there could be no procession and no distribution of branches, because the governor and the bishop could not agree on points of precedence.[3]

On the day of the Fête Dieu, however, there was a grand procession, which stopped from time to time at temporary altars, or *reposoirs*, placed at intervals along its course. One of these was in the fort, where the soldiers were drawn up, waiting the arrival of the procession. Laval demanded that they should take off their hats. Argenson assented, and the soldiers stood uncovered. Laval now insisted that they should kneel. The governor replied that it was their duty as soldiers to stand; whereupon the bishop refused to stop at the altar, and ordered the procession to move on.[4]

The above incidents are set down in the private journal of the superior of the Jesuits, which was not

1 *Journal des Jésuites, Février,* 1661.
2 *Ibid.*
3 *Ibid., Avril,* 1661.   4 *Ibid., Juin,* 1661.

meant for the public eye. The bishop, it will be seen, was, by the showing of his friends, in most cases the aggressor. The disputes in question, though of a nature to provoke a smile on irreverent lips, were by no means so puerile as they appear. It is difficult in a modern democratic society to conceive the substantial importance of the signs and symbols of dignity and authority at a time and among a people where they were adjusted with the most scrupulous precision, and accepted by all classes as exponents of relative degrees in the social and political scale. Whether the bishop or the governor should sit in the higher seat at table thus became a political question, for it defined to the popular understanding the position of Church and State in their relations to government.

Hence it is not surprising to find a memorial, drawn up apparently by Argenson, and addressed to the council of State, asking for instructions when and how a governor — lieutenant-general for the King — ought to receive incense, holy water, and consecrated bread; whether the said bread should be offered him with sound of drum and fife; what should be the position of his seat at church; and what place he should hold in various religious ceremonies; whether in feasts, assemblies, ceremonies, and councils of *a purely civil character*, he or the bishop was to hold the first place; and, finally, if the bishop could excommunicate the inhabitants or others for acts of a civil and political character, when the said acts were pronounced lawful by the governor.

The reply to the memorial denies to the bishop the power of excommunication in civil matters, assigns to him the second place in meetings and ceremonies of a civil character, and is very reticent as to the rest.[1]

Argenson had a brother, a counsellor of State, and a fast friend of the Jesuits. Laval was in correspondence with him, and, apparently sure of sympathy, wrote to him touching his relations with the governor. "Your brother," he begins, "received me on my arrival with extraordinary kindness;" but he proceeds to say, that, perceiving with sorrow that he entertained a groundless distrust of those good servants of God, the Jesuit fathers, he, the bishop, thought it his duty to give him in private a candid warning which ought to have done good, but which, to his surprise, the governor had taken amiss, and had conceived, in consequence, a prejudice against his monitor.[2]

Argenson, on his part, writes to the same brother, at about the same time. "The Bishop of Petræa is so stiff in opinion, and so often transported by his zeal beyond the rights of his position, that he makes no difficulty in encroaching on the functions of others; and this with so much heat that he will

---

1 *Advis et Résolutions demandés sur la Nouvelle France.*

2 *Lettre de Laval à M. d'Argenson, frère du Gouverneur, 20 Oct.,* 1659.

listen to nobody. A few days ago he carried off a servant girl of one of the inhabitants here, and placed her by his own authority in the Ursuline convent, on the sole pretext that he wanted to have her instructed, — thus depriving her master of her services, though he had been at great expense in bringing her from France. This inhabitant is M. Denis, who, not knowing who had carried her off, came to me with a petition to get her out of the convent. I kept the petition three days without answering it, to prevent the affair from being noised abroad. The Reverend Father Lalemant, with whom I communicated on the subject, and who greatly blamed the Bishop of Petræa, did all in his power to have the girl given up quietly, but without the least success, so that I was forced to answer the petition, and permit M. Denis to take his servant wherever he should find her; and if I had not used means to bring about an accommodation, and if M. Denis, on the refusal which was made him to give her up, had brought the matter into court, I should have been compelled to take measures which would have caused great scandal, — and all from the self-will of the Bishop of Petræa, who says that *a bishop can do what he likes*, and threatens nothing but excommunication." [1]

In another letter he speaks in the same strain of this redundancy of zeal on the part of the bishop,

---

[1] " — Qui dict *quun Evesque peult ce qu'il veult* et ne menace que dexcommunication."—*Lettre d'Argenson à son Frère,* 1659.

which often, he says, takes the shape of obstinacy and encroachment on the rights of others. "It is greatly to be wished," he observes, "that the Bishop of Petræa would give his confidence to the Reverend Father Lalemant instead of Father Ragueneau;"[1] and he praises Lalemant as a person of excellent sense. "It would be well," he adds, "if the rest of their community were of the same mind; for in that case they would not mix themselves up with various matters in the way they do, and would leave the government to those to whom God has given it in charge."[2]

One of Laval's modern admirers, the worthy Abbé Ferland, after confessing that his zeal may now and then have savored of excess, adds in his defence that a vigorous hand was needed to compel the infant colony to enter "the good path," — meaning, of course, the straitest path of Roman Catholic orthodoxy. We may hereafter see more of this stringent system of colonial education, its success, and the results that followed.

<hr>

[1] *Lettre d'Argenson à son Frère*, 21 *Oct.*, 1659.
[2] *Ibid.*, 7 *July*, 1660.

CHAPTER IX.

1658–1663.

LAVAL AND AVAUGOUR.

When Argenson arrived to assume the government, a curious greeting had awaited him. The Jesuits asked him to dine; vespers followed the repast; and then they conducted him into a hall, where the boys of their school — disguised, one as the Genius of New France, one as the Genius of the Forest, and others as Indians of various friendly tribes — made him speeches by turn, in prose and verse. First, Pierre du Quet, who played the Genius of New France, presented his Indian retinue to the governor, in a complimentary harangue. Then four other boys, personating French colonists, made him four flattering addresses, in French verse. Charles Denis, dressed as a Huron, followed, bewailing the ruin of his people, and appealing to Argenson for aid. Jean François Bourdon, in the character of an Algonquin, next advanced on the platform, boasted his courage, and declared that he was ashamed to cry like the Huron. The Genius of the Forest now appeared, with a retinue of wild Indians from the interior, who, being unable to speak French, addressed the governor in their native tongues, which the Genius proceeded to interpret. Two other boys, in the character of prisoners just escaped from the Iroquois, then came forward, imploring aid in piteous accents; and, in conclusion, the whole troop of Indians, from far and near, laid their bows and arrows at the feet of Argenson, and hailed him as their chief.[1]

Besides these mock Indians, a crowd of genuine savages had gathered at Quebec to greet the new "Onontio." On the next day — at his own cost, as he writes to a friend — he gave them a feast, consisting of "seven large kettles full of Indian corn, peas, prunes, sturgeons, eels, and fat, which they devoured, having first sung me a song, after their fashion."[2]

These festivities over, he entered on the serious business of his government, and soon learned that his path was a thorny one. He could find, he says, but a hundred men to resist the twenty-four hundred warriors of the Iroquois;[3] and he begs the proprietary

---

[1] *La Reception de Monseigneur le Vicomte d'Argenson par toutes les nations du pais de Canada à son entrée au gouvernement de la Nouvelle France; à Quebecq au Collège de la Compagnie de Jésus, le 28 de Juillet de l'année* 1658. The speeches, in French and Indian, are here given *verbatim*, with the names of all the boys who took part in the ceremony.

[2] *Papiers d'Argenson. Kebec, 5 Sept.,* 1658.

[3] *Mémoire sur le subject (sic) de la Guerre des Iroquois,* 1659.

company which he represented to send him a hundred more, who could serve as soldiers or laborers, according to the occasion.

The company turned a deaf ear to his appeals. They had lost money in Canada, and were grievously out of humor with it. In their view, the first duty of a governor was to collect their debts, which, for more reasons than one, was no easy task. While they did nothing to aid the colony in its distress, they beset Argenson with demands for the thousand pounds of beaver-skins, which the inhabitants had agreed to send them every year in return for the privilege of the fur-trade, — a privilege which the Iroquois war made for the present worthless. The perplexed governor vents his feelings in sarcasm. "They [the company] take no pains to learn the truth; and when they hear of settlers carried off and burned by the Iroquois, they will think it a punishment for not settling old debts, and paying over the beaver-skins."[1]   "I wish," he adds, "they would send somebody to look after their affairs here. I would gladly give him the same lodging and entertainment as my own."

Another matter gave him great annoyance. This was the virtual independence of Montreal; and here, if nowhere else, he and the bishop were of the same mind. On one occasion he made a visit to the place in question, where he expected to be received as governor-general; but the local governor, Maisonneuve,

---

[1] *Papiers d'Argenson*, 21 *Oct.*, 1659.

declined, or at least postponed, to take his orders
and give him the keys of the fort.   Argenson accordingly speaks of Montreal as "a place which makes so
much noise, but which is of such small account."[1]
He adds that, besides wanting to be independent, the
Montrealists want to monopolize the fur-trade, which
would cause civil war; and that the King ought to
interpose to correct their obstinacy.

In another letter he complains of d'Ailleboust, who
had preceded him in the government, though himself
a Montrealist.   Argenson says that, on going out to
fight the Iroquois, he left d'Ailleboust at Quebec, to
act as his lieutenant; that, instead of doing so, he
had assumed to govern in his own right; that he had
taken possession of his absent superior's furniture,
drawn his pay, and in other respects behaved as if he
never expected to see him again.   "When I returned,"
continues the governor, "I made him director in
the council, without pay, as there was none to
give him.   It was this, I think, that made him
remove to Montreal; for which I do not care, provided the glory of our Master suffer no prejudice
thereby."[2]

These extracts may, perhaps, give an unjust
impression of Argenson, who, from the general tenor
of his letters, appears to have been a temperate and
reasonable person.   His patience and his nervous

---

[1] *Papiers d'Argenson, 4 Août, 1659.*

[2] *Ibid.   Double de la lettre escripte par le Vaisseau du Gaigneur, parti le 6 Septembre (1658).*

system seem, however, to have been taxed to the
utmost. His pay could not support him. "The
costs of living here are horrible," he writes. "I
have only two thousand crowns a year for all my
expenses, and I have already been forced to run into
debt to the company to an equal amount."[1] Part of
his scanty income was derived from a fishery of eels,
on which sundry persons had encroached, to his great
detriment.[2] "I see no reason," he adds, "for staying
here any longer. When I came to this country, I
hoped to enjoy a little repose, but I am doubly
deprived of it, — on one hand by enemies without,
and incessant petty disputes within; and, on the
other, by the difficulty I find in subsisting. The
profits of the fur-trade have been so reduced that all
the inhabitants are in the greatest poverty. They
are all insolvent, and cannot pay the merchants their
advances."

His disgust at length reached a crisis. "I am
resolved to stay here no longer, but to go home next
year. My horror of dissension, and the manifest
certainty of becoming involved in disputes with
certain persons with whom I am unwilling to quarrel,
oblige me to anticipate these troubles, and seek some
way of living in peace. These excessive fatigues
are far too much for my strength. I am writing to
Monsieur the President, and to the gentlemen of the
Company of New France, to choose some other man

---

[1] *Papiers d'Argenson. Lettre à M. de Morangi, 5 Sept., 1658.*
[2] *Délibérations de la Compagnie de la Nouvelle France.*

for this government."[1]   And again, "If you take any interest in this country, see that the person chosen to command here has, besides the true piety necessary to a Christian in every condition of life, great firmness of character and strong bodily health. I assure you that without these qualities he cannot succeed. Besides, it is absolutely necessary that he should be a man of property and of some rank, so that he will not be despised for humble birth, or suspected of coming here to make his fortune; for in that case he can do no good whatever."[2]

His constant friction with the head of the Church distressed the pious governor, and made his recall doubly a relief.   According to a contemporary writer, Laval was the means of delivering him from the burden of government, having written to the President Lamoignon to urge his removal.[3]   Be this as it may, it is certain that the bishop was not sorry to be rid of him.

The Baron Dubois d'Avaugour arrived to take his place.   He was an old soldier of forty years' service,[4] blunt, imperative, and sometimes obstinate to perverseness, but full of energy, and of a probity which even his enemies confessed.   "He served a long time in Germany while you were there," writes the minis-

---

[1] *Papiers d'Argenson. Lettre à son Frère*, 1659.

[2] *Ibid. Lettre (à son Frère?)*, 4 *Nov.*, 1660. The originals of Argenson's letters were destroyed in the burning of the library of the Louvre by the Commune.

[3] Lachenaye, *Mémoire sur le Canada.*

[4] Avaugour, *Mémoire*, 4 *Août*, 1663.

Dubois d'Avaugour.

ter Colbert to the Marquis de Tracy, "and you must have known his talents, as well as his *bizarre* and somewhat impracticable temper." On landing, he would have no reception, being, as Father Lalemant observes, "an enemy of all ceremony." He went, however, to see the Jesuits, and "took a morsel of food in our refectory."[1] Laval was prepared to receive him with all solemnity at the Church; but the governor would not go. He soon set out on a tour of observation as far as Montreal, whence he returned delighted with the country, and immediately wrote to Colbert in high praise of it, observing that the St. Lawrence was the most beautiful river he had ever seen.[2]

It was clear from the first that, while he had a prepossession against the bishop, he wished to be on good terms with the Jesuits. He began by placing some of them on the council; but they and Laval were too closely united; and if Avaugour thought to separate them, he signally failed. A few months only had elapsed when we find it noted in Father Lalemant's private journal that the governor had dissolved the council and appointed a new one, and that other "changes and troubles" had befallen. The inevitable quarrel had broken out; it was a complex one, but the chief occasion of dispute was fortunate for the ecclesiastics, since it placed them, to a certain degree, morally in the right.

---

[1] Lalemant, *Journal des Jésuites, Septembre*, 1661.
[2] *Lettre d'Avaugour au Ministre*, 1661.

The question at issue was not new. It had agitated the colony for years, and had been the spring of some of Argenson's many troubles. Nor did it cease with Avaugour, for we shall trace its course hereafter, tumultuous as a tornado. It was simply the temperance question, — not as regards the colonists, though here, too, there was great room for reform, but as regards the Indians.

Their inordinate passion for brandy had long been the source of excessive disorders. They drank expressly to get drunk, and when drunk they were like wild beasts. Crime and violence of all sorts ensued; the priests saw their teachings despised and their flocks ruined. On the other hand, the sale of brandy was a chief source of profit, direct or indirect, to all those interested in the fur-trade, including the principal persons of the colony. In Argenson's time, Laval launched an excommunication against those engaged in the abhorred traffic; for nothing less than total prohibition would content the clerical party, and besides the spiritual penalty, they demanded the punishment of death against the contumacious offender. Death, in fact, was decreed. Such was the posture of affairs when Avaugour arrived; and, willing as he was to conciliate the Jesuits, he permitted the decree to take effect, although, it seems, with great repugnance. A few weeks after his arrival, two men were shot and one whipped, for selling brandy to Indians.[1] An extreme though

---

[1] *Journal des Jésuites, Octobre,* 1661.

partially suppressed excitement shook the entire settlement; for most of the colonists were, in one degree or another, implicated in the offence thus punished. An explosion soon followed; and the occasion of it was the humanity or good-nature of the Jesuit Lalemant.

A woman had been condemned to imprisonment for the same cause, and Lalemant, moved by compassion, came to the governor to intercede for her. Avaugour could no longer contain himself, and answered the reverend petitioner with characteristic bluntness. "You and your brethren were the first to cry out against the trade, and now you want to save the traders from punishment. I will no longer be the sport of your contradictions. Since it is not a crime for this woman, it shall not be a crime for anybody." [1] And in this posture he stood fast, with an inflexible stubbornness.

Henceforth there was full license to liquor-dealers. A violent reaction ensued against the past restriction, and brandy flowed freely among French and Indians alike. The ungodly drank to spite the priests and revenge themselves for the "constraint of consciences," of which they loudly complained. The utmost confusion followed, and the principles on which the pious colony was built seemed upheaved from the foundation. Laval was distracted with grief and anger. He outpoured himself from the pulpit in threats of divine wrath, and launched fresh excommunications

---

[1] La Tour, *Vie de Laval*, liv. v.

against the offenders; but such was the popular fury that he was forced to yield and revoke them.[1]

Disorder grew from bad to worse. "Men gave no heed to bishop, preacher, or confessor," writes Father Charlevoix. "The French have despised the remonstrances of our prelate, because they are supported by the civil power," says the superior of the Ursulines. "He is almost dead with grief, and pines away before our eyes."

Laval could bear it no longer, but sailed for France, to lay his complaints before the court, and urge the removal of Avaugour. He had, besides, two other important objects, as will appear hereafter. His absence brought no improvement. Summer and autumn passed, and the commotion did not abate. Winter was drawing to a close, when, at length, outraged Heaven interposed an awful warning to the guilty colony.

Scarcely had the bishop left his flock when the skies grew portentous with signs of the chastisement to come. "We beheld," gravely writes Father Lalemant, "blazing serpents which flew through the air, borne on wings of fire. We beheld above Quebec a great globe of flame, which lighted up the night, and threw out sparks on all sides. This same meteor appeared above Montreal, where it seemed to issue

---

[1] *Journal des Jésuites, Février*, 1662. The sentence of excommunication is printed in the Appendix to the *Esquisse de la Vie de Laval.* It bears date February 24. It was on this very day that he was forced to revoke it.

from the bosom of the moon, with a noise as loud as cannon or thunder; and after sailing three leagues through the air, it disappeared behind the mountain whereof this island bears the name."[1]

Still greater marvels followed. First, a Christian Algonquin squaw, described as "innocent, simple, and sincere," being seated erect in bed, wide awake, by the side of her husband, in the night between the fourth and fifth of February, distinctly heard a voice saying, "Strange things will happen to-day; the earth will quake!" In great alarm she whispered the prodigy to her husband, who told her that she lied. This silenced her for a time; but when, the next morning, she went into the forest with her hatchet to cut a fagot of wood, the same dread voice resounded through the solitude, and sent her back in terror to her hut.[2]

These things were as nothing compared with the marvel that befell a nun of the hospital, Mother Catherine de Saint-Augustin, who died five years later, in the odor of sanctity. On the night of the fourth of February, 1663, she beheld in the spirit four furious demons at the four corners of Quebec, shaking it with a violence which plainly showed their purpose of reducing it to ruins; "and this they would have done," says the story, "if a personage of admirable beauty and ravishing majesty [Christ], whom she saw in the midst of them, and who from

[1] Lalemant, *Relation*, 1663, 2.
[2] *Ibid.*, 1663, 6.

time to time gave rein to their fury, had not restrained them when they were on the point of accomplishing their wicked design." She also heard the conversation of these demons, to the effect that people were now well frightened, and many would be converted; but this would not last long, and they, the demons, would have them in time. "Let us keep on shaking," they cried, encouraging one another, "and do our best to upset everything."[1]

Now, to pass from visions to facts: "At half-past five o'clock on the morning of the fifth," writes Father Lalemant, "a great roaring sound was heard at the same time through the whole extent of Canada. This sound, which produced an effect as if the houses were on fire, brought everybody out of doors; but instead of seeing smoke and flame, they were amazed to behold the walls shaking, and all the stones moving as if they would drop from their places. The houses seemed to bend first to one side and then to the other. Bells sounded of themselves; beams, joists, and planks cracked; the ground heaved, making the pickets of the palisades dance in a way that would have seemed incredible had we not seen it in divers places.

"Everybody was in the streets; animals ran wildly about; children cried; men and women, seized with

---

[1] Ragueneau, *Vie de Catherine de St. Augustin*, liv. iv. chap. i. The same story is told by Juchereau, Lalemant, and Marie de l'Incarnation, to whom Charlevoix erroneously ascribes the vision, as does also the Abbé La Tour.

fright, knew not where to take refuge, expecting every moment to be buried under the ruins of the houses, or swallowed up in some abyss opening under their feet. Some, on their knees in the snow, cried for mercy, and others passed the night in prayer; for the earthquake continued without ceasing, with a motion much like that of a ship at sea, insomuch that sundry persons felt the same qualms of stomach which they would feel on the water. In the forests the commotion was far greater. The trees struck one against the other as if there were a battle between them; and you would have said that not only their branches, but even their trunks, started out of their places and leaped on one another with such noise and confusion that the Indians said that the whole forest was drunk."

Mary of the Incarnation gives a similar account, as does also Frances Juchereau de Saint-Ignace; and these contemporary records are sustained to some extent by the evidence of geology.[1] A remarkable effect was produced on the St. Lawrence, which was so charged with mud and clay that for many weeks the water was unfit to drink. Considerable hills and large tracts of forest slid from their places, some into

[1] Professor Sterry Hunt, whose intimate knowledge of Canadian geology is well known, tells me that the shores of the St. Lawrence are to a great extent formed of beds of gravel and clay resting on inclined strata of rock, so that earth-slides would be the necessary result of any convulsion like that of 1663. He adds that the evidence that such slides have taken place on a great scale is very distinct at various points along the river, especially at Les Eboulemens, on the north shore.

the river, and some into adjacent valleys. A number
of men in a boat near Tadoussac stared aghast at a
large hill covered with trees, which sank into the
water before their eyes; streams were turned from
their courses; water-falls were levelled; springs were
dried up in some places, while in others new springs
appeared. Nevertheless, the accounts that have
come down to us seem a little exaggerated, and sometimes ludicrously so; as when, for example, Mother
Mary of the Incarnation tells us of a man who ran
all night to escape from a fissure in the earth which
opened behind him and chased him as he fled.

It is perhaps needless to say that "spectres and
phantoms of fire, bearing torches in their hands,"
took part in the convulsion. "The fiery figure of a
man vomiting flames" also appeared in the air, with
many other apparitions too numerous to mention. It
is recorded that three young men were on their way
through the forest to sell brandy to the Indians,
when one of them, a little in advance of the rest, was
met by a hideous spectre which nearly killed him
with fright. He had scarcely strength enough to
rejoin his companions, who, seeing his terror, began
to laugh at him. One of them, however, presently
came to his senses, and said: "This is no laughing
matter; we are going to sell liquor to the Indians
against the prohibitions of the Church, and perhaps
God means to punish our disobedience." On this
they all turned back. That night they had scarcely
lain down to sleep when the earthquake roused

them, and they ran out of their hut just in time to escape being swallowed up along with it.[1]

With every allowance, it is clear that the convulsion must have been a severe one, and it is remarkable that in all Canada not a life was lost. The writers of the day see in this a proof that God meant to reclaim the guilty and not destroy them. At Quebec there was for the time an intense revival of religion. The end of the world was thought to be at hand, and everybody made ready for the last judgment. Repentant throngs beset confessionals and altars; enemies were reconciled; fasts, prayers, and penances filled the whole season of Lent. Yet, as we shall see, the Devil could still find wherewith to console himself.

It was midsummer before the shocks wholly ceased and the earth resumed her wonted calm. An extreme drought was followed by floods of rain, and then Nature began her sure work of reparation. It was about this time that the thorn which had plagued the Church was at length plucked out. Avaugour was summoned home. He took his recall with magnanimity, and on his way wrote at Gaspé a memorial to Colbert, in which he commends New France to the attention of the King. "The St. Lawrence," he says, "is the entrance to what may be made the

---

[1] Marie de l'Incarnation, *Lettre du* 20 *Août*, 1663. It appears from Morton, Josselyn, and other writers, that the earthquake extended to New England and New Netherlands, producing similar effects on the imagination of the people.

greatest state in the world;" and, in his purely military way, he recounts the means of realizing this grand possibility. Three thousand soldiers should be sent to the colony, to be discharged and turned into settlers after three years of service. During these three years they may make Quebec an impregnable fortress, subdue the Iroquois, build a strong fort on the river where the Dutch have a miserable wooden redoubt, called Fort Orange (Albany), and finally open a way by that river to the sea. Thus the heretics will be driven out, and the King will be master of America, at a total cost of about four hundred thousand francs yearly for ten years. He closes his memorial by a short allusion to the charges against him, and to his forty years of faithful service; and concludes, speaking of the authors of his recall, Laval and the Jesuits: "By reason of the respect I owe their cloth, I will rest content, Monseigneur, with assuring you that I have not only served the King with fidelity, but also, by the grace of God, with very good success, considering the means at my disposal."[1] He had, in truth, borne himself as a brave and experienced soldier; and he soon after died a soldier's death, while defending the fortress of Zrin, in Croatia, against the Turks.[2]

---

[1] Avaugour, *Mémoire, Gaspé,* 4 *Août,* 1663.

[2] *Lettre de Colbert au Marquis de Tracy,* 1664. *Mémoire du Roy, pour servir d'instruction au Sieur Talon.*

CHAPTER X.

1661–1664.

LAVAL AND DUMESNIL.

Though the proposals of Avaugour's memorial were not adopted, it seems to have produced a strong impression at court. For this impression the minds of the King and his minister had already been prepared. Two years before, the inhabitants of Canada had sent one of their number, Pierre Boucher, to represent their many grievances and ask for aid.[1] Boucher had had an audience of the young King, who listened with interest to his statements; and when in the following year he returned to Quebec, he was accompanied by an officer named Dumont, who had under his command a hundred soldiers for the colony, and was commissioned to report its con-

---

[1] To promote the objects of his mission, Boucher wrote a little book, *Histoire Véritable et Naturelle des Mœurs et Productions du Pays de la Nouvelle France.* He dedicates it to Colbert.

dition and resources.[1] The movement seemed to betoken that the government was wakening at last from its long inaction.

Meanwhile the Company of New France, feudal lord of Canada, had also shown signs of returning life. Its whole history had been one of mishap, followed by discouragement and apathy; and it is difficult to say whether its ownership of Canada had been more hurtful to itself or to the colony. At the eleventh hour it sent out an agent invested with powers of controller-general, intendant, and supreme judge, to inquire into the state of its affairs. This agent, Péronne Dumesnil, arrived early in the autumn of 1660, and set himself with great vigor to his work. He was an advocate of the Parliament of Paris, an active, aggressive, and tenacious person, of a temper well fitted to rip up an old abuse or probe a delinquency to the bottom. His proceedings quickly raised a storm at Quebec.

It may be remembered that, many years before, the company had ceded its monopoly of the fur-trade to the inhabitants of the colony, in consideration of that annual payment in beaver-skins which had been so tardily and so rarely made. The direction of the trade had at that time been placed in the hands of a council composed of the governor, the superior of the Jesuits, and several other members. Various changes had since taken place, and the trade was

---

[1] A long journal of Dumont is printed anonymously in the *Relation* of 1663.

now controlled by another council, established without the consent of the company,[1] and composed of the principal persons in the colony. The members of this council, with certain prominent merchants in league with them, engrossed all the trade, so that the inhabitants at large profited nothing by the right which the company had ceded;[2] and as the councillors controlled not only the trade, but all the financial affairs of Canada, while the remoteness of their scene of operations made it difficult to supervise them, they were able, with little risk, to pursue their own profit, to the detriment both of the company and the colony. They and their allies formed a petty trading oligarchy, as pernicious to the prosperity of Canada as the Iroquois war itself.

The company, always anxious for its beaver-skins, made several attempts to control the proceedings of the councillors and call them to account, but with little success, till the vigorous Dumesnil undertook the task; when, to their wrath and consternation, they and their friends found themselves attacked by wholesale accusations of fraud and embezzlement. That these charges were exaggerated there can be little doubt; that they were unfounded is incredible, in view of the effect they produced.

The councillors refused to acknowledge Dumesnil's

---

[1] *Registres du Conseil du Roy ; Reponse à la requeste presentée au Roy.*

[2] *Arrêt du Conseil d'État, 7 Mars,* 1657. Also *Papiers d'Argenson,* and *Extrait des Registres du Conseil d'État,* 15 *Mars,* 1656.

powers as controller, intendant, and judge, and declared his proceedings null.   He retorted by charging them with usurpation.   The excitement increased, and Dumesnil's life was threatened.

He had two sons in the colony.   One of them, Péronne de Mazé, was secretary to Avaugour, then on his way up the St. Lawrence to assume the government.   The other, Péronne des Touches, was with his father at Quebec.   Towards the end of August this young man was attacked in the street in broad daylight, and received a kick which proved fatal.   He was carried to his father's house, where he died on the twenty-ninth.   Dumesnil charges four persons, all of whom were among those into whose affairs he had been prying, with having taken part in the outrage; but it is very uncertain who was the immediate cause of Des Touches's death. Dumesnil, himself the supreme judicial officer of the colony, made complaint to the judge in ordinary of the company; but he says that justice was refused, the complaint suppressed by authority, his allegations torn in pieces, and the whole affair hushed.[1]

At the time of the murder, Dumesnil was confined

---

[1] Dumesnil, *Mémoire*. Under date August 31 the *Journal des Jésuites* makes this brief and guarded mention of the affair: "Le fils de Mons. du Mesnil . . . fut enterré le mesme iour, tué d'vn coup de pié par N." Who is meant by *N.* it is difficult to say. The register of the parish church records the burial as follows: —

"L'an 1661.   Le 30 Aoust a esté enterré au Cemetiere de Quebec Michel peronne dit Sr. des Touches fils de Mr. du Mesnil decedé le Jour precedent a sa Maison."

to his house by illness. An attempt was made to
rouse the mob against him, by reports that he had
come to the colony for the purpose of laying taxes;
but he sent for some of the excited inhabitants, and
succeeded in convincing them that he was their
champion rather than their enemy. Some Indians
in the neighborhood were also instigated to kill him,
and he was forced to conciliate them by presents.

He soon renewed his attacks, and in his quality of
intendant called on the councillors and their allies to
render their accounts, and settle the long arrears of
debt due to the company. They set his demands at
naught. The war continued month after month.
It is more than likely that when in the spring of
1662 Avaugour dissolved and reconstructed the
council, his action had reference to these disputes;
and it is clear that when in the following August
Laval sailed for France, one of his objects was to
restore the tranquillity which Dumesnil's proceedings had disturbed. There was great need; for,
what with these proceedings and the quarrel about
brandy, Quebec was a little hell of discord, the earthquake not having as yet frightened it into propriety.

The bishop's success at court was triumphant.
Not only did he procure the removal of Avaugour,
but he was invited to choose a new governor to
replace him.[1] This was not all; for he succeeded
in effecting a complete change in the government of
the colony. The Company of New France was called

[1] La Tour, *Vie de Laval*, liv. v.

upon to resign its claims;[1] and by a royal edict of
April, 1663, all power, legislative, judicial, and
executive, was vested in a council composed of the
governor whom Laval had chosen, of Laval himself,
and of five councillors, an attorney-general, and a
secretary, to be chosen by Laval and the governor
jointly.[2] Bearing with them blank commissions to
be filled with the names of the new functionaries,
Laval and his governor sailed for Quebec, where they
landed on the fifteenth of September. With them
came one Gaudais-Dupont, a royal commissioner
instructed to inquire into the state of the colony.

No sooner had they arrived than Laval and Mézy,
the new governor, proceeded to construct the new
council. Mézy knew nobody in the colony, and was,
at this time, completely under Laval's influence.
The nominations, therefore, were virtually made by
the bishop alone, in whose hands, and not in those of
the governor, the blank commissions had been
placed.[3] Thus for the moment he had complete control of the government; that is to say, the Church
was mistress of the civil power.

[1] See the deliberations and acts to this end in *Édits et Ordonnances concernant le Canada*, i. 30–32.

[2] *Édit de Création du Conseil Supérieur de Quebec.*

[3] *Commission octroyée au Sieur Gaudais. Mémoire pour servir
d'Instruction au Sieur Gaudais.* A sequel to these instructions, marked
"secret," shows that, notwithstanding Laval's extraordinary success
in attaining his objects, he and the Jesuits were somewhat distrusted. Gaudais is directed to make, with great discretion and
caution, careful inquiry into the bishop's conduct, and with equal
secrecy to ascertain why the Jesuits had asked for Avaugour's
recall.

Laval formed his council as follows: Jean Bourdon for attorney-general; Rouer de Villeray, Juchereau de la Ferté, Ruette d'Auteuil, Le Gardeur de Tilly, and Matthieu D'Amours for councillors; and Peuvret de Mesnu for secretary. The royal commissioner, Gaudais, also took a prominent place at the board.[1] This functionary was on the point of marrying his niece to a son of Robert Giffard, who had a strong interest in suppressing Dumesnil's accusations.[2] Dumesnil had laid his statements before the commissioner, who quickly rejected them, and took part with the accused.

Of those appointed to the new council, their enemy Dumesnil says that they were "incapable persons;" and their associate Gaudais, in defending them against worse charges, declares that they were "unlettered, of little experience, and nearly all unable to deal with affairs of importance." This was, perhaps, unavoidable; for except among the ecclesiastics, education was then scarcely known in Canada. But if Laval may be excused for putting

---

[1] As substitute for the *intendant*, an officer who had been appointed but who had not arrived.

[2] Dumesnil here makes one of the few mistakes I have been able to detect in his long memorials. He says that the name of the niece of Gaudais was *Marie Nau*. It was, in fact, *Michelle-Thérèse Nau*, who married Joseph, son of Robert Giffard, on the 22d of October, 1663. Dumesnil had forgotten the bride's first name. The elder Giffard was surety for Repentigny, whom Dumesnil charged with liabilities to the company, amounting to 644,700 livres. Giffard was also father-in-law of Juchereau de la Ferté, one of the accused.

incompetent men in office, nothing can excuse him for making men charged with gross public offences the prosecutors and judges in their own cause; and his course in doing so gives color to the assertion of Dumesnil that he made up the council expressly to shield the accused and smother the accusation.[1]

The two persons under the heaviest charges received the two most important appointments, — Bourdon, attorney-general; and Villeray, keeper of the seals. La Ferté was also one of the accused.[2] Of Villeray, the governor Argenson had written in 1659: "Some of his qualities are good enough, but confidence cannot be placed in him on account of his instability."[3] In the same year he had been ordered to France, "to purge himself of sundry crimes where-

---

[1] Dumesnil goes further than this, for he plainly intimates that the removing from power of the company, to whom the accused were responsible, and the placing in power of a council formed of the accused themselves, was a device contrived from the first by Laval and the Jesuits to get their friends out of trouble.

[2] Bourdon is charged with not having accounted for an immense quantity of beaver-skins which had passed through his hands during twelve years or more, and which are valued at more than 300,000 livres. Other charges are made against him in connection with large sums borrowed in Lauson's time on account of the colony. In a memorial addressed to the King in council, Dumesnil says that in 1662 Bourdon, according to his own accounts, had in his hands 37,516 livres belonging to the company, which he still retained.

Villeray's liabilities arose out of the unsettled accounts of his father-in-law, Charles Sevestre, and are set down at more than 600,000 livres. La Ferté's are of a smaller amount. Others of the council were indirectly involved in the charges.

[3] *Lettre d'Argenson, 20 Nov., 1659.*

with he stands charged."[1]   He was not yet free of
suspicion, having returned to Canada under an order
to make up and render his accounts, which he had
not yet done.   Dumesnil says that he first came to
the colony in 1651, as valet of the governor Lauson,
who had taken him from the jail at Rochelle, where
he was imprisoned for a debt of seventy-one francs,
"as appears by the record of the jail of date July
eleventh in that year."   From this modest beginning
he became in time the richest man in Canada.[2]   He
was strong in orthodoxy, and an ardent supporter of
the bishop and the Jesuits.   He is alternately praised
and blamed, according to the partisan leanings of the
writer.

Bourdon, though of humble origin, was, perhaps,
the most intelligent man in the council.   He was
chiefly known as an engineer, but he had also been a
baker, a painter, a syndic of the inhabitants, chief
gunner at the fort, and collector of customs for the
company.   Whether guilty of embezzlement or not,
he was a zealous devotee, and would probably have
died for his creed.   Like Villeray, he was one of
Laval's stanchest supporters, while the rest of the
council were also sound in doctrine and sure in
allegiance.

In virtue of their new dignity, the accused now
claimed exemption from accountability; but this was
not all.   The abandonment of Canada by the com-

---

[1] *Édit du Roy, 13 Mai, 1659.*
[2] *Lettre de Colbert à Frontenac, 17 Mai, 1674.*

pany, in leaving Dumesnil without support, and depriving him of official character, had made his charges far less dangerous. Nevertheless, it was thought best to suppress them altogether, and the first act of the new government was to this end.

On the twentieth of September, the second day after the establishment of the council, Bourdon, in his character of attorney-general, rose and demanded that the papers of Jean Péronne Dumesnil should be seized and sequestered. The council consented; and, to complete the scandal, Villeray was commissioned to make the seizure in the presence of Bourdon. To color the proceeding, it was alleged that Dumesnil had obtained certain papers unlawfully from the *greffe*, or record office. "As he was thought," says Gaudais, "to be a violent man," Bourdon and Villeray took with them ten soldiers, well armed, together with a locksmith and the secretary of the council. Thus prepared for every contingency, they set out on their errand, and appeared suddenly at Dumesnil's house between seven and eight o'clock in the evening. "The aforesaid Sieur Dumesnil," further says Gaudais, "did not refute the opinion entertained of his violence; for he made a great noise, shouted *robbers!* and tried to rouse the neighborhood, outrageously abusing the aforesaid Sieur de Villeray and the attorney-general, in great contempt of the authority of the council, which he even refused to recognize."

They tried to silence him by threats, but without

effect; upon which they seized him and held him fast in a chair, — "me," writes the wrathful Dumesnil, "who had lately been their judge." The soldiers stood over him and stopped his mouth, while the others broke open and ransacked his cabinet, drawers, and chest, from which they took all his papers, refusing to give him an inventory, or to permit any witness to enter the house. Some of these papers were private; among the rest were, he says, the charges and specifications, nearly finished, for the trial of Bourdon and Villeray, together with the proofs of their "peculations, extortions, and malversations." The papers were enclosed under seal, and deposited in a neighboring house, whence they were afterwards removed to the council-chamber, and Dumesnil never saw them again. It may well be believed that this, the inaugural act of the new council, was not allowed to appear on its records.[1]

On the twenty-first, Villeray made a formal report of the seizure to his colleagues; upon which, "by reason of the insults, violences, and irreverences therein set forth against the aforesaid Sieur de Villeray, commissioner, as also against the authority of the council," it was ordered that the offending Dumesnil should be put under arrest; but Gaudais, as he declares, prevented the order from being carried into effect.

---

[1] The above is drawn from the two memorials of Gaudais and of Dumesnil. They do not contradict each other as to the essential facts.

Dumesnil, who says that during the scene at his house he had expected to be murdered like his son, now, though unsupported and alone, returned to the attack, demanded his papers, and was so loud in threats of complaint to the King that the council were seriously alarmed. They again decreed his arrest and imprisonment, but resolved to keep the decree secret till the morning of the day when the last of the returning ships was to sail for France. In this ship Dumesnil had taken his passage, and they proposed to arrest him unexpectedly on the point of embarkation, that he might have no time to prepare and despatch a memorial to the court. Thus a full year must elapse before his complaints could reach the minister, and seven or eight months more before a reply could be returned to Canada. During this long delay the affair would have time to cool. Dumesnil received a secret warning of this plan, and accordingly went on board another vessel, which was to sail immediately. The council caused the six cannon of the battery in the Lower Town to be pointed at her, and threatened to sink her if she left the harbor; but she disregarded them, and proceeded on her way.

On reaching France, Dumesnil contrived to draw the attention of the minister Colbert to his accusations, and to the treatment they had brought upon him. On this Colbert demanded of Gaudais, who had also returned in one of the autumn ships, why he had not reported these matters to him. Gaudais made a lame attempt to explain his silence, gave his statement of the seizure of the papers, answered in vague terms some of Dumesnil's charges against the Canadian financiers, and said that he had nothing to do with the rest. In the following spring Colbert wrote as follows to his relative Terron, intendant of marine: —

"I do not know what report M. Gaudais has made to you, but family interests and the connections which he has at Quebec should cause him to be a little distrusted. On his arrival in that country, having constituted himself chief of the council, he despoiled an agent of the Company of Canada of all his papers, in a manner very violent and extraordinary; and this proceeding leaves no doubt whatever that these papers contained matters the knowledge of which it was wished absolutely to suppress. I think it will be very proper that you should be informed of the statements made by this agent, in order that, through him, an exact knowledge may be acquired of everything that has taken place in the management of affairs." [1]

Whether Terron pursued the inquiry does not appear. Meanwhile new quarrels had arisen at

---

[1] *Lettre de Colbert à Terron Rochelle*, 8 *Fév.*, 1664. "Il a spolié un agent de la Compagnie de Canada de tous ses papiers d'une manière fort violente et extraordinaire, et ce procédé ne laisse point à douter que dans ces papiers il n'y eût des choses dont on a voulu absolument supprimer la connaissance." Colbert seems to have received an exaggerated impression of the part borne by Gaudais in the seizure of the papers.

Quebec, and the questions of the past were obscured in the dust of fresh commotions. Nothing is more noticeable in the whole history of Canada, after it came under the direct control of the Crown, than the helpless manner in which this absolute government was forced to overlook and ignore the disobedience and rascality of its functionaries in this distant transatlantic dependency.

As regards Dumesnil's charges, the truth seems to be, that the financial managers of the colony, being ignorant and unpractised, had kept imperfect and confused accounts, which they themselves could not always unravel; and that some, if not all of them, had made illicit profits under cover of this confusion. That their stealings approached the enormous sum at which Dumesnil places them is not to be believed. But, even on the grossly improbable assumption of their entire innocence, there can be no apology for the means, subversive of all justice, by which Laval enabled his partisans and supporters to extricate themselves from embarrassment.

Note. — Dumesnil's principal memorial, preserved in the archives of the Marine and Colonies, is entitled *Mémoire concernant les Affaires du Canada, qui montre et fait voir que sous prétexte de la Gloire de Dieu, d'Instruction des Sauvages, de servir le Roy et de faire la nouvelle Colonie, il a été pris et diverti trois millions de livres ou environ.* It forms in the copy before me thirty-eight pages of manuscript, and bears no address, but seems meant for Colbert, or the council of state. There is a second memorial, which is little else than an abridgment of the first. A third, bearing the address *Au Roy et à nos Seigneurs du Conseil (d'État)*, and signed *Péronne Dumesnil*, is a petition for the payment of 10,132 livres due to him by the company for his services in Canada, " ou il a perdu son fils assassiné par les comptables du dit pays, qui n'ont voulu rendre compte au dit suppliant, Intendant, et ont pillé sa maison, ses meubles et papiers le 20 du mois de Septembre dernier, dont il y a acte."

Gaudais, in compliance with the demands of Colbert, gives his statement in a long memorial, *Le Sieur Gaudais Dupont à Monseigneur de Colbert*, 1664.

Dumesnil, in his principal memorial, gives a list of the alleged defaulters, with the special charges against each, and the amounts for which he reckons them liable. The accusations cover a period of ten or twelve years, and sometimes more. Some of them are curiously suggestive of more recent "rings." Thus Jean Gloria makes a charge of thirty-one hundred livres (francs) for fireworks to celebrate the King's marriage, when the actual cost is said to have been about forty livres. Others are alleged to have embezzled the funds of the company, under cover of pretended payments to imaginary creditors ; and Argenson himself is said to have eked out his miserable salary by drawing on the company for the pay of soldiers who did not exist.

The records of the Council preserve a guarded silence about this affair. I find, however, under date 20 Sept., 1663, " Pouvoir à M. de Villeray de faire recherche dans la maison *d'un nommé du Mesnil* des papiers appartenants au Conseil concernant Sa Majesté ;" and under date 18 March, 1664, " Ordre pour l'ouverture du coffre contenant les papiers de Dumesnil," and also an " Ordre pour mettre l'Inventaire des biens du Sr. Dumesnil entre les mains du Sr. Fillion."

CHAPTER XI.

1657–1665.

LAVAL AND MÉZY.

THE BISHOP'S CHOICE. — A MILITARY ZEALOT. — HOPEFUL BEGIN-
NINGS. — SIGNS OF STORM. — THE QUARREL. —DISTRESS OF MÉZY:
HE REFUSES TO YIELD; HIS DEFEAT AND DEATH.

WE have seen that Laval, when at court, had
been invited to choose a governor to his liking. He
soon made his selection. There was a pious officer,
Saffray de Mézy, major of the town and citadel of
Caen, whom he had well known during his long
stay with Bernières at the Hermitage. Mézy was the
principal member of the company of devotees formed
at Caen under the influence of Bernières and his
disciples. In his youth he had been headstrong and
dissolute. Worse still, he had been, it is said, a
Huguenot; but both in life and doctrine his conversion had been complete, and the fervid mysticism of
Bernières acting on his vehement nature had transformed him into a red-hot zealot. Towards the
hermits and their chief he showed a docility in
strange contrast with his past history, and followed

their inspirations with an ardor which sometimes
overleaped its mark.

Thus a Jacobin monk, a doctor of divinity, once
came to preach at the church of St. Paul at Caen;
on which, according to their custom, the brotherhood
of the Hermitage sent two persons to make report
concerning his orthodoxy. Mézy and another military zealot, "who," says the narrator, "hardly
know how to read, and assuredly do not know their
catechism," were deputed to hear his first sermon;
wherein this Jacobin, having spoken of the necessity
of the grace of Jesus Christ in order to the doing of
good deeds, these two wiseacres thought that he
was preaching Jansenism; and thereupon, after the
sermon, the Sieur de Mézy went to the proctor of
the ecclesiastical court and denounced him." [1]

His zeal, though but moderately tempered with
knowledge, sometimes proved more useful than on
this occasion. The Jacobin convent at Caen was
divided against itself. Some of the monks had
embraced the doctrines taught by Bernières, while
the rest held dogmas which he declared to be
contrary to those of the Jesuits, and therefore
heterodox. A prior was to be elected, and with the
help of Bernières his partisans gained the victory,
choosing one Father Louis, through whom the
Hermitage gained a complete control in the convent.
But the adverse party presently resisted, and com-

[1] Nicole, *Mémoire pour faire connoistre l'esprit et la conduite de la
Compagnie appellée l'Hermitage.*

plained to the provincial of their order, who came to Caen to close the dispute by deposing Father Louis. Hearing of his approach, Bernières asked aid from his military disciple, and De Mézy sent him a squad of soldiers, who guarded the convent doors and barred out the provincial.[1]

Among the merits of Mézy, his humility and charity were especially admired; and the people of Caen had more than once seen the town major staggering across the street with a beggar mounted on his back, whom he was bearing dry-shod through the mud in the exercise of those virtues.[2] In this he imitated his master Bernières, of whom similar acts are recorded.[3] However dramatic in manifestation, his devotion was not only sincere but intense. Laval imagined that he knew him well. Above all others, Mézy was the man of his choice; and so eagerly did he plead for him that the King himself paid certain debts which the pious major had contracted, and thus left him free to sail for Canada.

His deportment on the voyage was edifying, and the first days of his accession were passed in harmony. He permitted Laval to form the new council, and supplied the soldiers for the seizure of Dumesnil's papers. A question arose concerning Montreal, a subject on which the governors and the bishop rarely

---

[1] Nicole, *Mémoire pour faire connoistre l'esprit et la conduite de la Compagnie appellée l'Hermitage.*

[2] Juchereau, *Histoire de l'Hôtel-Dieu,* 149.

[3] See the laudatory notice of Bernières de Louvigny in the *Nouvelle Biographie Universelle.*

differed in opinion. The present instance was no exception to the rule. Mézy removed Maisonneuve, the local governor, and immediately replaced him, — the effect being, that whereas he had before derived his authority from the seigniors of the island, he now derived it from the governor-general. It was a movement in the interest of centralized power, and as such was cordially approved by Laval.

The first indication to the bishop and the Jesuits that the new governor was not likely to prove in their hands as clay in the hands of the potter, is said to have been given on occasion of an interview with an embassy of Iroquois chiefs, to whom Mézy, aware of their duplicity, spoke with a decision and haughtiness that awed the savages and astonished the ecclesiastics. He seems to have been one of those natures that run with an engrossing vehemence along any channel into which they may have been turned. At the Hermitage he was all devotee; but climate and conditions had changed, and he or his symptoms changed with them. He found himself raised suddenly to a post of command, or one which was meant to be such. The town major of Caen was set to rule over a region far larger than France. The royal authority was trusted to his keeping, and his honor and duty forbade him to break the trust. But when he found that those who had procured for him his new dignities had done so that he might be an instrument of their will, his ancient pride started again into life, and his headstrong temper broke out like a long-smothered fire. Laval stood aghast at the transformation. His lamb had turned wolf.

What especially stirred the governor's dudgeon was the conduct of Bourdon, Villeray, and Autcuil, those faithful allies whom Laval had placed on the council, and who, as Mézy soon found, were wholly in the bishop's interest. On the thirteenth of February he sent his friend Angoville, major of the fort, to Laval, with a written declaration to the effect that he had ordered them to absent themselves from the council, because, having been appointed "on the persuasion of the aforesaid Bishop of Petræa, who knew them to be wholly his creatures, they wish to make themselves masters in the aforesaid council, and have acted in divers ways against the interests of the King and the public for the promotion of personal and private ends, and have formed and fomented cabals, contrary to their duty and their oath of fidelity to his aforesaid Majesty."[1] He further declares that advantage had been taken of the facility of his disposition and his ignorance of the country to surprise him into assenting to their nomination; and he asks the bishop to acquiesce in their expulsion, and join him in calling an assembly of the people to choose others in their place. Laval refused; on which Mézy caused his declaration to be placarded about Quebec and proclaimed by sound of drum.

[1] *Ordre de M. de Mézy de faire sommation à l'Evêque de Petrée,* 13 *Fév.,* 1664. *Notification du dit Ordre, même date.* (Registre du Conseil Supérieur.)

The proposal of a public election, contrary as it was to the spirit of the government, opposed to the edict establishing the council, and utterly odious to the young autocrat who ruled over France, gave Laval a great advantage. "I reply," he wrote, "to the request which Monsieur the Governor makes me to consent to the interdiction of the persons named in his declaration, and proceed to the choice of other councillors or officers by an assembly of the people, that neither my conscience nor my honor, nor the respect and obedience which I owe to the will and commands of the King, nor my fidelity and affection to his service, will by any means permit me to do so."[1]

Mézy was dealing with an adversary armed with redoubtable weapons. It was intimated to him that the sacraments would be refused, and the churches closed against him. This threw him into an agony of doubt and perturbation; for the emotional religion which had become a part of his nature, though overborne by gusts of passionate irritation, was still full of life within him. Tossing between the old feeling and the new, he took a course which reveals the trouble and confusion of his mind. He threw himself for counsel and comfort on the Jesuits, though he knew them to be one with Laval against him, and though, under cover of denouncing sin in general, they had lashed him sharply in their sermons. There is something pathetic in the appeal

---

[1] *Réponse de l'Évêque de Petrée*, 16 *Fév.*, 1664.

he makes to them. For the glory of God and the service of the King, he had come, he says, on Laval's solicitation, to seek salvation in Canada; and being under obligation to the bishop, who had recommended him to the King, he felt bound to show proofs of his gratitude on every occasion. Yet neither gratitude to a benefactor nor the respect due to his character and person should be permitted to interfere with duty to the King, "since neither conscience nor honor permit us to neglect the requirements of our office and betray the interests of his Majesty, after receiving orders from his lips, and making oath of fidelity between his hands." He proceeds to say that, having discovered practices of which he felt obliged to prevent the continuance, he had made a declaration expelling the offenders from office; that the bishop and all the ecclesiastics had taken this declaration as an offence; that, regardless of the King's service, they had denounced him as a calumniator, an unjust judge, without gratitude, and perverted in conscience; and that one of the chief among them had come to warn him that the sacraments would be refused and the churches closed against him. "This," writes the unhappy governor, "has agitated our soul with scruples; and we have none from whom to seek light save those who are our declared opponents, pronouncing judgment on us without knowledge of cause. Yet as our salvation and the duty we owe the King are the things most important to us on earth, and as we hold them to be inseparable the one from the other; and as nothing is so certain as death, and nothing so uncertain as the hour thereof; and as there is no time to inform his Majesty of what is passing and to receive his commands; and as our soul, though conscious of innocence, is always in fear, — we feel obliged, despite their opposition, to have recourse to the reverend father casuists of the House of Jesus, to tell us in conscience what we can do for the fulfilment of our duty at once to God and to the King." [1]

The Jesuits gave him little comfort. Lalemant, their superior, replied by advising him to follow the directions of his confessor, a Jesuit, so far as the question concerned spiritual matters, adding that in temporal matters he had no advice to give.[2] The distinction was illusory. The quarrel turned wholly on temporal matters, but it was a quarrel with a bishop. To separate in such a case the spiritual obligation from the temporal was beyond the skill of Mézy, nor would the confessor have helped him.

Perplexed and troubled as he was, he would not reinstate Bourdon and the two councillors. The people began to clamor at the interruption of justice, for which they blamed Laval, whom a recent imposition of tithes had made unpopular. Mézy thereupon issued a proclamation, in which, after mentioning his opponents as the most subtle and artful persons

----

[1] *Mézy aux PP. Jésuites, Fait au Château de Québec ce dernier jour de Février*, 1664.

[2] *Lettre du P. H. Lalemant à Mr. le Gouverneur.*

in Canada, he declares that, in consequence of petitions sent him from Quebec and the neighboring settlements, he had called the people to the council-chamber, and by their advice had appointed the Sieur de Chartier as attorney-general in place of Bourdon.[1]

Bourdon replied by a violent appeal from the governor to the remaining members of the council;[2] on which Mézy declared him excluded from all public functions whatever, till the King's pleasure should be known.[3] Thus Church and State still frowned on each other, and new disputes soon arose to widen the breach between them. On the first establishment of the council, an order had been passed for the election of a mayor and two aldermen (*échevins*) for Quebec, which it was proposed to erect into a city, though it had only seventy houses and less than a thousand inhabitants. Repentigny was chosen mayor, and Madry and Charron aldermen; but the choice was not agreeable to the bishop, and the three functionaries declined to act, influence having probably been brought to bear on them to that end. The council now resolved that a mayor was needless, and the people were permitted to choose a syndic in his stead. These municipal elections were always so controlled by the authorities that the element of liberty which they seemed to represent was little but

---

[1] *Declaration du Sieur de Mézy*, 10 *Mars*, 1664.

[2] *Bourdon au Conseil*, 13 *Mars*, 1664.

[3] *Ordre du Gouverneur*, 13 *Mars*, 1664.

a mockery. On the present occasion, after an unaccountable delay of ten months, twenty-two persons cast their votes in presence of the council, and the choice fell on Charron. The real question was whether the new syndic should belong to the governor or to the bishop. Charron leaned to the governor's party. The ecclesiastics insisted that the people were dissatisfied, and a new election was ordered, but the voters did not come. The governor now sent messages to such of the inhabitants as he knew to be in his interest, who gathered in the council-chamber, voted under his eye, and again chose a syndic agreeable to him. Laval's party protested in vain.[1]

The councillors held office for a year, and the year had now expired. The governor and the bishop, it will be remembered, had a joint power of appointment; but agreement between them was impossible. Laval was for replacing his partisans, Bourdon, Villeray, Auteuil, and La Ferté. Mézy refused; and on the eighteenth of September he reconstructed the council by his sole authority, retaining of the old councillors only Amours and Tilly, and replacing the rest by Denis, La Tesserie, and Péronne de Mazé, the surviving son of Dumesnil. Again Laval protested; but Mézy proclaimed his choice by sound of drum, and caused placards to be posted, full, according to Father Lalemant, of abuse against the bishop. On this he was excluded from confession and absolu-

[1] *Registre du Conseil Supérieur.*

tion. He complained loudly; "but our reply was," says the father, "that God knew everything."[1]

This unanswerable but somewhat irrelevant response failed to satisfy him, and it was possibly on this occasion that an incident occurred which is recounted by the bishop's eulogist, La Tour. He says that Mézy, with some unknown design, appeared before the church at the head of a band of soldiers, while Laval was saying mass. The service over, the bishop presented himself at the door, on which, to the governor's confusion, all the soldiers respectfully saluted him.[2] The story may have some foundation, but it is not supported by contemporary evidence.

On the Sunday after Mézy's *coup d'état*, the pulpits resounded with denunciations. The people listened, doubtless, with becoming respect; but their sympathies were with the governor; and he, on his part, had made appeals to them at more than one crisis of the quarrel. He now fell into another indiscretion. He banished Bourdon and Villeray, and ordered them home to France.

They carried with them the instruments of their revenge, — the accusations of Laval and the Jesuits against the author of their woes. Of these accusations one alone would have sufficed. Mézy had appealed to the people. It is true that he did so

---

[1] *Journal des Jésuites, Octobre,* 1664.

[2] La Tour, *Vie de Laval,* liv. vii. It is charitable to ascribe this writer's many errors to carelessness.

from no love of popular liberty, but simply to make
head against an opponent; yet the act alone was
enough, and he received a peremptory recall.　Again
Laval had triumphed.　He had made one governor
and unmade two, if not three.　The modest Levite,
as one of his biographers calls him in his earlier days,
had become the foremost power in Canada.

Laval had a threefold strength at court, — his high
birth, his reputed sanctity, and the support of the
Jesuits.　This was not all, for the permanency of
his position in the colony gave him another advantage.　The governors were named for three years, and
could be recalled at any time; but the vicar apostolic
owed his appointment to the Pope, and the Pope
alone could revoke it.　Thus he was beyond reach
of the royal authority, and the court was in a certain
sense obliged to conciliate him.　As for Mézy, a man
of no rank or influence, he could expect no mercy.
Yet, though irritable and violent, he seems to have
tried conscientiously to reconcile conflicting duties,
or what he regarded as such.　The governors and
intendants, his successors, received, during many
years, secret instructions from the court to watch
Laval, and cautiously prevent him from assuming
powers which did not belong to him.　It is likely
that similar instructions had been given to Mézy,[1]

---

[1] The royal commissioner, Gaudais, who came to Canada with
Mézy, had, as before mentioned, orders to inquire with great secrecy
into the conduct of Laval. The intendant, Talon, who followed
immediately after, had similar instructions.

and that the attempt to fulfil them had aided to embroil him with one who was probably the last man on earth with whom he would willingly have quarrelled.

An inquiry was ordered into his conduct; but a voice more potent than the voice of the King had called him to another tribunal. A disease, the result perhaps of mental agitation, seized upon him and soon brought him to extremity. As he lay gasping between life and death, fear and horror took possession of his soul. Hell yawned before his fevered vision, peopled with phantoms which long and lonely meditations, after the discipline of Loyola, made real and palpable to his thought. He smelt the fumes of infernal brimstone, and heard the howlings of the damned. He saw the frown of the angry Judge, and the fiery swords of avenging angels, hurling wretches like himself, writhing in anguish and despair, into the gulf of unutterable woe. He listened to the ghostly counsellors who besieged his bed, bowed his head in penitence, made his peace with the Church, asked pardon of Laval, confessed to him, and received absolution at his hands; and his late adversaries, now benign and bland, soothed him with promises of pardon, and hopes of eternal bliss.

Before he died, he wrote to the Marquis de Tracy, newly appointed viceroy, a letter which indicates that even in his penitence he could not feel himself wholly in the wrong.[1] He also left a will in which the

---

[1] *Lettre de Mézy au Marquis de Tracy, 26 Avril, 1665.*

pathetic and the quaint are curiously mingled.
After praying his patron, Saint Augustine, with
Saint John, Saint Peter, and all the other saints, to
intercede for the pardon of his sins, he directs that
his body shall be buried in the cemetery of the poor
at the hospital, as being unworthy of more honored
sepulture. He then makes various legacies of piety
and charity. Other bequests follow, — one of which
is to his friend Major Angoville, to whom he leaves
two hundred francs, his coat of English cloth, his
camlet mantle, a pair of new shoes, eight shirts with
sleeve-buttons, his sword and belt, and a new blanket
for the major's servant. Felix Aubert is to have
fifty francs, with a gray jacket, a small coat of gray
serge, "which," says the testator, "has been worn for
a while," and a pair of long white stockings. And
in a codicil he further leaves to Angoville his best
black coat, in order that he may wear mourning for
him.[1]

His earthly troubles closed on the night of the
sixth of May. He went to his rest among the
paupers; and the priests, serenely triumphant, sang
requiems over his grave.

Note. — Mézy sent home charges against the bishop and the
Jesuits which seem to have existed in Charlevoix's time, but for
which, as well as for those made by Laval, I have sought in vain.

The substance of these mutual accusations is given thus by the
minister Colbert, in a memorial addressed to the Marquis de Tracy,
in 1665: "Les Jésuites l'accusent d'avarice et de violences; et lui

[1] *Testament du Sieur de Mézy.* This will, as well as the letter, is
engrossed in the registers of the council.

qu'ils voulaient entreprendre sur l'autorité qui lui a été commise par le Roy, en sorte que n'ayant que de leurs créatures dans le Conseil Souverain, toutes les résolutions s'y prenaient selon leurs sentiments."

The papers cited are drawn partly from the *Registres du Conseil Supérieur*, still preserved at Quebec, and partly from the Archives of the Marine and Colonies. Laval's admirer, the Abbé La Tour, in his eagerness to justify the bishop, says that the quarrel arose from a dispute about precedence between Mézy and the intendant, and from the ill-humor of the governor because the intendant shared the profits of his office. The truth is, that there was no intendant in Canada during the term of Mézy's government. One Robert had been appointed to the office, but he never came to the colony. The commissioner Gaudais, during the two or three months of his stay at Quebec, took the intendant's place at the council-board; but harmony between Laval and Mézy was unbroken till after his departure. Other writers say that the dispute arose from the old question about brandy. Towards the end of the quarrel there was some disorder from this source, but even then the brandy question was subordinate to other subjects of strife.

CHAPTER XII.

1662–1680.

LAVAL AND THE SEMINARY.

Laval's Visit to Court. — The Seminary. — Zeal of the Bishop : his Eulogists. — Church and State. — Attitude of Laval.

THAT memorable journey of Laval to court, which caused the dissolution of the Company of New France, the establishment of the Supreme Council, the recall of Avaugour, and the appointment of Mézy, had yet other objects and other results. Laval, vicar apostolic and titular Bishop of Petræa, wished to become in title, as in fact, Bishop of Quebec. Thus he would gain an increase of dignity and authority, necessary, as he thought, in his conflicts with the civil power; "for," he wrote to the cardinals of the Propaganda, "I have learned from long experience how little security my character of vicar apostolic gives me against those charged with political affairs: I mean the officers of the Crown, perpetual rivals and contemners of the authority of the Church."[1]

[1] For a long extract from this letter, copied from the original in the archives of the Propaganda at Rome, see Faillon, *Colonie Français*, iii. 432.

This reason was for the Pope and the cardinals. It may well be believed that he held a different language to the King. To him he urged that the bishopric was needed to enforce order, suppress sin, and crush heresy. Both Louis XIV. and the Queen Mother favored his wishes;[1] but difficulties arose, and interminable disputes ensued on the question whether the proposed bishopric should depend immediately on the Pope or on the Archbishop of Rouen. It was a revival of the old quarrel of Gallican and ultramontane. Laval, weary of hope deferred, at length declared that he would leave the colony if he could not be its bishop in title; and in 1674, after eleven years of delay, the King yielded to the Pope's demands, and the vicar apostolic became first Bishop of Quebec.

If Laval had to wait for his mitre, he found no delay and no difficulty in attaining another object no less dear to him. He wished to provide priests for Canada, drawn from the Canadian population, fed with sound and wholesome doctrine, reared under his eye, and moulded by his hand. To this end he proposed to establish a seminary at Quebec. The plan found favor with the pious King, and a decree signed by his hand sanctioned and confirmed it. The new seminary was to be a corporation of priests under a superior chosen by the bishop; and, besides

---

[1] *Anne d'Autriche à Laval*, 23 *Avril*, 1662; *Louis XIV. au Pape*, 28 *Jan.* 1664; *Louis XIV. au Duc de Créquy, Ambassadeur à Rome*, 28 *June*, 1664.

its functions of instruction, it was vested with distinct and extraordinary powers. Laval, an organizer and a disciplinarian by nature and training, would fain subject the priests of his diocese to a control as complete as that of monks in a convent. In France, the curé or parish priest was, with rare exceptions, a fixture in his parish, whence he could be removed only for grave reasons, and through prescribed forms of procedure. Hence he was to a certain degree independent of the bishop. Laval, on the contrary, demanded that the Canadian curé should be removable at his will, and thus placed in the position of a missionary, to come and go at the order of his superior. In fact, the Canadian parishes were for a long time so widely scattered, so feeble in population, and so miserably poor, that, besides the disciplinary advantages of this plan, its adoption was at first almost a matter of necessity. It added greatly to the power of the Church; and, as the colony increased, the King and the minister conceived an increasing distrust of it. Instructions for the "fixation" of the curés were repeatedly sent to the colony, and the bishop, while professing to obey, repeatedly evaded them. Various fluctuations and changes took place; but Laval had built on strong foundations, and at this day the system of removable curés prevails in most of the Canadian parishes.[1]

---

[1] On the establishment of the seminary. *Mandement de l'Évêque de Petrée, pour l'Établissement du Séminaire de Québec; Approbation du Roy* (*Édits et Ordonnances*, i. 33, 35); La Tour, *Vie de Laval*, liv.

Thus he formed his clergy into a family with himself at its head. His seminary, the mother who had reared them, was further charged to maintain them, nurse them in sickness, and support them in old age. Under her maternal roof the tired priest found repose among his brethren; and thither every year he repaired from the charge of his flock in the wilderness, to freshen his devotion and animate his zeal by a season of meditation and prayer.

The difficult task remained to provide the necessary funds. Laval imposed a tithe of one-thirteenth on all products of the soil, or, as afterwards settled, on grains alone. This tithe was paid to the seminary, and by the seminary to the priests. The people, unused to such a burden, clamored and resisted; and Mézy, in his disputes with the bishop, had taken advantage of their discontent. It became necessary to reduce the tithe to a twenty-sixth, which, as there was little or no money among the inhabitants, was paid in kind. Nevertheless, the scattered and impoverished settlers grudged even this contribution to the support of a priest whom many of them rarely saw; and the collection of it became a matter of the greatest difficulty and uncertainty. How the King came to the rescue, we shall hereafter see.

Besides the great seminary where young men were trained for the priesthood, there was the lesser semi-

vi.; *Esquisse de la Vie de Laval*, Appendix. Various papers bearing on the subject are printed in the Canadian *Abeille*, from originals in the archives of the seminary.

nary where boys were educated in the hope that they would one day take orders. This school began in 1668, with eight French and six Indian pupils, in the old house of Madame Couillard; but so far as the Indians were concerned it was a failure. Sooner or later they all ran wild in the woods, carrying with them as fruits of their studies a sufficiency of prayers, offices, and chants learned by rote, along with a feeble smattering of Latin and rhetoric, which they soon dropped by the way. There was also a sort of farm-school attached to the seminary, for the training of a humbler class of pupils. It was established at the parish of St. Joachim, below Quebec, where the children of artisans and peasants were taught farming and various mechanical arts, and thoroughly grounded in the doctrine and discipline of the Church.[1] The Great and Lesser Seminary still subsist, and form one of the most important Roman Catholic institutions on this continent. To them has recently been added the Laval University, resting on the same foundation, and supported by the same funds.

Whence were these funds derived? Laval, in order to imitate the poverty of the apostles, had divested himself of his property before he came to Canada; otherwise there is little doubt that in the fulness of his zeal he would have devoted it to his

---

[1] *Annales du Petit Séminaire de Quebec*, see *Abeille*, vol. i.; *Notice Historique sur le Petit Séminaire de Quebec, Ibid.*, vol. ii.; *Notice Historique sur la Paroisse de St. Joachim, Ibid.*, vol. i. The *Abeille* is a journal published by the seminary.

favorite object. But if he had no property he had influence, and his family had both influence and wealth. He acquired vast grants of land in the best parts of Canada. Some of these he sold or exchanged; others he retained till the year 1680, when he gave them, with nearly all else that he then possessed, to his seminary at Quebec. The lands with which he thus endowed it included the seigniories of the Petite Nation, the Island of Jesus, and Beaupré. The last is of great extent, and at the present day of immense value. Beginning a few miles below Quebec, it borders the St. Lawrence for a distance of sixteen leagues, and is six leagues in depth, measured from the river. From these sources the seminary still draws an abundant revenue, though its seigniorial rights were commuted on the recent extinction of the feudal tenure in Canada.

Well did Laval deserve that his name should live in that of the university which a century and a half after his death owed its existence to his bounty. This father of the Canadian Church, who has left so deep an impress on one of the communities which form the vast population of North America, belonged to a type of character to which an even justice is rarely done. With the exception of the Canadian Garneau, a liberal Catholic, those who have treated of him have seen him through a medium intensely Romanist, coloring, hiding, and exaggerating by turns both his actions and the traits of his character. Tried by the Romanist standard, his merits were great; though the extraordinary influence which he exercised in the affairs of the colony were, as already observed, by no means due to his spiritual graces alone. To a saint sprung from the *haute noblesse*, Earth and Heaven were alike propitious. When the vicar-general Colombière pronounced his funeral eulogy in the sounding periods of Bossuet, he did not fail to exhibit him on the ancestral pedestal where his virtues would shine with redoubled lustre. "The exploits of the heroes of the House of Montmorency," exclaims the reverend orator, "form one of the fairest chapters in the annals of Old France; the heroic acts of charity, humility, and faith achieved by a Montmorency form one of the fairest in the annals of New France. The combats, victories, and conquests of the Montmorency in Europe would fill whole volumes; and so, too, would the triumphs won by a Montmorency in America over sin, passion, and the Devil." Then he crowns the high-born prelate with a halo of fourfold saintship: "It was with good reason that Providence permitted him to be called Francis, for the virtues of all the saints of that name were combined in him, — the zeal of Saint Francis Xavier, the charity of Saint Francis of Sales, the poverty of Saint Francis of Assisi, the self-mortification of Saint Francis Borgia; but poverty was the mistress of his heart, and he loved her with incontrollable transports."

The stories which Colombière proceeds to tell of Laval's asceticism are confirmed by other evidence, and are, no doubt, true.   Nor is there any reasonable doubt that, had the bishop stood in the place of Brébeuf or Charles Lalemant, he would have suffered torture and death like them.   But it was his lot to strive, not against infidel savages, but against country-men and Catholics, who had no disposition to burn him, and would rather have done him reverence than wrong.

To comprehend his actions and motives, it is neces-sary to know his ideas in regard to the relations of Church and State.   They were those of the extreme ultramontanes, which a recent Jesuit preacher has expressed with tolerable distinctness.   In a sermon uttered in the Church of Notre Dame, at Montreal, on the first of November, 1872, he thus announced them: "The supremacy and infallibility of the Pope; the independence and liberty of the Church; *the subordination and submission of the State to the Church;* in case of conflict between them, the Church to decide, the State to submit: for whoever follows and defends these principles, life and a bless-ing; for whoever rejects and combats them, death and a curse."[1]

These were the principles which Laval and the

---

[1] This sermon was preached by Father Braun, S. J., on occasion of the "Golden Wedding," or fiftieth anniversary of Bishop Bourget of Montreal.   A large body of the Canadian clergy were present, some of whom thought his expressions too emphatic.   A translation by another Jesuit is published in the "Montreal Weekly Herald" of Nov. 2, 1872; and the above extract is copied *verbatim.*

Jesuits strove to make good. Christ was to rule in Canada through his deputy the bishop, and God's law was to triumph over the laws of man. As in the halcyon days of Champlain and Montmagny, the governor was to be the right hand of the Church, to wield the earthly sword at her bidding; and the council was to be the agent of her high behests.

France was drifting toward the triumph of the *parti dévot*, the sinister reign of petticoat and cassock, the era of Maintenon and Tellier, and the fatal atrocities of the dragonnades. Yet the advancing tide of priestly domination did not flow smoothly. The unparalleled prestige which surrounded the throne of the young King, joined to his quarrels with the Pope and divisions in the Church itself, disturbed, though they could not check, its progress. In Canada it was otherwise. The colony had been ruled by priests from the beginning, and it only remained to continue in her future the law of her past. She was the fold of Christ; the wolf of civil government was among the flock, and Laval and the Jesuits, watchful shepherds, were doing their best to chain and muzzle him.

According to Argenson, Laval had said, " A bishop can do what he likes; " and his action answered reasonably well to his words. He thought himself above human law. In vindicating the assumed rights of the Church, he invaded the rights of others, and used means from which a healthy conscience would have shrunk. All his thoughts and sympathies had

run from childhood in ecclesiastical channels, and he
cared for nothing outside the Church.   Prayer, meditation, and asceticism had leavened and moulded
him.   During four years he had been steeped in the
mysticism of the Hermitage, which had for its aim
the annihilation of self, and through self-annihilation
the absorption into God.[1]   He had passed from a life
of visions to a life of action.   Earnest to fanaticism,
he saw but one great object, — the glory of God on
earth.   He was penetrated by the poisonous casuistry
of the Jesuits, based on the assumption that all
means are permitted when the end is the service of
God; and as Laval, in his own opinion, was always
doing the service of God, while his opponents were
always doing that of the Devil, he enjoyed, in the
use of means, a latitude of which we have seen him
avail himself.

[1] See the maxims of Bernières published by La Tour.

SECTION THIRD.

THE COLONY AND THE KING.

CHAPTER XIII.

1661–1665.

ROYAL INTERVENTION.

FONTAINEBLEAU. — LOUIS XIV. — COLBERT. — THE COMPANY OF
THE WEST. — EVIL OMENS. — ACTION OF THE KING. — TRACY,
COURCELLE, AND TALON. — THE REGIMENT OF CARIGNAN-SALI-
ÈRES. — TRACY AT QUEBEC. — MIRACLES. — A HOLY WAR.

LEAVE Canada behind; cross the sea, and stand,
on an evening in June, by the edge of the forest of
Fontainebleau. Beyond the broad gardens, above
the long ranges of moonlit trees, rise the walls and
pinnacles of the vast château, — a shrine of history,
the gorgeous monument of lines of vanished kings,
haunted with memories of Capet, Valois, and
Bourbon.

There was little thought of the past at Fontainebleau
in June, 1661. The present was too dazzling and
too intoxicating; the future, too radiant with hope
and promise. It was the morning of a new reign;

the sun of Louis XIV. was rising in splendor, and
the rank and beauty of France were gathered to pay
it homage.   A youthful court, a youthful king; a
pomp and magnificence such as Europe had never
seen; a delirium of ambition, pleasure, and love, —
all this wrought in many a young heart an enchant-
ment destined to be cruelly broken.   Even old courtiers felt the fascination of the scene, and tell us of
the music at evening by the borders of the lake; of
the gay groups that strolled under the shadowing
trees, floated in gilded barges on the still water, or
moved slowly in open carriages around its borders.
Here was Anne of Austria, the King's mother, and
Marie Thérèse, his tender and jealous queen; his
brother, the Duke of Orleans, with his bride of sixteen, Henriette of England; and his favorite, that
vicious butterfly of the court, the Count de Guiche.
Here, too, were the humbled chiefs of the civil war,
Beaufort and Condé, obsequious before their triumphant master.   Louis XIV., the centre of all eyes, in
the flush of health and vigor, and the pride of new-
fledged royalty, stood, as he still stands on the
canvas of Philippe de Champagne, attired in a
splendor which would have been effeminate but for
the stately port of the youth who wore it.[1]

Fortune had been strangely bountiful to Louis

---

[1] On the visit of the court at Fontainebleau in the summer of
1661, see *Mémoires de Madame de Motteville, Mémoires de Madame de
La Fayette, Mémoires de l'Abbé de Choisy,* and Walckenaer's *Mémoires sur Madame de Sévigné.*

XIV. The nations of Europe, exhausted by wars and dissensions, looked upon him with respect and fear. Among weak and weary neighbors, he alone was strong. The death of Mazarin had released him from tutelage; feudalism in the person of Condé was abject before him; he had reduced his parliaments to submission; and in the arrest of the ambitious prodigal Fouquet, he was preparing a crushing blow to the financial corruption which had devoured France.

Nature had formed him to act the part of King. Even his critics and enemies praise the grace and majesty of his presence, and he impressed his courtiers with an admiration which seems to have been to an astonishing degree genuine. He carried airs of royalty even into his pleasures; and while his example corrupted all France, he proceeded to the apartments of Montespan or Fontanges with the majestic gravity of Olympian Jove. He was a devout observer of the forms of religion; and as the buoyancy of youth passed away, his zeal was stimulated by a profound fear of the Devil. Mazarin had reared him in ignorance; but his faculties were excellent in their way, and in a private station would have made him an efficient man of business. The vivacity of his passions and his inordinate love of pleasure were joined to a persistent will and a rare power of labor. The vigorous mediocrity of his understanding delighted in grappling with details. His astonished courtiers saw him take on himself the burden of administration, and work at it without

relenting for more than half a century. Great as
was his energy, his pride was far greater. As king
by divine right, he felt himself raised immeasurably
above the highest of his subjects; but while vindicating with unparalleled haughtiness his claims to
supreme authority, he was, at the outset, filled with
a sense of the duties of his high place, and fired by
an ambition to make his reign beneficent to France
as well as glorious to himself.

Above all rulers of modern times, Louis XIV. was
the embodiment of the monarchical idea. The
famous words ascribed to him, "I am the State,"
were probably never uttered; but they perfectly
express his spirit. "It is God's will," he wrote in
1666, "that whoever is born a subject should not
reason, but obey;"[1] and those around him were of
his mind. "The State is in the King," said Bossuet,
the great mouthpiece of monarchy; "the will of the
people is merged in his will. O Kings! put forth
your power boldly, for it is divine and salutary to
humankind."[2]

For a few brief years, this King's reign was indeed
salutary to France. His judgment of men, when
not obscured by his pride and his passion for flattery,
was good; and he had at his service the generals and
statesmen formed in the freer and bolder epoch that
had ended with his accession. Among them was
Jean Baptiste Colbert, formerly the intendant of

[1] *Œuvres de Louis XIV.*, ii. 283.

[2] Bossuet, *Politique tirée de l'Écriture sainte*, 670 (1843).

Mazarin's household, — a man whose energies matched his talents, and who had preserved his rectitude in the midst of corruption. It was a hard task that Colbert imposed on his proud and violent nature to serve the imperious King, morbidly jealous of his authority, and resolved to accept no initiative but his own. He must counsel while seeming to receive counsel, and lead while seeming to follow. The new minister bent himself to the task, and the nation reaped the profit. A vast system of reform was set in action amid the outcries of nobles, financiers, churchmen, and all who profited by abuses. The methods of this reform were trenchant and sometimes violent, and its principles were not always in accord with those of modern economic science; but the good that resulted was incalculable. The burdens of the laboring classes were lightened, the public revenues increased, and the wholesale plunder of the public money was arrested with a strong hand. Laws were reformed and codified; feudal tyranny, which still subsisted in many quarters, was repressed; agriculture and productive industry of all kinds were encouraged, roads and canals opened, trade was stimulated, a commercial marine created, and a powerful navy formed as if by magic.[1]

It is in his commercial, industrial, and colonial policy that the profound defects of the great minis-

----

[1] On Colbert, see Clément, *Histoire de Colbert;* Clément, *Lettres et Mémoires de Colbert;* Chéruel, *Administration monarchique en France*, ii. chap. vi.; Henri Martin, *Histoire de France*, xiii., etc.

ter's system are most apparent. It was a system of authority, monopoly, and exclusion, in which the government, and not the individual, acted always the foremost part. Upright, incorruptible, ardent for the public good, inflexible, arrogant, and domineering, he sought to drive France into paths of prosperity, and create colonies by the energy of an imperial will. He feared, and with reason, that the want of enterprise and capital among the merchants would prevent the broad and immediate results at which he aimed; and to secure these results he established a series of great trading corporations, in which the principles of privilege and exclusion were pushed to their utmost limits. Prominent among them was the Company of the West. The King signed the edict creating it on the twenty-fourth of May, 1664. Any person in the kingdom or out of it might become a partner by subscribing, within a certain time, not less than three thousand francs. France was a mere patch on the map, compared to the vast domains of the new association. Western Africa from Cape Verd to the Cape of Good Hope, South America between the Amazon and the Orinoco, Cayenne, the Antilles, and all New France, from Hudson's Bay to Virginia and Florida, were bestowed on it forever, to be held of the Crown on the simple condition of faith and homage. As, according to the edict, the glory of God was the chief object in view, the company was required to supply its possessions with a sufficient number of priests, and diligently to exclude

all teachers of false doctrine. It was empowered to
build forts and war-ships, cast cannon, wage war,
make peace, establish courts, appoint judges, and
otherwise to act as sovereign within its own domains.
A monopoly of trade was granted it for forty years.[1]
Sugar from the Antilles and furs from Canada were
the chief source of expected profit; and Africa was
to supply the slaves to raise the sugar. Scarcely was
the grand machine set in motion, when its directors
betrayed a narrowness and blindness of policy which
boded the enterprise no good. Canada was a chief
sufferer. Once more, bound hand and foot, she was
handed over to a selfish league of merchants, —
monopoly in trade, monopoly in religion, monopoly
in government. Nobody but the company had a
right to bring her the necessaries of life; and nobody
but the company had a right to exercise the traffic
which alone could give her the means of paying for
these necessaries. Moreover, the supplies which it
brought were insufficient, and the prices which it
demanded were exorbitant. It was throttling its
wretched victim. The Canadian merchants remon-
strated.[2] It was clear that if the colony was to live,
the system must be changed; and a change was
accordingly ordered. The company gave up its
monopoly of the fur-trade, but reserved the right to
levy a duty of one-fourth of the beaver-skins, and
one-tenth of the moose-skins; and it also reserved

<hr>

[1] *Édit d'Établissement de la Compagnie des Indes Occidentales.*
[2] *Lettre du Conseil Souverain à Colbert,* 1668.

the entire trade of Tadoussac, — that is to say, the trade of all the tribes between the lower St. Lawrence and Hudson's Bay. It retained, besides, the exclusive right of transporting furs in its own ships, — thus controlling the commerce of Canada, and discouraging, or rather extinguishing, the enterprise of Canadian merchants. On its part, it was required to pay governors, judges, and all the colonial officials out of the duties which it levied.[1]

Yet the King had the prosperity of Canada at heart; and he proceeded to show his interest in her after a manner hardly consistent with his late action in handing her over to a mercenary guardian. In fact, he acted as if she had still remained under his paternal care. He had just conferred the right of naming a governor and intendant upon the new company; but he now assumed it himself, the company, with a just sense of its own unfitness, readily consenting to this suspension of one of its most important privileges. Daniel de Rémy, Sieur de Courcelle, was appointed governor, and Jean Baptiste Talon intendant.[2] The nature of this duplicate

---

[1] *Arrêt du Conseil du Roy qui accorde à la Compagnie le quart des castors, le dixième des orignaux et la traite de Tadoussac: Instruction de Monseigneur de Tracy et à Messieurs le Gouverneur et l'Intendant.*

This company prospered as little as the rest of Colbert's trading companies. Within ten years it lost 3,523,000 livres, besides blighting the colonies placed under its control. (*Recherches sur les Finances,* cited by Clément, *Histoire de Colbert.*)

[2] *Commission de Lieutenant Général en Canada, etc., pour M. de Courcelle,* 23 *Mars,* 1665; *Commission d'Intendant de la Justice, Police, et Finances en Canada, etc., pour M. Talon,* 23 *Mars,* 1665.

government will appear hereafter. But before appointing rulers for Canada, the King had appointed a representative of the Crown for all his American domains. The Maréchal d'Estrades had for some time held the title of viceroy for America; and as he could not fulfil the duties of that office, being at the time ambassador in Holland, the Marquis de Tracy was sent in his place, with the title of lieutenant-general.[1]

Canada at this time was an object of very considerable attention at court, and especially in what was known as the *parti dévot*. The *Relations* of the Jesuits, appealing equally to the spirit of religion and the spirit of romantic adventure, had for more than a quarter of a century been the favorite reading of the devout, and the visit of Laval at court had greatly stimulated the interest they had kindled. The letters of Argenson, and especially of Avaugour, had shown the vast political possibilities of the young colony, and opened a vista of future glories alike for Church and for King.

So, when Tracy set sail he found no lack of followers. A throng of young nobles embarked with him, eager to explore the marvels and mysteries of the western world. The King gave him two hundred soldiers of the regiment of Carignan-Salières, and promised that a thousand more should follow. After spending more than a year in the West Indies,

---

[1] *Commission de Lieutenant Général de l'Amérique Méridionale et Septentrionale pour M. Prouville de Tracy*, 19 Nov., 1663.

where, as Mother Mary of the Incarnation expresses it, "he performed marvels and reduced everybody to obedience," he at length sailed up the St. Lawrence, and on the thirtieth of June, 1665, anchored in the basin of Quebec. The broad, white standard, blazoned with the arms of France, proclaimed the representative of royalty; and Point Levi and Cape Diamond and the distant Cape Tourmente roared back the sound of the saluting cannon. All Quebec was on the ramparts or at the landing-place, and all eyes were strained at the two vessels as they slowly emptied their crowded decks into the boats alongside. The boats at length drew near, and the lieutenant-general and his suite landed on the quay with a pomp such as Quebec had never seen before.

Tracy was a veteran of sixty-two, portly and tall, "one of the largest men I ever saw," writes Mother Mary; but he was sallow with disease, for fever had seized him, and it had fared ill with him on the long voyage. The Chevalier de Chaumont walked at his side, and young nobles surrounded him, gorgeous in lace and ribbons and majestic in leonine wigs. Twenty-four guards in the King's livery led the way, followed by four pages and six valets;[1] and thus, while the Frenchmen shouted and the Indians stared, the august procession threaded the streets of the Lower Town, and climbed the steep pathway that scaled the cliffs above. Breathing hard, they reached

---

[1] Juchereau says that this was his constant attendance when he went abroad.

the top, passed on the left the dilapidated walls of
the fort and the shed of mingled wood and masonry
which then bore the name of the Castle of St. Louis;
passed on the right the old house of Couillard and
the site of Laval's new seminary, and soon reached
the square betwixt the Jesuit college and the cathedral.   The bells were ringing in a frenzy of welcome. Laval in pontificals, surrounded by priests and
Jesuits, stood waiting to receive the deputy of the
King; and as he greeted Tracy and offered him the
holy water, he looked with anxious curiosity to see
what manner of man he was.   The signs were auspi-
cious.   The deportment of the lieutenant-general left
nothing to desire.   A *prie-dieu* had been placed for
him.   He declined it.   They offered him a cushion,
but he would not have it; and, fevered as he was,
he knelt on the bare pavement with a devotion that
edified every beholder.   *Te Deum* was sung, and a
day of rejoicing followed.

There was good cause.   Canada, it was plain, was
not to be wholly abandoned to a trading company.
Louis XIV. was resolved that a new France should
be added to the old.   Soldiers, settlers, horses, sheep,
cattle, young women for wives, were all sent out in
abundance by his paternal benignity.   Before the
season was over, about two thousand persons had
landed at Quebec at the royal charge.   "At length,"
writes Mother Juchereau, "our joy was completed by
the arrival of two vessels with Monsieur de Courcelle,
our governor; Monsieur Talon, our intendant, and

the last companies of the regiment of Carignan."
More state and splendor, more young nobles, more
guards and valets: for Courcelle, too, says the same
chronicler, "had a superb train; and Monsieur
Talon, who naturally loves glory, forgot nothing
which could do honor to the King." Thus a sun-
beam from the court fell for a moment on the rock of
Quebec. Yet all was not sunshine; for the voyage
had been a tedious one, and disease had broken out
in the ships. That which bore Talon had been a
hundred and seventeen days at sea,[1] and others were
hardly more fortunate. The hospital was crowded
with the sick; so, too, were the Church and the
neighboring houses; and the nuns were so spent with
their labors that seven of them were brought to the
point of death. The priests were busied in convert-
ing the Huguenots, a number of whom were detected
among the soldiers and emigrants. One of them
proved refractory, declaring with oaths that he would
never renounce his faith. Falling dangerously ill,
he was carried to the hospital, where Mother
Catherine de Saint-Augustin bethought her of a plan
of conversion. She ground to powder a small piece
of a bone of Father Brébeuf, the Jesuit martyr, and
secretly mixed the sacred dust with the patient's
gruel; whereupon, says Mother Juchereau, "this
intractable man forthwith became gentle as an angel,
begged to be instructed, embraced the faith, and

---

[1] *Talon au Ministre,* 4 *Oct.,* 1665.

abjured his errors publicly with an admirable fervor."[1]

Two or three years before, the Church of Quebec had received as a gift from the Pope the bodies or bones of two saints, — Saint Flavian and Saint Félicité. They were enclosed in four large coffers or reliquaries, and a grand procession was now ordered in their honor. Tracy, Courcelle, Talon, and the agent of the company bore the canopy of the Host. Then came the four coffers on four decorated litters, carried by the principal ecclesiastics. Laval followed in pontificals. Forty-seven priests, and a long file of officers, nobles, soldiers, and inhabitants, followed the precious relics amid the sound of music and the roar of cannon.[2]

"It is a ravishing thing," says Mother Mary, "to see how marvellously exact is Monsieur de Tracy at all these holy ceremonies, where he is always the first to come, for he would not lose a single moment of them. He has been seen in church for six hours together, without once going out." But while the lieutenant-general thus edified the colony, he betrayed no lack of qualities equally needful in his position. In Canada, as in the West Indies, he showed both vigor and conduct. First of all, he had been ordered to subdue or destroy the Iroquois; and the regiment of Carignan-Salières was the weapon

---

[1] Le Mercier tells the same story in the *Relation* of 1665.

[2] Compare Marie de l'Incarnation, *Lettre* 16 *Oct.*, 1666, with La Tour, *Vie de Laval*, chap. x.

placed in his hands for this end. Four companies of this corps had arrived early in the season; four more came with Tracy, more yet with Salières, their colonel, — and now the number was complete. As with slouched hat and plume, bandoleer, and shouldered firelock, these bronzed veterans of the Turkish wars marched at the tap of drum through the narrow street, or mounted the rugged way that led up to the fort, the inhabitants gazed with a sense of profound relief. Tame Indians from the neighboring missions, wild Indians from the woods, stared in silent wonder at their new defenders. Their numbers, their discipline, their uniform, and their martial bearing filled the savage beholders with admiration.

Carignan-Salières was the first regiment of regular troops ever sent to America by the French government. It was raised in Savoy by the Prince of Carignan in 1644, but was soon employed in the service of France; where, in 1652, it took a conspicuous part, on the side of the King, in the battle with Condé and the Fronde at the Porte St. Antoine. After the peace of the Pyrenees, the Prince of Carignan, unable to support the regiment, gave it to the King, and it was, for the first time, incorporated into the French armies. In 1664 it distinguished itself, as part of the allied force of France, in the Austrian war against the Turks. In the next year it was ordered to America, along with the fragment of a regiment formed of Germans, the whole being

placed under the command of Colonel de Salières.
Hence its double name.[1]

Fifteen heretics were discovered in its ranks, and
quickly converted.[2] Then the new crusade was
preached, — the crusade against the Iroquois, enemies
of God and tools of the Devil. The soldiers and
the people were filled with a zeal half warlike and
half religious. "They are made to understand,"
writes Mother Mary, "that this is a holy war, all for
the glory of God and the salvation of souls. The
fathers are doing wonders in inspiring them with
true sentiments of piety and devotion. Fully five
hundred soldiers have taken the scapulary of the
Holy Virgin. It is we [the Ursulines], who make
them; it is a real pleasure to do such work;" and
she proceeds to relate a "beau miracle," by which
God made known his satisfaction at the fervor of
his military servants.

[1] For a long notice of the regiment of Carignan-Salières
(Lorraine), see Susane, *Ancienne Infanterie Française*, v. 236. The
portion of it which returned to France from Canada formed a
nucleus for the reconstruction of the regiment, which, under the
name of the regiment of Lorraine, did not cease to exist as a separate organization till 1794. When it came to Canada it consisted,
says Susane, of about a thousand men, besides about two hundred
of the other regiment incorporated with it. Compare *Mémoire du
Roy pour servir d'instruction au Sieur Talon*, which corresponds very
nearly with Susane's statement.

[2] Besides these, there was Berthier, a captain. "Voilà," writes
Talon to the King, "le 16me converti; ainsi votre Majesté mois-
sonne déjà à pleines mains de la gloire pour Dieu, et pour elle bien
de la renommée dans toute l'étendue de la Chrétienté." (*Lettre du
7 Oct.*, 1665.)

The secular motives for the war were in themselves strong enough; for the growth of the colony absolutely demanded the cessation of Iroquois raids, and the French had begun to learn the lesson that in the case of hostile Indians no good can come of attempts to conciliate, unless respect is first imposed by a sufficient castigation. It is true that the writers of the time paint Iroquois hostilities in their worst colors. In the innumerable letters which Mother Mary of the Incarnation sent home every autumn, by the returning ships, she spared no means to gain the sympathy and aid of the devout; and, with similar motives, the Jesuits in their printed *Relations* took care to extenuate nothing of the miseries which the pious colony endured. Avaugour too, in urging the sending out of a strong force to fortify and hold the country, had advised that, in order to furnish a pretext and disarm the jealousy of the English and Dutch, exaggerated accounts should be given of danger from the side of the savage confederates. Yet, with every allowance, these dangers and sufferings were sufficiently great.

The three upper nations of the Iroquois were comparatively pacific; but the two lower nations, the Mohawks and Oneidas, were persistently hostile; making inroads into the colony by way of Lake Champlain and the Richelieu, murdering and scalping, and then vanishing like ghosts. Tracy's first step was to send a strong detachment to the Richelieu to build a picket fort below the rapids of Chambly,

which take their name from that of the officer in
command.   An officer named Sorel soon afterwards
built a second fort on the site of the abandoned
palisade work built by Montmagny, at the mouth of
the river, where the town of Sorel now stands; and
Salières, colonel of the regiment, added a third fort,
two or three leagues above Chambly.[1]   These forts
could not wholly bar the passage against the nimble
and wily warriors who might pass them in the night,
shouldering their canoes through the woods.   A
blow, direct and hard, was needed, and Tracy
prepared to strike it.

Late in the season an embassy from the three
upper nations — the Onondagas, Cayugas, and
Senecas — arrived at Quebec, led by Garacontié, a
famous chief whom the Jesuits had won over, and
who proved ever after a stanch friend of the French.
They brought back the brave Charles Le Moyne of
Montreal, whom they had captured some three
months before, and now restored as a peace-offering,
taking credit to themselves that "not even one of his
nails had been torn out, nor any part of his body
burnt."[2]   Garacontié made a peace speech, which, as
rendered by the Jesuits, was an admirable specimen of
Iroquois eloquence; but while joining hands with him
and his companions, the French still urged on their
preparations to chastise the contumacious Mohawks.

---

[1] See the map in the *Relation* of 1665. The accompanying text
of the *Relation* is incorrect.

[2] *Explanation of the eleven Presents of the Iroquois Ambassadors,*
N. Y. Colonial Docs., ix. 37.

CHAPTER XIV.

1666, 1667.

THE MOHAWKS CHASTISED.

The governor, Courcelle, says Father Le Mercier, "breathed nothing but war," and was bent on immediate action. He was for the present subordinate to Tracy, who, however, forbore to cool his ardor, and allowed him to proceed. The result was an enterprise bold to rashness. Courcelle, with about five hundred men, prepared to march in the depth of a Canadian winter to the Mohawk towns, — a distance estimated at three hundred leagues. Those who knew the country vainly urged the risks and difficulties of the attempt. The adventurous governor held fast to his purpose, and only waited till the St. Lawrence should be well frozen. Early in January, it was a solid floor; and on the ninth the march began. Officers and men stopped at Sillery, and knelt in the little mission chapel before the shrine of

Saint Michael, to ask the protection and aid of the warlike archangel; then they resumed their course, and, with their snow-shoes tied at their backs, walked with difficulty and toil over the bare and slippery ice. A keen wind swept the river, and the fierce cold gnawed them to the bone. Ears, noses, fingers, hands, and knees were frozen; some fell in torpor, and were dragged on by their comrades to the shivering bivouac. When, after a march of ninety miles, they reached Three Rivers, a considerable number were disabled, and had to be left behind; but others joined them from the garrison, and they set out again. Ascending the Richelieu, and passing the new forts at Sorel and Chambly, they reached at the end of the month the third fort, called Ste. Thérèse. On the thirtieth they left it, and continued their march up the frozen stream.

About two hundred of them were Canadians, and of these seventy were old Indian-fighters from Montreal, versed in wood-craft, seasoned to the climate, and trained among dangers and alarms. Courcelle quickly learned their value, and his "Blue Coats," as he called them, were always placed in the van.[1] Here, wrapped in their coarse blue capotes, with blankets and provisions strapped at their backs, they strode along on snow-shoes, which recent storms had made indispensable. The regulars followed as they could. They were not yet the tough and experienced woodsmen that they and their descend-

---

[1] Dollier de Casson, *Histoire du Montréal*, A. D. 1665, 1666.

ants afterwards became; and their snow-shoes embarrassed them, burdened as they were with the heavy loads which all carried alike, from Courcelle to the lowest private.

Lake Champlain lay glaring in the winter sun, a sheet of spotless snow; and the wavy ridges of the Adirondacks bordered the dazzling landscape with the cold gray of their denuded forests. The long procession of weary men crept slowly on under the lee of the shore; and when night came they bivouacked by squads among the trees, dug away the snow with their snow-shoes, piled it in a bank around them, built their fire in the middle, and crouched about it on beds of spruce or hemlock,[1] — while, as they lay close packed for mutual warmth, the winter sky arched them like a vault of burnished steel, sparkling with the cold diamond lustre of its myriads of stars. This arctic serenity of the elements was varied at times by heavy snow-storms, and before they reached their journey's end the earth and the ice were buried to the unusual depth of four feet. From Lake Champlain they passed to Lake George[2] and the frigid glories of its snow-wrapped mountains, thence crossed to the Hudson, and groped their way through the woods in search of the Mohawk towns. They

---

[1] One of the men, telling the story of their sufferings to Daniel Gookin, of Massachusetts, indicated this as their mode of encamping. See Mass. Hist. Coll. first series, i. 161.

[2] *Carte des grands lacs, Ontario et autres . . . et des pays traversez par MM. de Tracy et Courcelle pour aller attaquer les agniés* [Mohawks], 1666.

soon went astray; for thirty Algonquins, whom they had taken as guides, had found the means of a grand debauch at Fort Ste. Thérèse, drunk themselves into helplessness, and lingered behind. Thus Courcelle and his men mistook the path, and, marching by way of Saratoga Lake and Long Lake,[1] found themselves, on Saturday the twentieth of February, close to the little Dutch hamlet of Corlaer, or Schenectady. Here the chief man in authority told them that most of the Mohawks and Oneidas had gone to war with another tribe. They however caught a few stragglers, and had a smart skirmish with a party of warriors, losing an officer and several men. Half frozen and half starved, they encamped in the neighboring woods, where, on Sunday, three envoys appeared from Albany, to demand why they had invaded the territories of his Royal Highness the Duke of York. It was now that they learned for the first time that the New Netherlands had passed into English hands, a change which boded no good to Canada. The envoys seemed to take their explanations in good part, made them a present of wine and provisions, and allowed them to buy further supplies from the Dutch of Schenectady. They even invited them to enter the village, but Courcelle declined, — partly because the place could not hold them all, and partly because he feared that his men, once seated in a chimney-corner, could never be induced to leave it.

Their position was cheerless enough; for the vast

---

[1] *Carte . . . des pays traversez par MM. de Tracy et Courcelle, etc.*

beds of snow around them were soaking slowly under a sullen rain, and there was danger that the lakes might thaw and cut off their retreat. "Ye Mohaukes," says the old English report of the affair, "were all gone to their Castles with resolution to fight it out against the french, who, being refresht and supplyed wth the aforesaid provisions, made a shew of marching towards the Mohaukes Castles, but with faces about, and great sylence and dilligence, return'd towards Cannada." "Surely," observes the narrator, "so bould and hardy an attempt hath not hapned in any age."[1] The end hardly answered to the beginning. The retreat, which began on Sunday night, was rather precipitate. The Mohawks hovered about their rear, and took a few prisoners; but famine and cold proved more deadly foes, and sixty men perished before they reached the shelter of Fort Ste. Thérèse. On the eighth of March, Courcelle came to the neighboring fort of St. Louis or Chambly. Here he found the Jesuit Albanel acting as chaplain; and, being in great ill humor, he charged him with causing the failure of the expedition by detaining the Algonquin guides. This singular notion took such possession of him, that, when a few days after he met the Jesuit Frémin at Three Rivers, he embraced him ironically, saying, at the same time, "My father, I am the unluckiest gentleman in the world; and

[1] *A Relation of the Govern^r. of Cannada, his March with 600 Volunteirs into ye Territoryes of His Royall Highnesse the Duke of Yorke in America.* See Doc. Hist. N. Y. i. 71.

you, and the rest of you, are the cause of it." [1] The pious Tracy and the prudent Talon tried to disarm his suspicions, and with such success that he gave up an intention he had entertained of discarding his Jesuit confessor, and forgot or forgave the imagined wrong.

Unfortunate as this expedition was, it produced a strong effect on the Iroquois by convincing them that their forest homes were no safe asylum from French attacks. In May, the Senecas sent an embassy of peace; and the other nations, including the Mohawks, soon followed. Tracy, on his part, sent the Jesuit Bêchefer to learn on the spot the real temper of the savages, and ascertain whether peace could safely be made with them. The Jesuit was scarcely gone when news came that a party of officers hunting near the outlet of Lake Champlain had been set upon by the Mohawks, and that seven of them had been captured or killed. Among the captured was Leroles, a cousin of Tracy; and among the killed was a young gentleman named Chasy, his nephew.

On this the Jesuit envoy was recalled; twenty-four Iroquois deputies were seized and imprisoned; and Sorel, captain in the regiment of Carignan, was sent with three hundred men to chastise the perfidious Mohawks. If, as it seems, he was expected to attack their fortified towns or "castles," as the English call them, his force was too small. This

---

1 *Journal des Jésuites, Mars,* 1666.

time, however, there was no fighting. At two days from his journey's end, Sorel met the famous chief called the Flemish Bastard, bringing back Leroles and his fellow-captives, and charged, as he alleged, to offer full satisfaction for the murder of Chasy. Sorel believed him, retraced his course, and with the Bastard in his train returned to Quebec.

Quebec was full of Iroquois deputies, all bent on peace or pretending to be so. On the last day of August there was a grand council in the garden of the Jesuits. Some days later, Tracy invited the Flemish Bastard and a Mohawk chief named Agariata to his table, when allusion was made to the murder of Chasy. On this the Mohawk, stretching out his arm, exclaimed in a braggart tone, "This is the hand that split the head of that young man." The indignation of the company may be imagined. Tracy told his insolent guest that he should never kill anybody else; and he was led out and hanged in presence of the Bastard.[1] There was no more talk of peace. Tracy prepared to march in person against the Mohawks with all the force of Canada.

On the day of the Exaltation of the Cross, "for whose glory," says the chronicler, "this expedition

---

[1] This story rests chiefly on the authority of Nicholas Perrot, *Mœurs des Sauvages*, 113. La Potherie also tells it, with the addition of the chief's name. Colden follows him. The *Journal des Jésuites* mentions that the chief who led the murderers of Chasy arrived at Quebec on the sixth of September. Marie de l'Incarnation mentions the hanging of an Iroquois at Quebec, late in the autumn, for violating the peace.

is undertaken," Tracy and Courcelle left Quebec with thirteen hundred men. They crossed Lake Champlain, and launched their boats again on the waters of St. Sacrament, now Lake George. It was the first of the warlike pageants that have made that fair scene historic. October had begun, and the romantic wilds breathed the buoyant life of the most inspiring of American seasons, when the blue-jay screams from the woods, the wild duck splashes along the lake, and the echoes of distant mountains prolong the quavering cry of the loon; when weather-stained rocks are plumed with the fiery crimson of the sumach, the claret hues of young oaks, the amber and scarlet of the maple, and the sober purple of the ash; or when gleams of sunlight, shot aslant through the rents of cool autumnal clouds, chase fitfully along the glowing sides of painted mountains. Amid this gorgeous euthanasia of the dying season, the three hundred boats and canoes trailed in long procession up the lake, threaded the labyrinth of the Narrows, — that sylvan fairy-land of tufted islets and quiet waters, — and landed at length where Fort William Henry was afterwards built.[1]

About a hundred miles of forests, swamps, rivers, and mountains still lay between them and the Mohawk towns. There seems to have been an Indian path, for this was the ordinary route of the Mohawk and Oneida war-parties; but the path was narrow, broken, full of gullies and pitfalls, crossed

[1] *Carte . . . des pays traversez par MM. de Tracy et Courcelle, etc.*

by streams, and in one place interrupted by a lake which they passed on rafts. A hundred and ten "Blue Coats," of Montreal, led the way, under Charles Le Moyne; Repentigny commanded the levies from Quebec. In all there were six hundred Canadians, six hundred regulars, and a hundred Indians from the missions, who ranged the woods in front, flank, and rear, like hounds on the scent. Red or white, Canadians or regulars, all were full of zeal. "It seems to them," writes Mother Mary, "that they are going to lay siege to Paradise, and win it and enter in, because they are fighting for religion and the faith."[1] Their ardor was rudely tried. Officers as well as men carried loads at their backs, whence ensued a large blister on the shoulders of the Chevalier de Chaumont, in no way used to such burdens. Tracy, old, heavy, and infirm, was inopportunely seized with the gout. A Swiss soldier tried to carry him on his shoulders across a rapid stream; but midway his strength failed, and he was barely able to deposit his ponderous load on a rock. A Huron came to his aid, and bore Tracy safely to the farther bank. Courcelle was attacked with cramps, and had to be carried for a time like his commander. Provisions gave out, and men and officers grew faint with hunger. The Montreal soldiers had for chaplain a sturdy priest, Dollier de Casson, as large as Tracy and far stronger; for the incredible story is told of him that when in good

---

[1] Marie de l'Incarnation, *Lettre du* 16 *Oct.*, 1666.

condition he could hold two men seated on his extended hands.[1] Now, however, he was equal to no such exploit, being not only deprived of food, but also of sleep, by the necessity of listening at night to the confessions of his pious flock; and his shoes, too, had failed him, nothing remaining but the upper leather, which gave him little comfort among the sharp stones. He bore up manfully, being by nature brave and light-hearted; and when a servant of the Jesuits fell into the water, he threw off his cassock and leaped after him. His strength gave out, and the man was drowned; but a grateful Jesuit led him aside, and requited his efforts with a morsel of bread.[2] A wood of chestnut-trees full of nuts at length stayed the hunger of the famished troops.

It was Saint Theresa's day when they approached the lower Mohawk town. A storm of wind and rain set in; but, anxious to surprise the enemy, they pushed on all night amid the moan and roar of the forest, — over slippery logs, tangled roots, and oozy mosses, under dripping boughs and through saturated bushes. This time there was no want of good guides; and when in the morning they issued from the forest, they saw, amid its cornfields, the palisades of the Indian stronghold. They had two small pieces of cannon brought from the lake by relays of men, but they did not stop to use them. Their twenty

---

[1] Grandet, *Notice manuscrite sur Dollier de Casson*, extract given by J. Viger in appendix to *Histoire du Montréal* (Montreal, 1868).

[2] Dollier de Casson, *Histoire du Montréal*, A. D. 1665, 1666.

drums beat the charge, and they advanced to seize
the place by *coup-de-main*. Luckily for them, a
panic had seized the Indians: not that they were
taken by surprise, for they had discovered the
approaching French, and, two days before, had sent
away their women and children in preparation for a
desperate fight; but the din of the drums, which
they took for so many devils in the French service,
and the armed men advancing from the rocks and
thickets in files that seemed interminable, so wrought
on the scared imagination of the warriors that they
fled in terror to their next town, a short distance
above. Tracy lost no time, but hastened in pursuit.
A few Mohawks were seen on the hills, yelling and
firing too far for effect. Repentigny, at the risk of his
scalp, climbed a neighboring height, and looked down
on the little army, which seemed so numerous as it
passed beneath, "that," writes the superior of the Ursulines, "he told me that he thought the good angels
must have joined with it: whereat he stood amazed."

The second town or fort was taken as easily as
the first; so, too, were the third and the fourth.
The Indians yelled, and fled without killing a man;
and still the troops pursued, following the broad
trail which led from town to town along the valley
of the Mohawk. It was late in the afternoon when
the fourth town was entered,[1] and Tracy thought

---

[1] Marie de l'Incarnation says that there were four towns in all.
I follow the *Acte de prise de possession*, made on the spot. Five are
here mentioned.

that his work was done; but an Algonquin squaw who had followed her husband to the war, and who had once been a prisoner among the Mohawks, told him that there was still another above. The sun was near its setting, and the men were tired with their pitiless marching; but again the order was given to advance. The eager squaw showed the way, holding a pistol in one hand and leading Courcelle with the other; and they soon came in sight of Andaraqué, the largest and strongest of the Mohawk forts. The drums beat with fury, and the troops prepared to attack; but there were none to oppose them. The scouts sent forward reported that the warriors had fled. The last of the savage strongholds was in the hands of the French.

"God has done for us," says Mother Mary, "what he did in ancient days for his chosen people, — striking terror into our enemies, insomuch that we were victors without a blow. Certain it is that there is miracle in all this; for if the Iroquois had stood fast, they would have given us a great deal of trouble and caused our army great loss, seeing how they were fortified and armed, and how haughty and bold they are."

The French were astonished as they looked about them. These Iroquois forts were very different from those that Jogues had seen here twenty years before, or from that which in earlier times set Champlain and his Hurons at defiance. The Mohawks had had counsel and aid from their Dutch friends, and adapted their savage defences to the rules of European art. Andaraqué was a quadrangle formed of a triple palisade, twenty feet high, and flanked by four bastions. Large vessels of bark filled with water were placed on the platforms of the palisade for defence against fire. The dwellings which these fortifications enclosed were in many cases built of wood, though the form and arrangement of the primitive bark-lodge of the Iroquois seems to have been preserved. Some of the wooden houses were a hundred and twenty feet long, with fires for eight or nine families. Here, and in subterranean *caches*, was stored a prodigious quantity of Indian-corn and other provisions; and all the dwellings were supplied with carpenters' tools, domestic utensils, and many other appliances of comfort.

The only living things in Andaraqué, when the French entered, were two old women, a small boy, and a decrepit old man, who, being frightened by the noise of the drums, had hidden himself under a canoe. From them the victors learned that the Mohawks, retreating from the other towns, had gathered here, resolved to fight to the last; but at sight of the troops their courage failed, and the chief was first to run, crying out, "Let us save ourselves, brothers! the whole world is coming against us!"

A cross was planted, and at its side the royal arms. The troops were drawn up in battle array, when Jean Baptiste du Bois, an officer deputed by

Tracy, advancing sword in hand to the front, proclaimed in a loud voice that he took possession in the name of the King of all the country of the Mohawks; and the troops shouted three times, *Vive le Roi*.[1]

That night a mighty bonfire illumined the Mohawk forests; and the scared savages from their hiding-places among the rocks saw their palisades, their dwellings, their stores of food, and all their possessions turned to cinders and ashes. The two old squaws captured in the town threw themselves in despair into the flames of their blazing homes. When morning came, there was nothing left of Andaraqué but smouldering embers, rolling their pale smoke against the painted background of the October woods. *Te Deum* was sung and mass said; and then the victors began their backward march, — burning, as they went, all the remaining forts, with all their hoarded stores of corn, except such as they needed for themselves. If they had failed to destroy their enemies in battle, they hoped that winter and famine would do the work of shot and steel.

While there was distress among the Mohawks, there was trouble among their English neighbors, who claimed as their own the country which Tracy had invaded. The English authorities were the more disquieted, because they feared that the lately conquered Dutch might join hands with the French

---

[1] *Acte de prise de possession*, 17 *Oct.*, 1666.

against them. When Nicolls, governor of New York, heard of Tracy's advance, he wrote to the governors of the New England colonies, begging them to join him against the French invaders, and urging that if Tracy's force were destroyed or captured, the conquest of Canada would be an easy task. There was war at the time between the two Crowns; and the British court had already entertained this project of conquest, and sent orders to its colonies to that effect. But the New England governors — ill prepared for war, and fearing that their Indian neighbors, who were enemies of the Mohawks, might take part with the French — hesitated to act, and the affair ended in a correspondence, civil if not sincere, between Nicolls and Tracy.[1] The treaty of Bréda, in the following year, secured peace for a time between the rival colonies.

The return of Tracy was less fortunate than his advance. The rivers, swollen by autumn rains, were difficult to pass; and in crossing Lake Champlain two canoes were overset in a storm, and eight men were drowned. From St. Anne, a new fort built early in the summer on Isle La Motte, near the northern end of the lake, he sent news of his success to Quebec, where there was great rejoicing and a solemn thanksgiving. Signs and prodigies had not been wanting to attest the interest of the upper and nether powers in the crusade against the myrmidons

---

[1] See the correspondence in *N. Y. Col. Docs.*, iii. 118–156. Compare *Hutchinson Collection*, 407, and *Mass. Hist. Coll.*, xviii. 102.

of hell.   At one of the forts on the Richelieu, "the soldiers," says Mother Mary, "were near dying of fright.   They saw a great fiery cavern in the sky, and from this cavern came plaintive voices mixed with frightful howlings.   Perhaps it was the demons, enraged because we had depopulated a country where they had been masters so long, and had said mass and sung the praises of God in a place where there had never before been anything but foulness and abomination."

Tracy had at first meant to abandon Fort St. Anne; but he changed his mind after returning to Quebec.   Meanwhile the season had grown so late that there was no time to send proper supplies to the garrison.   Winter closed, and the place was not only ill-provisioned, but was left without a priest. Tracy wrote to the superior of the Sulpitians at Montreal to send one without delay; but the request was more easily made than fulfilled, for he forgot to order an escort, and the way was long and dangerous. The stout-hearted Dollier de Casson was told, however, to hold himself ready to go at the first opportunity.   His recent campaigning had left him in no condition for braving fresh hardships, for he was nearly disabled by a swelling on one of his knees. By way of cure he resolved to try a severe bleeding, and the Sangrado of Montreal did his work so thoroughly that his patient fainted under his hands. As he returned to consciousness, he became aware that two soldiers had entered the room.   They told him that they were going in the morning to Chambly, which was on the way to St. Anne; and they invited him to go with them. "Wait till the day after to-morrow," replied the priest, "and I will try." The delay was obtained; and on the day fixed the party set out by the forest path to Chambly, a distance of about four leagues. When they reached it, Dollier de Casson was nearly spent; but he concealed his plight from the commanding officer, and begged an escort to St. Anne, some twenty leagues farther. As the officer would not give him one, he threatened to go alone, on which ten men and an ensign were at last ordered to conduct him. Thus attended, he resumed his journey after a day's rest. One of the soldiers fell through the ice, and none of his comrades dared help him. Dollier de Casson, making the sign of the cross, went to his aid, and, more successful than on the former occasion, caught him and pulled him out. The snow was deep; and the priest, having arrived in the preceding summer, had never before worn snow-shoes, while a sack of clothing, and his portable chapel which he carried at his back, joined to the pain of his knee and the effects of his late bleeding, made the march a purgatory.

He was sorely needed at Fort St. Anne. There was pestilence in the garrison. Two men had just died without absolution, while more were at the point of death, and praying for a priest. Thus it happened that when the sentinel descried far off, on the ice of Lake Champlain, a squad of soldiers approaching, and among them a black cassock, every officer and man not sick or on duty came out with one accord to meet the new-comer. They overwhelmed him with welcome and with thanks. One took his sack, another his portable chapel, and they led him in triumph to the fort. First he made a short prayer, then went his rounds among the sick, and then came to refresh himself with the officers. Here was La Motte de la Lucière, the commandant; La Durantaye, a name destined to be famous in Canadian annals; and a number of young subalterns. The scene was no strange one to Dollier de Casson, for he had been an officer of cavalry in his time, and fought under Turenne;[1] a good soldier, without doubt, at the mess table or in the field, and none the worse a priest that he had once followed the wars. He was of a lively humor, given to jests and mirth; as pleasant a father as ever said *Benedicite*. The soldier and the gentleman still lived under the cassock of the priest. He was greatly respected and beloved; and his influence as a peace-maker, which he often had occasion to exercise, is said to have been remarkable. When the time demanded it, he could use arguments more cogent than those of moral suasion. Once, in a camp of Algonquins, when, as he was kneeling in prayer, an insolent savage came to interrupt him, the father, without rising, knocked the intruder flat by a blow of his fist; and the other

[1] Grandet, *Notice manuscrite sur Dollier de Casson,* extracts from copy in possession of the late Jacques Viger.

Indians, far from being displeased, were filled with admiration at the exploit.[1]

His cheery temper now stood him in good stead; for there was dreary work before him, and he was not the man to flinch from it. The garrison of St. Anne had nothing to live on but salt pork and half-spoiled flour. Their hogshead of vinegar had sprung a leak, and the contents had all oozed out. They had rejoiced in the supposed possession of a reasonable stock of brandy; but they soon discovered that the sailors, on the voyage from France, had emptied the casks and filled them again with salt-water. The scurvy broke out with fury. In a short time, forty out of the sixty men became victims of the loathsome malady. Day or night, Dollier de Casson and Forestier, the equally devoted young surgeon, had no rest. The surgeon's strength failed, and the priest was himself slightly attacked with the disease. Eleven men died; and others languished for want of help, for their comrades shrank from entering the infected dens where they lay. In their extremity some of them devised an ingenious expedient. Though they had nothing to bequeath, they made wills in which they left imaginary sums of money to those who had befriended them; and thenceforth they found no lack of nursing.

In the intervals of his labors, Dollier de Casson would run to and fro for warmth and exercise on a

---

[1] Grandet, *Notice manuscrite sur Dollier de Casson,* cited by Faillon, *Colonie Française,* iii. 395, 396.

certain track of beaten snow, between two of the
bastions, reciting his breviary as he went, so that
those who saw him might have thought him out of
his wits.   One day La Motte called out to him as he
was thus engaged, "Eh, Monsieur le curé, if the
Iroquois should come, you must defend that bastion.
My men are all deserting me, and going over to you
and the doctor."   To which the father replied, "Get
me some litters with wheels, and I will bring them
out to man my bastion.   They are brave enough
now; no fear of their running away."   With banter
like this, they sought to beguile their miseries; and
thus the winter wore on at Fort St. Anne.[1]

Early in spring they saw a troop of Iroquois
approaching, and prepared as well as they could to
make fight; but the strangers proved to be ambassadors of peace.   The destruction of the Mohawk
towns had produced a deep effect, not on that nation
alone, but also on the other four members of the
league.   They were disposed to confirm the promises
of peace which they had already made; and Tracy
had spurred their good intentions by sending them
a message that unless they quickly presented themselves at Quebec, he would hang all the chiefs whom
he had kept prisoners after discovering their treach-

---

[1] The above curious incidents are told by Dollier de Casson, in his
Histoire du Montréal, preserved in manuscript in the Mazarin Library
at Paris.   He gives no hint that the person in question was himself,
but speaks of him as *un ecclésiastique*.   His identity is, however,
made certain by internal evidence, by a passage in the *Notice* of
Grandet, and by other contemporary allusions.

ery in the preceding summer. The threat had its effect: deputies of the Oneidas, Onondagas, Cayugas, and Senecas presently arrived in a temper of befitting humility. The Mohawks were at first afraid to come; but in April they sent the Flemish Bastard with overtures of peace, and in July a large deputation of their chiefs appeared at Quebec. They and the rest left some of their families as hostages, and promised that if any of their people should kill a Frenchman, they would give them up to be hanged.[1]

They begged, too, for blacksmiths, surgeons, and Jesuits to live among them. The presence of the Jesuits in their towns was in many ways an advantage to them; while to the colony it was of the greatest importance. Not only was conversion to the Church justly regarded as the best means of attaching the Indians to the French and alienating them from the English; but the Jesuits living in the midst of them could influence even those whom they could not convert, soothe rising jealousies, counteract English intrigues, and keep the rulers of the colony informed of all that was passing in the Iroquois towns. Thus, half Christian missionaries, half political agents, the Jesuits prepared to resume the hazardous mission of the Iroquois. Frémin and Pierron were ordered to the Mohawks, Bruyas to the Oneidas, and three others were named for the

---

[1] *Lettre du Père Jean Pierron, de la Compagnie de Jésus, escripte de la Motte* [Fort Ste. Anne] *sur le lac Champlain, le 12me d'aoust,* 1667.

remaining three nations of the league. The troops had made the peace; the Jesuits were the rivets to hold it fast, — and peace endured without absolute rupture for nearly twenty years. Of all the French expeditions against the Iroquois, that of Tracy was the most productive of good.

NOTE. — On Tracy's expedition against the Mohawks compare Faillon, *Histoire de la Colonie Française au Canada*, iii.

END OF VOL. I.